Hector Sanguino was born in Convención (North of Santander), Colombia. He is the author of *A True Odyssey* and the author of other novels written in Spanish, including *Un Bello Sueño* – a children's story, *Las Pistas del Diablo*, *La Misión de los Elegidos*, *Las Manchas del Diamante* and *The Effects of Betrayal* – a biographical novel.

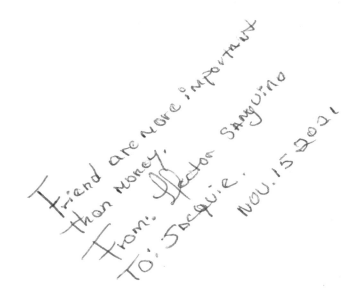

Friend are more important than money.
From: Hector Sanguino
To: Jacquie. NOV. 15 2021

Hector Sanguino

THE EFFECTS OF BETRAYAL

AUSTIN MACAULEY PUBLISHERS™

LONDON * CAMBRIDGE * NEW YORK * SHARJAH

A CIP catalogue record for this title is available from the British Library.

ISBN 9781528976985 (Paperback)
ISBN 9781398427730 (ePub e-book)

www.austinmacauley.com

First Published 2021
Austin Macauley Publishers Ltd
Level 37, Office 37.15, 1 Canada Square
Canary Wharf
London
E14 5AA

Table of Contents

Do not give up your dream, even if people think it is impossible, fight for it!

Hector Sanguino

In memory of all the
friends and family in my life.
May God keep their souls in heaven.

Author's Note

The author, out of respect for the privacy of the people involved, changed all names and locations where the events took place. Any resemblance to real people, events or places is just coincidence.

Prologue

This is a story based on real events, where the effects of betrayal create unending consequences, which, in both the short-term and long-term, end with vengeance.

In this emotional novel, the true story is mixed with small doses of fantasy, where, through fictional characters, the author recreates the adventures of Jorge Sotomayor and the people involved in his story.

Sotomayor's misfortune begins at the pinnacle of his profession. His fast climb as a boss augured in his life a bright future; however, in time, his life would collapse like a castle of cards. In a fatal car accident, his wife was fatally wounded, and his mother was critically wounded and only days later, would fall into a vegetative state. These circumstances forced Sotomayor to lose everything, including his morals.

His inner malice, in addition to the fatal circumstances, would bring Sotomayor to be the witness to a massacre. As this attack was unexpected, he was unable to intervene in defence of his friends; however, he was able to capture in his mobile phone, the images of their murders, which were executed by the men of Tancredo Moreira. An unknown drug trafficker at the time; he was currently making his first moves in politics, and years later, he would be destined to become a powerful politician.

Sotomayor, in his longing for financial security, is forced to go into the dark world of drug trafficking. There he establishes small drug cartels, which after a few months, he leaves in the hands of his partners. After each dissociation, he would settle in another city and begin a new cartel.

Through his charitable deeds and generosity among the poorer ones, he became well known and referred to with endearing names. Some nicknamed him "the Angel," others "Godfather," "Saint," "the Saint," or "the Monk." These pseudonyms would indirectly protect him from the harassment of Baena and Guerrero, two detectives who were obsessed to capture him. With this, Sotomayor not only managed to evade the authorities, but also managed to keep his most dangerous enemies away, who always had a very difficult time recognising him.

Another person who sometimes had the same trouble was Ludiela, Sotomayor's lover and the most beloved female mule, who was obsessed by her gambling addiction and the erotic passion burning with desire that had always made her look for him. That strong sentiment, manifested in a strange love, made her the only person able to discover him through his characters. Although on occasion when she found him despite his excellent characterisations, even she had her doubts that it was Sotomayor.

Another of the tricks of Sotomayor, which was successful was the cocaine trafficking, using 'mules' of generally old age.

'Mules', drug traffickers, who carry attached to their bodies, small amount of cocaine.

These people, after becoming popular at the borders, were responsible for smuggling in the cocaine to neighbouring countries. Their ages and the shameless way that they carried it were immune to inspection. These strategies would fill his enemies with helplessness, who were unable to kill or even just capture him. Frustrated, this would awaken in them all kinds of jealousies.

Sotomayor, wishing to avoid unexpected encounters with those hunting for him, decided to immigrate to Panama. There, through a friend, he obtained the house of fashions 'Le Fallèle' and took on a new character, Marlon de la Roca. With this, Sotomayor changed the way he sent cocaine to other countries and, from that moment, the cocaine would be smuggled by young women. However, months later, the ambition of five of these mules would betray him. These women, creating their own cartel, named 'Divas,' bravely took over Sotomayor's clients.

The modality that would be used by these women in their drug trafficking was the most extreme or dangerous, known in the mafia as 'Poisoned Mule' (because in these cases, all of them carried the cocaine inside their stomach, vagina and anus).

Weeks later, during one of their travels, the plane in which the 'Divas' were transporting cocaine was abducted by Islamic terrorists.

The overwhelming fear of Lorena, the Divas' boss and the most ambitions cartel's member, who was carrying inside her body more than two kilograms of cocaine, caused her to forget the rule disallowing her from consuming any food or drink. She, subdued by her nerves, drank two glasses of cognac, making one of the capsules camouflaged in her stomach explode. Minutes later, Lorena was overwhelmed with strong pain and quickly died. That situation provoked in the authorities an immediate reaction, with Interpol quickly working to dismantle and capture all the Divas' cartel members.

Despite this, none of these women linked to Sotomayor during the investigation. However, the detectives would eventually discover Oscar de la Roca, his secret identity.

Sotomayor became fearful of the detectives' harassment, eventually taking refuge in El Paso, a border town between Colombia and Brazil.

El Paso is an area that, due to its strategic location, Sotomayor believed was very safe for his needs because it was in the middle of the jungle, did not have a defined nationality and the best part was that it did not have any military authorities. The law there was executed by civilians who, for a period of six months, shared its administration between both countries.

These advantages ensured that Sotomayor, for the first time as a drug trafficker, established his permanent residence there. Also, at the same time, he created and purchased a company in the wood industry and started exporting to the United States. After that, with his undercover partners, he created the 'Poppy Cartel.'

Sotomayor's generosity and his contribution to the inhabitants of El Paso increased their gratitude towards Sotomayor's life, and so he was named 'the Saint,' an alias which indirectly would move him far away from his persecutors.

The robbery's coincidence with a lottery prize would make the killers sent by the Poppy Cartel to kill Manamu, the most loyal bodyguard to Sotomayor. But Zé Maria, his twin brother, and another cartel member, would discover that his brother was innocent.

That knowledge pushed him to start an investigation, finding evidence that pointed directly to Zeledon Lindarte as suspect number one. The reason of this link was because Zeledon was a businessman who, in the days that the robbery occurred, unexpectedly sold all his properties and moved away with no destination in mind. That caused Zé Maria to hunt Zeledon and his family, after assuming Zeledon is guilty.

Months later, in the city of Bahia, Sotomayor, Ludiela and the detectives, Baena and Guerrero, would be killed by order of Tancredo Moreira, a corrupt politician who thought that, with their deaths, they would take his secret to their graves. However, when he didn't find the evidence that incriminated him as the mastermind of his crimes, Tancredo discovered that it was passed into the hands of Dirceu Figuereiro, alias 'the Poet,' who was considered by Sotomayor as his best emergent man. A person by which Tancredo Moreira was willing to pay his weight in gold to the killer who could end his life. That offer provoked, in Dirceu, a death persecution that pushed him to immigrate to another country.

His strange situation eventually brought him to Toronto, Canada, where he will meet his friend Zeledon. There Dirceu would witness the drama of his friend's life, the treachery of his wife Olmeda.

Meanwhile, while Dirceu lived in the city of Toronto, he learnt through Facebook that in El Paso, his friend Fernanda had a confidential envelope for him. An envelope which Sotomayor gave to her days before his murder and ensured she promised to deliver personally to Dirceu if something unexpected were to happen to his life.

Months after his arrival to Toronto, Dirceu and Fernanda would forge their revenge against the politician. Nevertheless, it was exceedingly difficult because Dirceu had a high price on his head and needed to provide the evidence to the Brazilian prosecutor's office in Brasilia, where Tancredo's killers were searching for Dirceu, as if they were searching for needle in a haystack.

After avoiding many obstacles, Dirceu was successful. The day that he arrived, with surprise, he noticed that the director was Larissa, the woman who years back was his fiancée and the same person who, based on suspicion that Dirceu was the killer of her brother, condemned him to a degrading future, despite being innocent.

That reunion between both is to bring a great repercussion in their present life and ensured that their hidden feelings surfaced. But Dirceu's pride and Larissa's responsibility as prosecutor general in that moment, guaranteed that neither of them would initiate the first step to reconciliation. Therefore, Dirceu without options would eventually leave and lose her forever.

Months after their last meeting, Larissa, based on the pain of losing her soulmate, pushed her to resign from her position as prosecutor general of Brazil and immigrate to Canada. Her mission there was to recover Dirceu's love and start together a new life.

Sotomayor's Decisión and Falcão's Murder

Months after his mother's funeral, one afternoon while Sotomayor was watching the sunset fall, his sadness would grow worse. He knew that he wouldn't see his wife waiting for him to share dinner together, nor would he find his mother in front of the television screen focused on her favourite soap opera – an excuse which his mother told, just to stay awake until his arrival. She knew that her son didn't like to find her asleep in the old rocking chair. But that routine since months ago suddenly changed. For that reason, when Sotomayor parked his car in front of his house and got out of it, although he didn't see the house lights on, he imagined with nostalgia that his wife was waving her hands through the window.

Dejected by his memory, Sotomayor went up the entrance steps, turned the lights on and slumped heavily on the couch. He knew that it would be the last week that he would see the house standing. The house payment's deadline was coming up, and he didn't have a way to pay the debt. Therefore, the lender without a doubt would sell the house to a construction company.

At that moment, Sotomayor felt that his world had just collapsed and that everything was against him. In six months, he had been in several tragic circumstance in his life. His wife died in a car accident, which also caused fatal trauma to his mother that left her in a coma until the end of her days. And lastly but not least, an expired contract made him lose his job, ensuring that he would lose all hope. Even though his luck was against him, his desire to get his mother out of a vegetative state pushed Sotomayor to appeal to all possible resources. Optimistic that doctors could assist with his mother's recovery, he brought her to the best specialists in the country. He spent all his money, all his savings and much more that he didn't have. That's why he was left without money and with many debts to pay to the bank and his friends when his mother died.

With her death, Sotomayor began to fight the clinic expenses where his mother had spent her last months. In addition, the burial cost and other obligations acquired further complicated his situation. This eventually led him to borrow money from 'day pay' mafia loan sharks. Faster and easy help, but illegal, with high interests and extremely dangerous collection agents. As a guarantee, Sotomayor would leave the house deed, his most prized treasure.

Although the house's price for Sotomayor wasn't especially important, he did not want to lose the property. Sotomayor didn't care about the material value, but of most significance for him was the great sentimental value in where he kept his mother's memories, his childhood years, and the happiest moments beside his wife.

Without a job, the days passed faster and faster and Sotomayor couldn't pay the stipulated payments. The debts would grow more and the money that the loan shark lent wasn't able to cover the amount borrowed. So, the collection agents and hired killers began to hunt down Sotomayor.

One afternoon, Sotomayor was trying to mislead the gunmen who harassed him, and put on his face a false moustache, changed his hair colour, and wore green contact lenses. Also, he wore a dirty hat and took off the heel from his left boot. This behaviour made him look like an old lame man when he was walking; it was hugely different from the Sotomayor's image that many people knew. With his improvised disguise, he passed the collection agents and lender's gunmen, but none of them managed to recognise him. His disguise misled even his lender, to whom minutes later, Sotomayor would surprise with his character.

After a long talk between both, the lender agreed to forgive to him the interest of the debt in exchange for the furniture and house appliances. Also, the lender gave him a week more without interest to recover the house for the agreed amount. However, finding a job in less than seven days and getting all this money would be impossible for him because at that moment. Sotomayor didn't know where to go for help. He felt that he was very in debt with his friends and if he would them annoy again, it would be impertinent. He was aware that although everyone would help him, he wouldn't collect enough money to pay a part of his mortgage. For this reason, Sotomayor desperately decided to go towards the Brazil's border.

While he was there, he met with his ex-brother-in-law, who lent him some money and talked to him about a possibility of getting the rest in a few weeks if his friend, Falcão, a cocaine trafficker, accepts him as his personal bodyguard. That job option wasn't very eye-catching for Sotomayor. However, if the trafficker could lend the rest of the money, it would be the most viable attempt to recover the place of his most precious memories.

Two days later, his ex-brother-in law notified him that Falcão accepted him in his small organisation.

The good news filled Sotomayor with happiness, who, thankful for his solved problem, would exert an organised work ethic in the cartel. His accounting experience quickly won Falcão's confidence. That would quickly lead him to know through the account's books, the secret society between Tancredo Moreira and his boss Falcão.

After his first month in the organisation, Sotomayor received the loan from Falcão. With that money on his hands, Sotomayor thought he would recover his property. He was optimistic that he would get back the agreement and looked for his lender. But when he tried to pay off the debt, he would be shocked; the house already had been demolished. This sad news gave Sotomayor a blow to the head and with that, he felt that his life did not have meaning because his misfortune would condemn him to carry his sadness forever.

In the lender's office, Sotomayor took fate's evil games as something ironic because at that moment, he had the means to pay his debt, but with that money, he couldn't stop the destruction of the place where all his memories from yesterday were reposed. Although Falcão's loan in that moment was no longer necessary, Sotomayor felt that he owed a favour and decided despite the danger, continued at Falcão's service.

There in that small Cartel, as the days passed, Sotomayor learnt through his boss everything related to the quality of the drug, the easiest way to transport it and how to manage the buyers.

While Sotomayor learnt all about cocaine, in the bordering country, the election season was approaching and the political candidates in the provinces of Brazil flooded the streets and avenues with their canvas and banners painted in hundreds of colours. Each political leader, displaying their flag colour proudly, announced through criers, radio and television to have a solution for the town's problems.

That morning when the politicians' display started, Tancredo Moreira, as aspirant to the assembly of his province, during the first hour's morning, would be surprised by two phone calls one after the other.

In the first call, Falcão, his secret partner, told him that the coca crops in their chemical process had produced fifty-nine kilos of cocaine, and this would be sold the next day. For that reason, it is urgent that next Saturday they have a meeting, because they need to discuss the new cocaine price and give the share of his profits, Falcão concluded.

The other call was issued from the central office of his political party and, it wouldn't be as positive as the previous one.

In this call, the party's secretary notified him that his nomination as political candidate from that moment was cancelled, apparently due to the arbitrary way that he would solve problems and the falsity with which he intended to reach the political seat. Thus, the members of his party based on these anomalies, saw no future in him. They are in an agreement to suspend him from their campaign for two years, the party secretary informed him.

When Tancredo heard this decision, he didn't say anything, but–wouldn't accept his fate. He knew that if he accepted their verdict, he would have a premature political death, and his desire was to occupy a high rank in the government of his country. He immediately started to search for alliances and, while looking for help, he went to his corrupt colleagues and a week later, with an independent party, he would be thrown into the political world again.

From that moment, Tancredo realised that if he wanted to make it to the top, he needed to change his bad image. However, to achieve this goal, he would need to invest much more money; although he counted on the contributions from his new collaborators, he knew that this money wouldn't be enough.

The deficit kept the candidate analysing the problem. A few minutes later, he concluded that the solution was in his hands. Immediately after, he called his men and in agreement with them, he planned to kill Falcão's cartel and then, he would take the money from them. He knew that Falcão's cartel, after the cocaine was sold, would be carrying a big amount of money with them. The amount that, Tancredo supposed, was enough to cover for the deficit in his campaign.

That early Saturday morning, Tancredo and his gunmen embarked in two official vans towards their target. Once they arrived, five of the ten killers, including the politician, left the first van and waited for the arrival of the rest of their partners to go over the plan again.

After the interruption, five of them camouflaged in thick vegetation, waiting for the other partners to contact Falcão's cartel to put their plan in action.

While the gunmen Tancredo's plan in action, Falcão's escorts at the other end of the mountain still waited impatiently for the cocaine's buyers. After many encounters, it was the first time that they hadn't arrived on time. A break down in the aircraft fuel hoses would be the cause of the forty-five minutes of delay the buyer explained to them.

After a brief explanation, they reviewed the cocaine's purity in which five kilos of the fifty-nine packets would be rejected by the buyers because the cocaine didn't have the required quality.

After completing the sale, Falcão received the money and each group departed.

The buyers were worried about the unexpected weather change, so they quickly camouflaged the cocaine and left as soon as possible in their helicopter, while Falcão and his escorts, in their three Toyota Ranger vans, headed down the mountain way to their next meeting.

That morning, for their safety and trying to dodge the storm that was impending from the northern part of the firmament, Falcão ordered his men to take the south trail. Also, for the sake of better security, he ordered that the cartel's money and the impure cocaine be transported in the vehicle driven by Sotomayor. However, his last order wouldn't come to fruition, because seven kilometres arriving, Sotomayor's car tire suffered a puncture. These circumstances forced Falcão to transfer the escorts and money to a second vehicle and ordered Sotomayor to be left in charge to fix the tire as soon as possible, because he needed to be on time to Tancredo's meeting, Falcão concluded.

Fifteen minutes later, when his work was finished, Sotomayor tried to reach his companions. He accelerated his vehicle to make up for lost time. Although he hurried, he would only arrive once the meeting was almost over.

From a distance, Sotomayor noticed the two parked vans, but when he did not see his friends, he suspected that something unusual was happening. Curious by his intuition, Sotomayor camouflaged the cocaine and proceeded to investigate.

Cautiously, he crossed the forest until he was only a few metres from the meeting. At this moment, several men carrying powerful weapons and wearing ski masks came out of the thick vegetation. Initially, Sotomayor thought that these were the Tancredo's bodyguards securing the perimeter. So, he walked towards these guys without fear. However, as soon as he was about to enter the small, deforested area, he heard Tancredo asking his boss:

"Falcão, where is the five kilograms of impure cocaine?"

"In a van being driven by Sotomayor," Falcão answered.

Tancredo was disappointed to hear this and sent four of his bodyguards to intercept the vehicle and pick up the drug. This attitude in the politician seemed strange to Sotomayor who decided to hide again. Then, he took his cell phone and started filming.

Seconds later, Tancredo picked up his share of money from Falcão's hands and said goodbye to him. Immediately after his departure, the masked men that Sotomayor observed minutes before pointed their guns towards Falcão's cartel and started shooting.

The bursts of gunfire at close range quickly killed the bodyguards and Falcão.

After confirming that all were dead, the killers took off their ski masks and made a phone call to Tancredo. When he and his escort returned to the crime scene and saw the corpses, the politician was very pleased, saying:

"Very good job, guys!"

Both, the unexpected attack, and Tancredo's satisfaction was filmed on Sotomayor's mobile phone.

While the first killers' group executed a part of plan, the rest of the assassins, who were looking for Sotomayor, although found the van, returned without success.

This eventually caused Tancredo to assume that Sotomayor, the last of Falcão's bodyguards, had been a witness to the killings. Thus, all off Tancredo's men went out searching for him because they knew that he wouldn't be far away.

When Sotomayor heard that they were hunting for him, with much caution and fear, he started to flee between the thick vegetation. Unfortunately, a few minutes later, his right hand was struck by a branch, which made him drop the cell phone. The noise alerted the assassins, who focused their attack on that area. Luckily, the knowledge of the area helped Sotomayor escape. Although the assassins followed his footsteps for several hours, they couldn't reach him. So, the indignant politician ordered a bounty against Sotomayor who, fearful of an unavoidable response from Tancredo, immigrated to the other side of Brazil.

According to Sotomayor, if he escaped intact from that attack, it was because due to his wife and mother's interventions, who interceded for him from heaven. They, in advance, sent indirect signals to him and tried to move him far away from the danger. Although the signals were evident from the moment in which the house was demolished, he was overwhelmed by his worries and couldn't interpret these signals on time. Even so, these signals didn't stop there because through the threat of a storm that delayed the buyers and the tire's puncture that would prevent him to be on time, his loved ones showed from heaven that they were watching him.

Melquiades' Death

As the days passed, Tancredo Moreira demonstrated to the people around his province that he is doing good things, but on the other hand, he secretly plotted revenge against the politicians who didn't like how he approached politics. His next target would be Melquiades Duarte, president of Tancredo's former political party. His assassination was to take place one week after Falcão and his bodyguards were killed.

The three men that Tancredo put in charge would be chosen among the same killers who executed the murders of Falcão's cartel. Carrying, with them, pistols with silencers and hiding in the darkness of the night, they would cross the neighbour's garden and jump on the roof of Melquiades' residence. Then, using the latest technology from the roof, they would block the security cameras. This strategy, in a matter of minutes, would give the killers access to the interior of Melquiades' house. There, without obstacles and stealthy like felines, they started to check room by room, murdering the occupants. With that silent and effective action, the killers made sure that they didn't leave witnesses.

Minutes later, the group's leader made a call to his boss and assured him that the politician's traitor, his wife, the housekeeper and his two bodyguards were dead.

The man on the other side of the line, in an attempt to avoid repeating the same mistake of the previous massacre, ordered them to search the mansion again from the basement to the attic. With this precaution, Tancredo wanted to prevent any kind of surprise.

After twenty minutes of searching, the group's leader proceeded to make a second call. With much confidence, he assured him that everything was under control. Immediately in response, the man on the other end of the line asked him, "Are you sure?"

"Of course, Mr Moreira. From tonight, Melquiades will no longer be an impediment to your future negotiations because we shut his mouth forever," the group's leader confirmed again.

Tancredo reminded them to take from them all valuables, as well as their cell phones and not to forget to plunder the safe deposit box, which was behind the imitation Picasso picture. With that, according to Tancredo's thinking, the authorities would be certain that the motives of their murders were related with a robbery.

However, their mission, although seemed perfect for them, had left two loose ends.

The first, a mobile phone that one of the victims, a few second before his death dropped and it slipped under the sofa without his murderer noticing it.

The second was a pest exterminator who was in the residence's attic, looking inside the ventilation because of a strange noise that, according to the homeowner, kept them from sleeping in the mornings.

That night, the exterminator, having located the burrow and stationing himself between the space of the first floor and the attic, put the traps and waited patiently for the furtive guests to arrive. The man was so focused on his task that he could hear clearly what was happening on the main floor. His ears at that moment caught the footsteps of some people who, through the window terrace, entered very stealthily into the house.

Moments after their interruptions, the exterminator could hear the sounds when the bodies of the victims, one by one, heavily fell to the ground, dragging in agony to death, several objects around each of them.

As the sudden sounds were unexpected, it alarmed the exterminator somewhat.

His true fear started when, from a distance, he heard a conversation in which the group's leader assured to the unknown person on the phone that all the occupants of the house had been eliminated. This phrase made him realise that something very serious was happening. For that reason, the exterminator immediately turned off his mobile phone. Then, very cautiously, he searched through the ventilation channel for the piece of pressed wood or ceiling tile quadrant by where he was entering. This piece was placed a few metres behind him, as he could pass the wood's piece from that side to the other end. There, very gently from inside the ventilation's surface channel, he screwed and tried to hide the evidence that was inside.

The killers' boss, when he entered the kitchen and noticed the patch on the ceiling, tried to verify why that wood's piece was placed in the opposite way. However, when he tried to move the quadrant, he realised that it was adjusted, but he didn't think that from inside, someone had been listening to the entire incriminating conversation.

During his minutes of panic, the exterminator heard a conversation again when the murderers' leader, through his mobile phone, once again called his boss stating in a very relaxed voice:

"Mr Moreira, don't be worried about anything, with the jewels, mobile phones, money and the weapons, we will certainly fool the authorities."

Immediately after finishing their short talk, the killers one by one left the mansion and went to the Rose's Zone of the municipality, where they would find a supposed guilty person.

With the killers' departures, the house was very calm. After one and a half hours of terror, normality had returned. Regardless, the exterminator didn't move for a few minutes more because he wanted to be sure that the assassins hadn't noticed his presence.

With his nerves under control, the exterminator thought for a moment to use a public telephone to report the situation to the authorities. However, when he went down and saw the five corpses on the floor, he was afraid to call the police. He knew that if he made a call, he would reveal his name, and those who had murdered these people would try to keep him quiet forever. At that moment, his instinct to survive would lead him to erase all the evidence that indicated that he had been in the mansion.

The fact that the exterminator didn't know about the security camera made him think that his measures be successful.

After placing the ceiling block back correctly, he cleaned his tracks and put his cup in pocket where he had previously taken coffee, then he searched for the mobile phones to erase the recorded messages that he had sent to his employer Melquiades that early evening. However, this would not be possible, since supposedly all the phones were stolen.

Under those circumstances, the exterminator decided that the best option was to keep the secret and decided to flee. He chose to confuse the prosecutors.

Twelve hours after the murders at the Melquiades house, the continuous calls to her boss without answer alarmed his secretary who was very worried and gave a warning to the authorities. With her call, the police would be present to verify what is happening. When they got access into the mansion and discovered the corpses, the restricted the area and called the prosecutor's office.

Because the crime occurred at a border town, the investigators in charge were detectives Baena and Guerrero.

They immediately arrived at the scene of the crime and began to collect the evidence. When they finished their inspection, everything according to the detectives pointed to a robbery. A job of professionals, since the killers hadn't left witnesses nor any trace that would incriminate them. In addition, the ballistics tests informed them that the cartridges of calibre ten millimetres found at the scene of the crime were from illegal weapons, because the ammunition was prohibited in the country. Despite this, they had to find something that would put them on track to the killers. They began with the medical examiner, who determined that the deaths had occurred between 9:30 pm and 10 pm the day before.

Until that moment, the evidence that Baena and Guerrero had in their hands was very little. They only had the records from the security cameras, where they could see a man with a motorcycle without licence plate, wearing a wide hat and a terrible coverall and carried a medium suitcase on his shoulder.

The man was greeted by Melquiades' bodyguards who, through the back door of the garage, gave him access to the mansion. He arrived at 8 pm, but the video didn't show if this man left before 9:45 pm or after because during that time, the security cameras suffered a malfunction and stopped recording.

The detectives, thus, assumed that this person must have been inside of the house minutes after the murders, but that was just an estimation.

The track on which they focused was not very forceful, and although the video showed the suspect, in that moment, it would be impossible to recognise his face due to his large hat, which was covering his face. Hoping for a positive outcome, the detectives continued to search for any possible evidence. Baena picked up the house phone and concentrated on the messages from weeks ago. Minutes later, he would find the following voicemail.

"Mr Duarte, it's the exterminator. I wanted to tell you that I cannot come this week. But I will be there next Sunday the 23rd, at 8 pm," the man said.

Immediately after Baena listened to the voicemail, he searched for the phone number of the person who had left the message. However, seconds later, he would be disappointed because the call was made from a public phone.

On the other hand, Guerrero would have more luck, because after reviewing thoroughly under the old sofa, he found a mobile phone from one of the victims. In this phone, it had registered a dozen calls made by Melquiades' secretary and a text message without answer sent that Sunday night, at 8:57 pm. The message said the following words: *Mr Duarte, the causes of the noise during the early hours weren't from rats as you thought. The noise came from a couple of raccoons who are making their burrow at the end of the attic.*

While Baena and Guerrero found this evidence, a drug addict who was sleeping in the area close to the Melquiades' house was astonished to finding his dirty backpack with a great sum of money, jewels, mobile phones and two pistols. Arrogant for his luck, the drug addict took a bundle of bills and put them in his pockets. Then, he walked towards the most expensive restaurant in the area. When he attempted to enter the restaurant door, the security guards obstructed his entrance.

"Sorry, sir, but you cannot enter because this is a private place, just for executives and businessmen," they said.

The drug addict reacted with anger, pulling out from his dirty pockets a bundle of bills, proudly showing his money to them.

"I don't care! I will pay for everyone inside the restaurant," the drug addict answered.

"Sorry, sir, but you are not allowed to be here regardless," the security said again.

After the rejection, the drug addict became furious. Still under the effects of drugs, he took a pistol with a silencer from his backpack and began to shoot without any control. Unable to control the weapon, in less than one minute, he unloaded all the fifteen shots around his feet.

Afterwards, the unharmed guards subdued the man and handed him to the police, who would inevitably find in his belongings, a backpack with many things stolen from somewhere. However, during his interrogation, he swore to God that he never participated in any kind of robbery and that these objects mealy appeared in his baggage, as if it were magic trick; the drug addict insisted on this again and again.

After collecting the evidence, the police proceeded to analyse the pistol's serial number, indicating to them that the weapon was not official and less, it belonged to a legal military force.

When the police finished interrogating the drug addict, the detectives were notified by the police about the situation and the man would be taken to the Melquiades' house, where, after being questioned by Baena, the addict's innocence would be confirmed.

His responses and the guards' reports corroborated that his innocence was very evident because the instant in which the gun had been fired by him, the force of the shots had dominated his arm and that inexperience confirmed to Baena that the suspect had never in his life pulled the trigger of a gun.

The detective pointed out that this was a planned strategy by the true culprits to divert the investigation, because the work done at Melquiades' house was undoubtedly executed by professionals, Baena concluded.

Hours later, with the number that appeared on the mobile phone screen found by Guerrero; the detectives knew that the message was sent from a mobile phone registered by the name of Gustavo Espino. Based on that information, they initiated a search to locate his residence, but it wouldn't be enough, because when they arrived at the Gustavo's address, they were surprised to find that the man and his two small children had recently undertaken a trip, according to his neighbours.

Until that moment, all evidence pointed to Gustavo as either an accomplice, eyewitness or a possible assassin. But this man, with no criminal history against him, dedicated to his extermination job, a widower with two young children, didn't have the profile of a hired killer. They didn't have any doubt that he was a key witness to protect. Thus, in front of the press, the detectives omitted knowing of his existence, because any suspicious comment about him would seal his fate.

Regardless, they had to find him to be able to clarify the truth, and the best way to do it was to place a search against him, where they would accuse him as the killer of his wife.

Although they both knew that this was a false accusation, since his wife's death was caused by cancer, they also knew this was the safest option in order to protect him.

Days later, after analysing their other options, the detectives proposed a link with the crime to the politician, Tancredo Moreira, because weeks before, this politician had been fired by Mr Duarte's political party; thus, he would have motive. However, this was just a hypothesis without evidence to support it, and so the detectives brushed off their theory, since the suspect was a very influential person and was already being investigated by their colleagues in Brazil. Besides that, he was out of their jurisdiction and, without an order, they couldn't intervene in that case anyway.

While the detectives confirmed Gustavo's presence at the scene of the crime, he and his two minor children, Raul, and Juliana, arrived at the North Brazilian border. There, under a false identity, they settled in the municipality of El Paso, where the three supposedly would begin a new life.

The Preliminary Investigation and My Meeting with the Monk

Twenty-five days after Falcão and his bodyguards were killed, their relatives complained about their strange disappearances, causing the SIB (Intelligence Service of Brazil) to order their secret agents, Vinicio Braga and I, Dirceu Figuereiro, to initiate the investigation about their vanishings.

According to all of them, the facts pointed to a possible massacre.

The morning that we were notified about this case, we were celebrating together with Larissa, my fiancée, our wedding engagement, and her promotion as regional director of public prosecutions. The party, between our colleagues and friends that night, was very short for us. That's why we extended the party until early morning of the following day, and we continued enjoying with too much euphoria. But this immense joy would be eradicated by the fateful news. From a long time ago, at the border, a disappearance wouldn't happen of this magnitude.

That day, while we were feeling the hangover effects touring our bodies, we introduced ourselves to the SIB chiefs. There, they annexed the primary report and the statements obtained from their relatives' complaints to our file, where they confirmed that a month ago, in the town of Tabatinga, an area between Brazil and Colombia, was the last time that they saw the men alive.

They all confessed in their declaration that these people were linked to drug trafficking, and all seven were working for a small drug trafficker named Falcão, who was also included as missing. In addition to the vital information, the declarants provided the photographs of their relatives to the SIB and they proposed their own theories. According to them, the motive of their disappearance was a robbery because in talks with his relatives' days before, they warned that, in this area, due to the ambition from other cartels, it was necessary to be under maximum alert in order to protect the money from the cocaine sale.

After the information was collected, we analysed the motives of these alleged disappearances and compared these with the murders occurred on the other side of the Brazilian border with the Duarte family and their employees. The similarities between these events made us concluded that the same people were involved in both assassinations.

Hours after receiving written statements by complainants, we began the search around a rural zone in that municipality. In that same day, we obtained information on the vans in which the deceased were mobilized. These vans were found hundreds of kilometres away from the village, covered by tree branches at the bottom of a cliff.

As the surrounding farmers mentioned, we knew that days ago in the glen, a great shooting occurred, and that date coincided with the disappearance of Falcão and his bodyguards.

The circumstantial evidence led us to the place where the massacre supposedly had been carried out; hundreds of ten-millimetre cartridges, dispersed on the spot and bullets embedded in the trees, confirmed our theory.

As we advanced in the investigation, Tancredo Moreira was back in the province's capital. Knowing that we were investigating the murders, he started to plan a trap for us with anticipation. The trap that he started with a supposed local labourer, who very convincingly told us that he had seen, several weeks ago, armed men digging a great pit in a mountain point known as El Mineirão, a small village located almost ten kilometres of the population of Ipiranga.

Based on their story, we arrived at the place. After entering the most mountainous part of the terrain, I felt a small prick in the neck.

Seconds later, a heavy sleep began, and during my drowsiness, I watched as my companion collapsed. When I woke up from the sedative effect, a sharp pain in my chest warned me that I was injured. Exhausted by the blood loss, I slowly inclined my head and, as soon as I turned around, I saw myself with my pistol in my right hand and, besides my body, there was a backpack full of money. As well as this, I saw my colleague and brother-in-law, Vinicio, dying on the ground. He was severely wounded and died within seconds of his awakening.

At that moment, the police arrived and from their location, they ordered me, to throw the pistol far from my hands. Upon their request, they proceeded to lift our bodies, and we were taken to the hospital of the municipality.

In their report, the police would notify my bosses the cause of my detention. According to them, I had murdered my colleague because I tried to keep the money from the blackmail, which I supposedly received from the person that we were investigating that day, because when I recovered from the wounds, the Internal Affairs officers of the SIB already had done their investigation and they had new evidence that condemned me. Among them, an amount in my savings account of 500 million of cruzados, and a video from weeks ago where I was coming out of the bank with a bulky luggage. Conspiracy that, for them, was the biggest proof of my culpability.

The evidence led them to suspend me for six months and, as a security measure, l would be detained until they finished the investigation.

On the other hand, during their investigation, the forensic team would find proof of my innocence because of the high doses of chloroform found in our blood tests, showing them that we had been wounded after the drug's somniferous effects. Another piece of evidence in my favour was that they didn't find gunpowder samples on my left or right hands, ultimately disproving the Internal Affairs Office charges against me as the killer. In addition to that, the date that appeared in the video, showed that it was a montage, because that day at the same time, I was in the director's office, receiving an honourable mention for my excellent work as a researcher. Under those circumstances, I was declared innocent and returned to my work. Despite this, my colleagues and girlfriend, sister of the deceased, didn't believe in my innocence. That led me to move away from the institution and turn my life into a real chaos for eighteen months.

The crisis of losing the woman that I loved and the contempt of my co-workers lead me to the world of antidepressants, drugs and alcohol. However, that disappointment later would give me something positive, because without thinking, the alcohol filled me with emotion and made my mind create phrases of romanticism mixed with spite that would turn into poetry. At that moment, exclaiming stanzas such as these whenever I would be drunk, I thought would soothe pain in my soul.

I remembered the first part of this poem dedicated to Larissa that I started one morning while I was at home, sad and sober. My thoughts took me to the cupboard, from where I extracted a bottle of liquor and drank a shot, which turned into continuous drinks one after the other. Once under the effects of alcohol, I took a sheet of my notebook and began to write.

With this first stanza, I wanted to say to Larissa that her departure would cause my death, since it never crossed by my mind that at some point, she would think of leaving me, and since I knew that her journey would have no return, with her farewell, I would die just as the sun that will die with the afternoon, because in the prison of her love, she would imprison my heart, with shackles tied to a passion that runs through my blood and doomed to the memory of the last kiss, which like a bonfire still burns on my lips.

With her abandonment, I knew that the sun will be hidden, and at night, the stars will stop shining, and if she could ask the moon, what is the cause of my sadness? The moon would be shaking her base and would answer her, "Because you're abandoning him! And your absence will cause his death!"

The moon, very worried, would also say to her, "Understand that leaving him would be just like taking his life, because from that wound he would never recover, since in his heart you will leave a dagger that, little by little, would start to kill him. With that dagger in his heart, he would be a few steps into the abyss, in the deepest of a maze without an exit. And during that chaos, he would struggle to get up, because his optimism is dying, consumed by your memory.

"If he gave you everything from his life and with love, he made castles near the sea, he thought that he would be your king and you, the queen, who from her balcony, would dominate his kingdom.

"I don't know, if this was a little bit or a lot, but all that he had in his life, he wanted to put at your feet and create with illusion, a thousand ways to love you.

"However, the dreams that he placed on your hands, would die as leaves when fall from tree. With that, destiny showed him, how sad his ending would be.

"Because with your departure, you would leave him alone and without hope, condemned to the flames of the bonfire, living only of longing, and remembering his years of spring, observing with sadness that in dry leaves very soon his tree will remain. If you killed his joy with your falsehood and, turned in a chimera, that dream that he thought would last an eternity.

"Today that you have decided to leave, he will try not to cry, although he will drown with his tears and his blood in his veins will stop circulating. However, he knows that when you start your journey, you can never reach him because his tears would increase the sea level, and in its waters, he will be shipwrecked, since with your departure, without a doubt will mark the end because if you are not here, his life is like a mirror in the darkness."

In about four hours of thinking about her, there was not much that I would capture, but it was enough to drink the contents of some bottles of rum until I fell asleep from the drunkenness.

The next day, as soon as I woke up, I started to formulate poetry. Wanting to express with verses all that suffering that was carried in my soul, I continuous expressing like as moon, and I wrote a second stanza.

Second Stanza

"Even through his pain, he wants you to be happy forever, he doesn't care that your happiness means his pain and insomnia for many days. And it wouldn't surprise me, if during this agony, his heart tired from so much suffering, could stop beating at dawn. In the moment that his dreams died, you would cut the illusion of being together forever.

"For your love, although he did all the impossible, it wasn't possible to stop you, since your love was consumed like water in the desert. With your decision, you would leave him to starboard and in the middle of a storm, so when he saw the ship without a helmsman, his heart would break into a thousand pieces.

"But his pain wouldn't disturb the feelings that he carries inside, and he will always be thinking of the best desire for you. However, seeing that you are not there, he will realize that, without you, he had nothing, and it will be like a rainbow without colours, an oasis in the middle of the sun, or like a spring without the aroma of the flowers. Your memories are so impregnated in all the things that you have left him, that even the roses in his garden feel your abandonment and with your departure, all of them have wilted.

"This sadness is so great that, he caused with his walking the echo in the mountain that silences his voice and made the nightingale fill with the feeling of his pain, turning its cheerful sing into a moan."

The moon, sad about his suffering, asked her:

"What will he do about his sorrow? If in the end nothing that he did for you was worth it, since in its summer till the swallows were confused. Those that made nests beside his tree, waiting to see its flowers to continue their travel, however, only autumn would come, and all of them would die, waiting for his spring."

I remember that to make the third part of this poem was easy, since drinking, and writing during my drunkenness became routine. This meant that in the first days of my pity, it did not only cloud my mind with alcohol, but also, it emanated the inspiration to do the third stanza, a stanza that based in the moon thought started with her name.

Third Stanza

"Larissa, because you are far, you cannot see that with your goodbye, his eyes were reflecting sorrow that, till the mountains, purple flowers were sprouted for him. Of black would the lilies' leaves be dyed, and all the carnations' buds would die with the dew of the morning. Same as these, he will also die of thirst, as a shipwreck in the middle of an immense sea, full of memories.

"That is why, sometimes many people see life as unjust and carried away by the passions of the heart, they didn't realise that love is beautiful and think of death as a way out. Regardless, I know your absence will cause the same in him, because from this moment, his heart will stop beating. Because without you, he will be living on as a mere grain of sand lost in the desert, like a sun that is hidden from noon, like a phonic singer in the middle of a concert, like a fictional story without fantasy!

"But in the meantime, he will continue to wander with his grief, tormented by your memories and just making castles in the air. Because you took possession of his joy and without him thinking to join his heart to your passion, is a prisoner in your love jail. And although he reproaches you and condemns you, he still waits for you to return his love, since believing in your lies has left him empty-handed. That is why, he is afraid of beginning the night and not seeing the light of a new day. This feeling has made him a coward, who is afraid to open his heart, because it is full of memories, that just speak about your love."

As my crisis became bigger, my soul was overwhelmed by my feelings of yesterday, and would continue from the depths emanating the sad phrases that hurt me. During those moments inspired by my nostalgia, my poetry became more extensive, by which, in a poetic way I would relate the chronology of my suffering based on the moon's thoughts and finished my pity, with the following stanzas.

Second Last Stanza

"I know that you do not understand that even in his soul, the fire of his passion for you still burns with great intensity that even in its ashes, you can make a great bonfire. And as he knows that you have a heart of stone, when hearing its lament, you will not feel any pain. Even though your pride will have to prostrate to his bed, but that attitude will be for him a passing illusion, a summer that died when the last flower falls. Dry leaves that will drag the wind without any direction.

"At the beginning, all for him was like a colour of rose, he never thought that with summer's arrival, the rose would wither. Because with your departure, you left him, like a fish aground in the sand that is slowly dying while the fisher enjoys his condemnation.

My inspiration in those days didn't stop; the pain that emanate from my soul would feed my mind, and the alcohol would feed my body. These two mixtures would give to me the force to still be alive. However, sensing that my end was close, I wrote down in these verses, what I considered to be the last part of the poem.

Last Stanzas

"Today because you don't see him cry, you are thinking that he is feeling better. But as his eyes can emanate more tears even after having cried so much, yesterday he shed so many tears to comfort his pain that the rivers were overflowed because of it.

"However, the tears that his eyes sprout today, are stained with blood that sprout because they are going to die like the sun at dusk. His disconsolate heart knows that your absence will be too great, because with your departure, you showed him that your love was just a fraud. And though his soul continues spoiled by your forgetfulness, he will recognise that in those days, a good thing and sad thing had happened. The good thing from his past, was to know you, but the sad thing of the present, would be lose you.

The moon without doubt, would say to her, "I know that you, wherever you go, will think that he is very happy, since you don't distinguish the feeling between love and falsehood. You don't know how hard it is for him to live without you because day after day, he is consumed by his solitude. And although with the loneliness the body never dies, he recognises that his soul is buried and the person who lives in the middle of that superficial calm, is the same as being dead. But, when he cannot welcome you, it will make you an incredibly sad woman, since when you returned you will find him lifeless. Due to that, you will feel a wound in the heart, and you are crying for him will double, one for your pain and another for his departure, since when you want to find him, you will know that this minstrel was reduced to ashes. Then, your eyes will cry, and your cynical smile will be erased from your face. Because you will no longer find the debris of his body, nor his sorrows, nor his *laughter, since all your memories with him were carried away by the breeze," the moon concluded.*

By declaiming these stanzas of sadness wherever I arrived, I converted my verses into poetry and because of the feeling with which I interpreted them, I was nicknamed 'the Poet,' a pseudonym by which many people would know me.

While the spite was evolving my life, Sotomayor became the most sought-after unknown drug trafficker on the border. His need to outwit the persecutors led him to create his own characters and small cartels, which after a few months would be dismantled and then he would settle in another city with a new character so that his enemies wouldn't be able to find to him. But even with his cunning plans, Sotomayor knew that he lacked a person to trust; someone who would secretly keep him informed of what was happening around him.

That weakness in his structure and the fact that we had the same enemy in common would lead him to seek an alliance with me, and although at the time of his arrival, I was in a great depressive crisis, he knew all the things about my past and saw me as the ideal person to carry out this kind of work for him.

That day, hours before Sotomayor found me, I had ingested Valium and ethyl alcohol because, when the 'Monk,' a pseudonym with which Sotomayor was known as in the commune found me, I, the Poet would be doped and in the middle of a convulsion caused by the mixed effects of the two substances.

Under Sotomayor's order, I was immediately taken out of the dump and taken to a specialist clinic in the centre of the city. There, in two months, psychologists and toxicologists stripped me of addiction, and I recovered from the psychological trauma and would learn from that moment to see life differently.

After my treatment, I was discharged and walked towards the outside the clinic to start a new life. That afternoon, the Monk was waiting for me at the clinic's entrance. When I saw him again, with the intention to express my gratitude, I walked with him to his car. When I wanted to do it, he clarified me with much optimism:

"Do not worry, Poet, that helping you was in my plans," he said.

Intrigued by his words, I got into the car and asked:

"So, my meeting with you wasn't a coincidence?"

"No," the Monk answered, "because I have been looking for you, since the day you stopped looking for me," the Monk confirmed.

His answer confused me even more. So, I asked a new question.

"What was the reason that you were searching for me?"

Sotomayor showed a small smile and replied:

"My determination to find you was because I know of you and the excellent work that you did as an agent of the SIB, and I need a person with those qualities to exercise a secret watch over my surroundings. If you accept the proposal, you will have money, vehicles and armed men at your disposal. In addition, I would give you the possibility of revenge on those who placed the trap, where Vinicio appeared dead, as well as the person who stipulated the order of the murder," Sotomayor said.

Astonished, I asked, "How can I get revenge on them if I have no idea who they were?"

"Easy," Sotomayor said, "and even better, you will not have the need to look for them. They will come to your hands looking for me, because the assassins who mowed down the life of your partner Vinicio, are part of the same group that is hunting me. Their obsession is to eliminate me because I was an eyewitness to the murder of Falcão and his escorts. We both have the same enemy in common, and both of you and I are obliged to avenge both deaths."

After few seconds of silence, I asked a new question:

"Of the disappeared bodyguards, who are you?"

"I am Jorge Sotomayor," he responded.

When I heard his name in amazement, I exclaimed:

"But your appearance is nothing like the man I was looking for!"

"You are right," Sotomayor told me. "However, thanks to my characters, I have managed to mislead the harassment of the authorities and the persecution from Tancredo Moreira, the mastermind of the murders mentioned."

Knowing the name of the person who caused my misfortune comforted my soul and, under that circumstance, I accepted the alliance with Sotomayor. Once the agreement was reached, we both arrived at a parking lot, where he handed me the keys to a pickup truck and, inside of it, there was enough money to buy everything I needed, including security personnel. With them under my command, five days later, a secret service agency would be installed in the commune, working exclusively for the Monk.

Baena's Failures

After several months of following the footsteps of her lover, the tiredness was evident in her eyes. Even though Ludiela wanted to keep going, she knew that she was close to her goal to find Sotomayor. The only impediment was transportation; although she had her own vehicle, she had decided to leave it in a parking lot of the city. It wasn't advisable to reach the dangerous commune by driving a BMW sport car; it would be more viable to take a taxi. However, when she looked at her watch, Ludiela noticed that it read 9:30 pm, the deadline for someone to rush to the commune. As the minutes passed, Ludiela's hope started to vanish, and her situation became more difficult.

In her eagerness to achieve to get transportation, Ludiela had already requested the service of several taxi drivers, who, upon hearing the address, immediately refused to transport her to her destination. Invaded by her anxiety, she made one final attempt. Moments after her call, the taxi parked outside and Ludiela without knowing if the driver would take her, opened the back door, and got into the vehicle.

"Where is the lady going?" the taxi driver asked.

"To the club in the East Commune," she replied without hesitate.

The young woman's response made the taxi driver a little nervous, since it was after ten o'clock at night, an hour which only someone in very much need would take such a risk.

At that moment, although Ludiela was talking to the right person, the driver thought for a few seconds about the trip. Trying to evade her, he warned her that the place at that hour is very dangerous. However, the taxi driver after contemplating his economic crisis that he is going through at that moment decided to take advantage of the situation of his client and offered to take her but only to the main street of the commune, under a condition of receiving triple pay and being paid in advance. Ludiela accepted the condition without protest.

Immediately as the taxi arrived at its destination, Ludiela left the vehicle and was guided by the sound of the music that she was hearing from the distance, which directed her steps to reaching her objective. Not even five minutes of her walk had passed when two men, pointing their pistols, came towards her with the intention of raping her.

With their left hands, they clung to her throat, making it impossible for Ludiela to scream. She was defenceless, and they pushed her against the wall and began to caress her private parts. But from one moment to the next, when the criminals had her under their control, they liberated her and started to run, as if they had seen the devil.

Ludiela was surprised and turned her head, and from a distance, she observed four people: among them was the man nicknamed 'The Godfather.' Although his physiognomy and tone of voice were quite different from the man that she was looking for, she had no doubt that it was Sotomayor.

Moments after having rescued her from the clutches of his attackers, one of her saviours took Ludiela by the shoulders and brought her to a private vehicle that would take them to the nightclub. There, after a few minutes, when she and her saviour was alone, Ludiela, loaded with questions, went to strip the Godfather of his disguise. Ludiela, with the certainty of not being in wrong, clasped him in her arms.

Minutes after their passionate hug, an allergic reaction over the Sotomayor's body started from the perfume that Ludiela would leave on his skin. That unease, accompanied by continuous sneezing and strong nasal congestion, would be confused with the symptoms of a cold.

Sotomayor, somewhat disconcerted by the interruption of the moment, smiled a smile that was combined with sarcasm and joy. The mixture of these two attitudes was because the emotion that Sotomayor felt at that time. Because Ludiela, besides being his ex-trafficker and drug mule, was also his favourite lover and the only person who, in all his false identities, had been able to follow his footsteps and discover his true personality. With that virtue in her, ironically, life showed Sotomayor that he wasn't as cunning as he believed.

He acknowledged that, thanks to Ludiela's obsession, he had, on more than one occasion, frustrated his pursuers and avoided his capture, since Ludiela's presence was an indicator that the detectives and Tancredo Moreira's paid killers weren't too far from him.

After Sotomayor's allergic reaction, Ludiela took a shower and, from the bath, went out wrapped in a tiny towel, which, in front of Sotomayor, fell from her body as if it was magic, leaving the intimate parts in the open. Then followed by kisses and caresses, they ended up in bed.

After a passionate labour of sex, where the two satiated their bodies with pleasure until exhaustion, Sotomayor understood that to manage and control the high erotic voltage in Ludiela, he needed to resort to certain sexual supports.

Because of his adrenaline, Sotomayor remained active and awake while Ludiela, defeated by fatigue, would be in a deep sleep.

At that moment, Sotomayor took advantage of the circumstances and left, on the bed, a bag full of money and the property title under her full name, and also left a note talking about his passion for her, which, according to him, was comparable with the blood that circulated in his veins. But even though he wanted her so much, he had to get away from her again, since he didn't want Tancredo Moreira to pursue or hurt her for revenge.

In the rest of his notes, he explained to her that the purpose of the donation was to keep her occupied for a while. He knew well that, in a month at the latest, her addiction to gambling, the need for easy money and her memories would awaken her obsession of him, and again, she would begin to look for him. Because of this, the Godfather, in the final part of the paragraph, advised her not to look for him again, since the next time she wouldn't have the same luck. For this reason, he recommended that she manage the property and the money carefully and not to worry about their origins, as they were acquired totally legally.

That warning, stipulated by Sotomayor in his note, would cause an opposite effect in Ludiela, and more than some advice, she would take it as a challenge.

The departure of her benefactor would leave Ludiela very sad and quite worried. She thought that, since the Godfather wasn't around, she would be at the mercy of the common delinquency that operated in the sector, but she was wrong, since Sotomayor would not abandon her to her fate. In fact, he left me in charge of protecting her in secret.

A week after the sudden visit of Ludiela, the commune would be besieged by a military convoy. I remembered that on this day, while the military provided security, the detectives started their search.

That Wednesday December 31st, camouflaged in the darkness of the night, each military group was assigned a task.

As silent as felines, they interrupted the bustle in the commune, with a unit of detectives, led by Baena, stormed the club in search of Sotomayor, alias 'the Godfather,' a nickname that was extremely popular in this place because to almost all infants there, Sotomayor was their godfather.

During the military harassment, the club was filled with customers. Some danced to the rhythm of reggaetón, while others in the bar were relieving the stress of the week.

Among these, there were several impatient drunks, waiting for the clock to mark midnight to go out and receive the New Year with shots to the air.

At the other end of the nightclub in the DJ booth, current owner of the club, Ludiela, was stricken by her memories. As soon as the year's end approached, she looked sadly into the distance, and the first image that come to her mind was Sotomayor. At that moment, her wish was to be beside him and start the New Year together. As Ludiela and all the people there waited the farewell bustle for the old year. When they heard the sudden sound of shots, they confusingly assumed it was the welcome to the New Year. But a deep voice with a military tone made them fall into reality.

Immediately after, the military personnel ordered all of them to lie flat on the ground.

Instantly after his demand, dozens of detectives, with guns in their hand, interrupted the atmosphere of celebration and proceeded to check, one by one, the customers inside the club.

After completing an exhaustive search, the prosecutors found several criminals among patrons who called themselves by the aliases 'the Monk' and 'the Godfather.' Hearing this at first made the prosecutors happy, as these were the same appellations that the people who knew to Sotomayor had given him during his initial stages of drug trafficking.

Following these characters, Baena and his second in command, Detective Guerrero, had begun searching for him years ago. However, when they investigated the people under arrest, the detectives found that none were the real Sotomayor, the person for who the operation was carried out to find. Unfortunately for them, days before, Sotomayor had dismantled his previous cartel and settled with a new character, in another city.

The detectives, with no other options, focused on Ludiela, trying to pin her to something illegal; nevertheless, they didn't find any irregularities regarding the property ownership. Because of that, they gave up their attempt but didn't remove her from their list of suspects.

At the confirmation of her innocence, Sotomayor's secret man would communicate to him what had happened.

When Sotomayor listened to the details, he ordered me to move away from the commune and wait for his call. He knew from experience that, after what had occurred, Ludiela had found the perfect excuse to sell the place and without doubt, she would waste all the money at the casino.

With the frustrating raid, Detective Baena and his partner, Detective Guerrero, added a new failure to the long list of attempts of capturing Sotomayor. But even though their faces, at that moment, didn't look disappointed, they hoped that at their next pursuit would achieve their goal. They would follow his footsteps, and, despite the misfortune, they wouldn't give up.

Simultaneously with the new frustration of the two detectives, hundreds of miles away, Sotomayor was creating a new character and making contacts to start a new cartel.

After finding the people that he was looking for, 'the Angel' became the new nickname of Sotomayor, and he entrusted his contacts with the task of finding a shelter where he could rest safely for a while.

Twenty-four hours after the Angel's request, his new partners, with the acquisition of El Oasis farm, gave the solution to them boss' needs.

That afternoon, when Sotomayor received the location of his future refuge, he was filled with nostalgic memories since that area was where he began his footsteps as a drug trafficker, and he knew the place like the back of his hand. That advantage was going to be another point for him against his pursuers. But although this building was a strategic site for the Angel's purpose, it would be necessary for his partners to construct a refuge inside that would provide them with a secure place in the event of an attack by the authorities, because his new partners, Richard and Eric, recommended for him to stay in the capital for forty-five days longer at least.

Because of that commitment, his two new partners, leading a group of men, would do something that, months later, would put them directly in the hands of Detectives Baena and Guerrero.

That morning, Eric, Richard and several of their escorts, in pursuit of their goal, left in two vans towards to the dam construction.

They arrived close to the dam in the hours of dusk and at the precise moment when a heavy downpour started to fall.

Their goal at that time was to intercept one of the vehicles driven by the workers returning from the city. Then, Sotomayor's partners would kidnap its occupants and would take them to the El Oasis farm.

With that intention, they hid themselves together with the vans in a shortcut of the road. There, stealthily, they waited until they confirmed that the two first vehicles we were moving away.

Clear to proceed, they proceeded to intercept the last of the vehicles. As they made their attempt, the driver of the third vehicle, when seeing the vans were beginning to drive off course and reversing, had no choice but to break suddenly to avoid an accident. This action alarmed the passengers in the truck, who were with the vehicle covered by the tent, making it impossible to observe what was happening.

Intrigued by the situation, the engineer and his six workers stepped off the vehicle one by one. As they went down, they were captured by a group of men who, during the heavy rain, forced them inside their vans.

Seconds after the abduction, they were subjected to an inspection had their communication devices seized and finally, would have their faces covered with black bags.

Then, they kidnapped the workers, who thought that it was a reprisal of the guerrilla against the construction company for refusing to pay the *vaccine*, 'the taxes that companies must pay to local illegal gangs.' Based on their assumptions, the engineer and the workers began to beg.

They explained to their captors that they were simply subcontractors, practically regular workers, and so they had very little relationship with the company's top officials, so their abductions wouldn't cause the construction company any negative effect.

Nevertheless, despite their pleas and attempts to clarify their situation, the kidnappers didn't seem to change their attitude. Without further options, the eight workers left their liberation in the abductors' hands.

Richard, the kidnappers' leader, chose the truck driver from the group and put him inside the cabin, and then handcuffed his hands against a plastic door handle. After confirming that he was well tied, he retreated to the front of the vehicle, raised the hood, and detached the power distributor from the engine, throwing it down the mountain.

Richard and Eric's vans were ready, so they left with the abductees for the El Oasis farm. As they drove away, the handcuffed driver inside the vehicle redoubled his efforts to break the plastic handle.

After some time, he achieved his goal and, although he continued with his hand's chains, he was free to walk wherever he wanted.

At that moment, the driver had two options: to take the road by foot to the nearest village, which was about twenty kilometres away or continue to the dam construction. Without thinking too much, he leaned towards the most viable possibility and began a long journey on foot.

After walking almost six kilometres, he met with his workmates, who, thinking that the truck was stuck in mud, came back to help. When they found out what happened, they became worried and returned to the dam. From there, they notified the authorities about the kidnappings and contacted the relatives of their abducted comrades.

Hours later, a squadron of special forces, under the control of the detectives Baena and Guerrero, arrived in the zone. Upon their arrival, reporters and relatives of the victims would also arrive.

With the perimeter secured, the military ordered the journalists to begin their reporting.

Simultaneously with their report, Baena and Guerrero added the driver's interrogation, who, through his story, described the faces of the kidnappers in detail, as well as the cars used, weapons they used and the kind of clothing that the kidnappers were wearing.

Once collecting the evidence, the detectives went over their options. Due to their hypotheses, Baena and Guerrero initiated the investigation based on the evidence from the driver.

With the little that they knew of the zone, they took a map and looked for relevant routes. Then, taking its length, they divided it into an equal number of interceptions, where through these, the kidnappers could have access to one hundred percent of the rural farms, and at the same time to enter the mountain zone.

Given the circumstances, it was very difficult for detectives to find, at that moment, a direct clue that would lead them to release the abductees. With no other options, the two focused their inquiry on the city, surrounding towns, villages, and settlements.

In those places, the home phones of each worker kidnapped and relatives, as well as the construction company phones, would be intercepted. With this, the detectives sought to capture communication that would provide enough evidence.

On the other hand, Baena and Guerrero, based on satellite photographs and the description that they had of the vans and their occupants, would place about a hundred of their men at strategic locations. Even though the days were passing, the evidence that they were looking for wasn't appearing, since most of the vehicles arrived at the different towns were of the same make and model as those used by the captors. As well as that none of their license plates coincided with the serial that the detectives' infiltrators had in their possession.

At the same time as the detectives proceeded with their investigation, the seven hostages, guarded by their kidnappers, would discover the reason for their kidnaps – to build an underground refuge with a secret entrance from the pool inside the farm, hidden from the authority's eyes.

Before starting the job, Richard and Eric promised the captives that after finishing the task, the seven would be released. But they wouldn't leave with empty hands, since each of them would take a large sum of money.

After the pact, the engineer designed what would be the shelter and made a list of materials and machinery to use.

Five hours after his request, the materials and tools arrived at the Oasis farm. With this, they started the excavation and the process of their future deaths.

There at the Oasis farm, at the end of each day, the captives would be locked up in an immense hall, where, despite their limitation, they had some privileges. One of these was television. During their captivity, through the newscasts, they watched their relatives and friends begging to the captors so that they respected their lives and freed them. These messages and the eagerness to be free soon made the engineer and the workers double their work. Because of this attitude, the work finished in record time, and in recognition of their work, each would supposedly receive the money that Richard and Eric had promised.

The moment filled with emotions and happiness for six of the kidnapped for two reasons.

The first was obviously the fact that they would soon be free. And the second, because they would receive, from their captors, enough money to set up their own business.

Although they all felt that feeling, the happiness of the youngest one kidnapped would be threefold. The extra motive of his enthusiasm was that with the money that he would receive, he could finish university, and at the same time, it was enough to pay the lawyer that could help his innocent brother currently serving time at La Modelo prison, 'Colombia's largest penitentiary.'

However, their happiness would not last long, since Richard and Eric didn't want anyone else, other than Sotomayor, to know of the existence of the shelter. In advance, they had planned for their death, in which they included their four escorts.

The day they were to be freed; the group of the kidnaps were embarked in two vans. There with black bags, the captors again would cover their heads. The two leaders told their men that they should leave them in the same place where they were kidnapped.

At that moment, none of the builders, and much less their custodians, would think that they were about to meet their death.

Minutes later, hundreds of bullets would finish their lives. The workers would be killed first by their custodians and then, Richard and Eric would kill the killers. Sotomayor never would know about this event because his partners keep it a secret, and before he came, they would hire new personal security.

Five weeks after the murders, Baena and Guerrero, through satellite photographs and videos taken by the phantom plane, captured images of armed civilians near the Oasis farm. In the filming, these people appeared to be wearing military clothing and assault rifles. Next to them, there were several vans like the one described by the ex-released driver.

The fact that these men carried long-range weapons related them directly to the guerrillas, paramilitaries, or drug traffickers. Based on that hypothesis, the detectives focused their attention on the farm and ordered the pilot of the phantom plane to perform a thorough spying on the area.

On the other hand, communication experts intercepted radio waves and managed to listen to a conversation where the escorts, referring to the boss, called him by the name of 'the Angel.' That alias, to the detectives, didn't leave the slightest doubt that it referred to Sotomayor. This made them certain that they were close to achieving their objective. Thinking of his capture, they conducted the perfect plan.

Baena's hypothesis made sense because Sotomayor, in his different good-natured personages, had been a genius to pass unnoticed. A makeup teacher whose real identity only a few people knew.

Another point in his favour had been his generosity, and thus in each city where he arrived, the community would give him different pseudonyms that indirectly protected him from his persecutors.

Some of them in the past had called him "the Protector," others "the Apostle" or "the Angel" because in his arrival to create his new cartel, Sotomayor would always adopt a new character and a humble attitude.

He thought he would leave his security to his secret man, spying around his community to alert to any eventuality. Besides this, Sotomayor was a very astute person. Although he would choose large capitals as the centre of his illicit operations, he didn't stay in that city for more than one year. He just ensured that his new cartel was ready, before looking for a humble person, who after an agreement, became his partner and would be left in charge of the business.

In his agreement, Sotomayor, or the alias by he would be called by the community, was to provide the supplies to his partner in a safe place, as well as drug mules, and at the same time would take the money controlled by drug sales.

As remuneration for their services, the partner would receive thirty percent of the earnings. However, the partners, in the rest of their activities were free to proceed as they wished.

In their personal decisions, the Angel never had any participation, and whenever they respected his agreements, he didn't place any obstacle on them. And so, after stipulating the rules to comply, Sotomayor would retire to another city, because he didn't want to give the capos, the bosses of other illicit organizations, such as Tancredo Moreira, the chance to kill him, nor a chance for the authorities to capture him.

The fact that Sotomayor moved away from the city, where he founded his cartel and changed his character in each place that he arrived, was a strategy, so that his partners did not recognise him when faced with his presence. Because if he left them at his leisure, he would know about each one, until the slightest transaction they made on the cocaine. Intelligently, when he made the agreement with them, he gave, to his partners, a temporary code for safety, which would be modified by him, an hour before every delivery. To access the international payment of shipments, they had to enter that code with a password that was registered in the database of their personal computer.

At the same time, the drug mules that Sotomayor had hired at different borders were elderly people who were very professional in their work, and although the cross-border travel of these senior citizens were made several times a day, they only would carry out their deliveries once a week.

Their professionalism as traffickers would allow them to import the drug into neighbouring countries in an uncomplicated way: Transported by ground, they travelled on motorcycles and camouflaged in varied materials such as fertiliser bags, into the bike's pipe and other parts which didn't generate much suspicion from police.

Occasionally the border guards, when making a routine check, with suspicion asked them:

"What are you carrying in these fertiliser bags?"

He or she, exhibiting on their face a gesture of mocking surprise, responded, "A few pounds of cocaine!"

Of course, because of the grace with which they said it, the border guards never believed them. The insinuation sometimes made the guards angry and in response to their nonsense, they treated the elderly drug mules with degrading phrases and, in the middle of their anger, warned them.

"Stupid old folk, if you really were to carry cocaine, you never would simply betray yourself, and by now, you would be trembling with fear."

Another of the Angel's wiles were that after establishing his new cartel, he would cut all association with everyone he knew beforehand and change his partners, as soon as possible.

Sotomayor's strategy meant that in few weeks, he would give a status as capos to his prior partners, relegating all their responsibilities to them. The only ones that he didn't renew until that moment were his drug trafficking mules, although in each cocaine travel, it was ordered to them to change the modality of the deliveries. With that audacity, Sotomayor had always managed to confuse the authorities, as well as his dangerous enemies. However, at that time, according to the thinking of Baena and Guerrero, Sotomayor's luck had taken a turn against him, because this time they worked on new, solid information.

That afternoon of the burning sun, special forces, under their command, entered very stealthily in the properties of the Oasis farm. They knew that if they wanted to capture Sotomayor, they could not make mistakes, for with the least of these, Sotomayor would escape again. Due to their precautions, the advances of troops were coordinated through satellite photographs and monitored from a computer centre in the capital. For that reason, each step-in pursuit of its goal was assured. This led the detectives to think that, as the minutes passed, the capture of Jorge Sotomayor, alias 'the Angel,' would be more imminent. However, within eight hundred metres from the farm, the special forces encountered the first obstacle, a security cordon.

Baena's order was to neutralise the sentinels but would forbid the troops to use regular weapons. Just in an extreme case, they would use a pistol with silencer because they had to capture them alive. This impediment forced the command to stalk them until obtaining the key phrase that they would be reporting every ten minutes from sentinels.

Immediately upon obtaining the information, they would have less of that time to subdue them and avoid them and would alert to their colleagues in the second security ring. Baena didn't want to give Sotomayor, as well as his partners, the chance to escape because they were essential pieces for a possible conviction against his capo. That's why the detectives had a plan to take all the traffickers by surprise. Due to the order, four of Baena's men left the group to fulfil their mission. Without altering the silence of the mountains, they walked slowly along the small stretch of thick vegetation. Like felines stalking their prey, the small commando hoped to get the key phrase to forge the attack. Simultaneously with their stalking, the mobile phones from the sentinels started to ring. During the call, by communicating the key phrase, "The plague is in calm," they reported to their boss that so far, all is well. As soon as they finished the call, a coordinated attack on the vigilantes began.

As the onslaught would certainly be fulminated, Baena's men rushed on the four sentinels in order to not to give them the opportunity to use their weapons. Instantly after their attacks, Baena and the rest of his men elsewhere would continue their advance, confident that the commando in charge of the mission had managed to subdue them.

While Baena and his command secured the surroundings of the farm, there on the small hill, the commando and sentinels entered a fierce melee, since the bandits had great knowledge in martial arts, and so it would be impossible for the commando to immobilize them immediately. For that reason, the fight would last for almost eight minutes.

After that time, the commando through a phone call told Baena, as did Guerrero, that their missions were successful. At the same time of their report, the prosecutors gave them the order to contact through the radios of the captured, the Sotomayor's escorts at the other end. Immediately to the request, the person in charge to do it, would send the same key phrase of minutes ago. "The plague is in calm."

With that strategy, the prosecutors thought that they wouldn't find obstacles and predicted that his task would be a successful mission, but something had happened that the prosecutors at that time weren't considering. This was that every ten minutes, the Angel's sentinels had to report to his boss with a different key phrase, so that when they sent the same phrase twice, the Angel's personal escorts were alarmed and deduced that something out of the ordinary was happening.

Moments later, the Angel's guards went out to secure the perimeter, entering a fierce gunfight against the special forces.

When the Angel and his partners, who were in the pool at the same, Richard and Eric, heard the shots, they immediately took their backpacks where they carried their personal computer, weapons and money. Then, they followed the capo's steps who, through his mobile phone, sent a secret code, and automatically one side of the pool opened a secret shelter, which would pass unnoticed in the eyes of his pursuers.

After an hour's fight, the bullets stopped as the numerical superiority and military strategy had managed to subdue the capo's personal escorts. Immediately to their captures, Detective Baena and his men searched the farm of Sotomayor. There was not a centimetre of land that went unsearched. However, the result would be negative. The reason for their failure was that three of the fourteen people who knew of the existence of the shelter were inside the secret tunnel. The other eleven were buried in a common grave, since the partners of Sotomayor, as security measure, killed the engineer, his workers and even their hired help to kidnap the workers. For that reason, they felt safe in that place; nobody apart from them knew that it existed. As well as that, in their hiding place, they had closed circuit television with cameras hidden in strategic points that kept them informed of all the steps that Baena and his men were taking. There, the three also had enough food to survive for several weeks. With those measures, the confidence of leaving unharmed became more viable with each passing hour.

While in the shelter, optimism took over the three, but with Baena and Guerrero, determination of achieving Sotomayor's capture would keep them on their feet. They knew that Sotomayor, or the Angel, hadn't been able to circumvent the ambush of their commandos, and the presence of special forces on the Oasis farm would last for several days.

Baena's obsession with finding Sotomayor led his men to dig pits in various parts of the land, in search of a possible shelter underground. Not satisfied with this, Baena passed one by one the Sotomayor's bodyguards through a polygraph, achieving a new disappointment when none of them would provide the answer to his problem.

While Baena exhausted all viable options, his men, using heat sensors, inspected each of the rooms of the building, its ceilings, and the floor. Even with this exhaustive task, the result to find Sotomayor was negative.

They finished the rigorous inspection, so the Detective Guerrero ordered the drainage of the swimming pool and personally entered. Optimistically, he took his weapon and with the revolver handle began to hit both the walls and the bottom.

Soon after, one of his men detected on the left side of the pool a source of heat; exalted by the discovery, he notified Baena that it might be emanated by the temperature of people inside. They immediately began the excavation. Nevertheless, after making some holes in three places that were perforated, the sensors continued to emit the same signal in all its surroundings, because they were digging over the thermal regulators of the water that supplied the swimming pool.

After four days of searching, Baena and their men retreated from the farm. But it wouldn't be remained unguarded, the farm would be patrolled by guards twenty-four hours a day with a police squad.

When Sotomayor observed that Baena and their men had retreated, he knew now that the harassment to find them was going to be less rigorous, it would be easier for him to sneak away, since he counted on his cunning and knowledge of the area and the darkness of the night. On top of that, I, as his secret man, would closely coordinate his escape.

Because Sotomayor was the obsession of the detectives, his partners, Eric, and Richard, gave him the option to leave first, agreeing between the three that two hours later, the next person who was leaving the shelter would be Richard and four hours later Eric, the last of them.

After the agreement, the Angel took the computers and, in a CD, extracted all the information that incriminated him and their partners as drug traffickers.

After the work was done, he grabbed all the parts of the database, shattered them, and dumped these down the toilet.

Sotomayor waited that the small fragments were absorbed by the pressure of the water; when this task was finished, he decided that it was time to leave.

Seconds before he did it, he warned his companions that if, after the stipulated time and half an hour extra more, the shelter wasn't invaded, it meant that he had managed to reach a safe place. Because of this recommendation, Sotomayor left them two maps with the most viable routes for their escapes and began his adventure.

As the Angel left, his partners waited in refuge, with the assurance that they would go unharmed.

After the minutes passed, the clock struck ten o'clock, and the shelter continued to be safe. This indicated that luck was on their side; it was the right moment for the second of the three to escape from the danger.

Richard, very stealthy, went outside, jumped the security wall, and guided in the light of the moon, directed his steps towards one of the wooded areas that surrounded the farm. However, minutes after his escape began, he was surprised by one of the officers who guarded the area.

Immediately upon his capture, Richard tried to bribe him. He put his hand in his backpack to get money. However, the lieutenant thought that his intention was to take out a weapon, an action that provoked the reaction of the officer, who immediately shot first.

That discharge made the friction of the bullet cause Richard a slight wound at the top of his head.

Seconds after his wound, his body would collapse face down on the ground. Instantly, the officer with great caution and without dropping his gun, directed his steps towards the victim.

Already in front of him, and confirming that he was unconscious, he proceeded to examine him, finding among his belongings a backpack full of money, one 10mm gold Beretta pistol, a laptop and a map that, by the strokes drawn on it, accurately divulged the hiding place of his partners.

The lieutenant, driven by his ambition, extracted the weapon from the victim's backpack and placed it in Richard's right hand. Then he took Richard's finger, pinned it to the trigger and fired two shots into the air. After that, he took his pistol and killed him with a shot in the head. When he confirmed that he was dead, he stripped his valuables and belongings and hid them, thinking to return to them later.

A few minutes after that attack, the rest of his fellow police officers arrived. When they saw the deceased, they confused him with Sotomayor and began to extend questions.

The officer argued that he acted in self-defence and in the performance of his duty. In addition, he clarified to them that the body lying on the ground wasn't the person that they were thinking about.

However, the lieutenant affirmed to them that it was one of the capo partners and, according to him, the person that would be the link to find the hiding Sotomayor place. The reason for his certainty was the information that he found on the map, by which the officer told them that the capo and his companions were still sheltered in the farm; more precisely, inside of the pool's shelter, at the right side.

One of the police officers, seconds after of Lieutenant's insinuation, with surprise, exclaimed, "But, Lieutenant, the swimming pool already was checked by Detective Baena's men and they didn't find anything."

"Because they were searching in the wrong place," the officer responded sarcastically.

After the revelation, the officer knew that if the people inside the shelter came out alive, when they see the corpse of their friend without his personal backpack, they would probably start to ask, "Why doesn't he have his backpack?"

The officer thought that they, although surprised and sad, without doubt they will ask him, "Officer! Where is our partner's backpack?"

According to the lieutenant, the rest of Richard's partners inside the shelter will also have to die.

The lieutenant, with the intention of eliminating them, put himself to the front of the mission. After finding the supposed hiding place, he ordered their men to break down the wall.

After half an hour of arduous work, the obstacle would be eliminated. With free access to the shelter, the lieutenant began to forge his plan in his mind.

While he made up his mind, Eric, at the other end of the shelter and behind the dividing wall of that sophisticated refuge, was preparing to surrender to authority. But when he thought to leave the refuge, he heard the order given by the officer to kill all persons inside the shelter.

That order made Richard take his pistol Beretta from his personal backpack, turn off the lighting and prepare to defend himself.

Immediately to the lieutenant's order, the second in command of the platoon opposed his decision and with an energetic tone, he expressed to him, "But Lieutenant! Why not give them the opportunity to surrender?"

The officer, hearing that his subordinate contradicted his order, replied furiously, "Because my experience tells me that they aren't willing to do it. They prefer a tomb in their homeland than being extradited to another country."

After the reprimand to his subordinate, the angry officer, added, "Now, is it clear, Sergeant?"

"Yes sir!" he answered.

After their words, they went into action. However, at that moment, the darkness of the shelter prevented the officer visualising the target. He took his flashlight and with his pistol in his hand, entered first, shooting without any direction.

While he did this, Eric, guided by the flashlight light, shot at the offensive. With his reaction, he managed to wound the lieutenant lightly on one of his legs. The wound made him fall against the floor, and he suffered a fracture in his neck.

Seconds after that event, the sergeant of the squadron took command and personally, with one of their men, entered the shelter.

The two of them, without making a single shot and just protecting themselves with the darkness of the area, with much caution, dragged the injured officer outside.

After putting him outside safely and requesting medical assistance, the sergeant ordered his subordinates to abort the mission because the shelter had a narrow strategic entrance, and it was dark inside; the person at the other end had all the advantages.

Because of his strategy, the sergeant entered a dialogue with the alleged drug traffickers, to whom he promised to respect their lives if they didn't resist.

Eric's response was immediate: he said that they were willing to surrender, but on one condition – he required that Detective Baena would be the person who capture them.

When the agreement was reached, an outcome started where both parties were going to benefit.

According to the sergeant, with the agreement, he would be a winner because by capturing one of the most wanted men in the country, he would earn some extra money. Besides that, with his mediation in his capture, it would give him a sudden rise in his career. However, the sergeant was wrong, and Eric would eventually be the most favoured, since after falling into Baena's hands, Eric would protect his more valuable treasure, his own life.

The determination of the sergeant objected to the initial order issued by the lieutenant, who, even after being wounded and unable to move, continued to demand them to carry out a fatal attack.

At that moment, his cries were interrupted by the noise of a helicopter of the Red Cross, in which some paramedics arrived, along with detectives Baena and Guerrero. With their faces covered by balaclavas, they hoped to make the most important capture of their entire career.

Immediately after they arrived, the two detectives walked their way towards to the pool. There, the sergeant reported to them about the situation was and informed them that the reason for not having called them earlier was because the officer in charge of mission didn't allow it.

After the report, the sergeant left the command to the order of detective who immediately took the small megaphone and introduced himself as Baena and ordered the fugitives to leave the shelter with their hands up.

Seconds later, the sophisticated shelter was illuminated again and Eric stepped outside. At that time, everyone there waited for more than one person. However, as the minutes passed and they didn't see the rest of the traffickers appear, Baena and Guerrero asked surprisingly, "Where is the Angel?"

"Is he not thinking of surrendering to us?"

As the cameras inside of shelter didn't cover the area where his murder occurred, Eric, without knowing that Richard was killed by the lieutenant, answered no, because to him, the Angel and Richard escaped a long time ago.

"I have been in this shelter alone," Eric said.

The detectives, doubting his words, jumped into the pool, handcuffed him, and proceeded to enter the shelter. In that construction, they would find high technology but not the man that they were looking for.

After verifying the area, Baena ordered that Richard's corpse and the wounded officer be transported by helicopter to the polyclinic.

Minutes later, he would inform Eric about his partner's death.

After the helicopter's departure, the sergeant gave the prosecutors a report on the finding of the corpse and the events that occurred with the shelter's taking.

But in his report, the sergeant didn't mention the backpack with the money, nor the valued things that Richard carried with him.

At that moment, Eric, who listened to the story, understood why the lieutenant wanted to kill them. For convenience, Eric would take his hypothesis to prison and was convinced that from there, he would discover the truth.

While Eric's theory was beginning to take shape, he was held incommunicado and subjected to intense interrogations by Baena and Guerrero, who through him, tried endlessly to get the evidence that would lead to the capture of the Angel and the rest of the organisation. However, even with the promises offered, they didn't achieve a positive result.

Because of that, the detectives focused their research on Eric's personal computer. They were optimists to think they would find the information that Eric had denied them on the hard disk. To his surprise, the device had disappeared, and the SD cards did not contain even the slightest documentation that related to Eric or his companions, with the drug trafficking or other crimes.

For that reason, when they did not find the evidence, they couldn't continue with Eric's harassment. Without more options, under the charge of illegal weapons possession, they were obliged to send him to a maximum-security prison.

Two weeks later, Eric, enjoying the privileges that the law offered to him as a prisoner, would learn through his external contacts that the lieutenant to whom he wounded had been discharged because he ordered his partners outside to follow him very carefully. He also warned them to be alert, for if the lieutenant returned to the Oasis farm to recover the loot, it would confirm that he had been the killer of his partner, and under the same circumstances, the officer was to die.

However, the days passed, and the lieutenant didn't make any suspicious trip outside the city.

After a month of waiting, the lieutenant was finally fully recovered, and with that, he would begin the process of his death.

The morning before he would be killed, the officer took his private car and drove towards the Oasis farm, without knowing that from a distance, he was followed by Eric's men.

An hour after his trip, the lieutenant entered the grounds of the Oasis, parked his car, and headed towards the mountainous area.

Ten minutes later, he arrived. Then, crossing beneath the thorny ferns, he would excavate for a couple minutes and picked up the loot – loot that would only be caressed in his hands for a few seconds, before immediately to his happiness, several shots would end his life.

Sotomayor's Arrival to Panama and the Coincidence

Sotomayor, without knowing the fate of his last two partners, settled in Panama City. There, with a fake name and a new persona, he made the difficult decision to leave the drug trade for a while, because he planned to buy one hundred percent of the shares of a bankrupt tailoring agency called Le Fallèle.

As Sotomayor didn't want to arouse any suspicions, he adopted the persona of an effeminate man, which would allow him to avoid a list of questions in front of the owners.

His feminine tone of voice, his waxed eyebrows, the colour of his hair, his diamond ring and his tightly fitted jeans would be the first impressions to the previous proprietors.

The day after Sotomayor bought the Le Fallèle agency, he paid off the debts accumulated by the previous administration and gave the company a new image. Then, he personally contacted the formerly fired designers and rehired them in their usual positions.

While that was going on in Sotomayor's life, things began to get complicated for Eric in prison, as the detectives had managed to link him to the San Francisco Cartel, and he would face possible extradition to the United States. His lawyer, in his attempt to avoid Eric's extradition, recommended him to take advantage of the anticipated confession and plead guilty of kidnapping and murdering the seven builders, because if he was able to be covered by that law, the judge couldn't charge him for two crimes at the same time. With no other option, Eric accepted the deal.

In his interrogation, Eric didn't omit any details. He revealed how their murders were carried out and the place where the bodies were buried.

With this confession, the judge suspended the extradition process and Eric was charged with multiple murders. The news of his confession and the announcement that Eric would be in jail for a long time were watered among the prisoners, like rain in wintertime. These comments came fast to Fabian's ears, a brother of one of the builders who Eric had killed months ago. Since no one in the courtyard knew the blood ties between them, it helped Fabian find an effortless way to take his revenge.

Due to his secret intention, two days later, Eric was found dead in one of the prison bathrooms. No one would know for now who was his executioner.

While Richard and Eric in Colombia had a fatal end, Sotomayor, in Panama City, had the luck in his favour and everything was coming out as he wanted. He had already managed to get the tailoring company registered under the fictitious name of Marlon de la Roca, a pseudonym with which he would patent his future collections at the chamber of commerce.

Days later, through a televised interview, De la Roca announced his project and the opening of his renovated clothing store, Le Fallèle. Since the moment that he announced it, his extravagant way of dressing caused great controversy in his critics who watched his business on the TV because just as his image was, his collections would be same they thought.

With their criticism, they predicted a total failure. But as Sotomayor's idea was to innovate in fashion and, at the same time, find an opportunity for his secret purpose, he continued with his project.

As an optimist, he suggested to his designers that his brand should be inspired by ordinary people because the models wouldn't be the usual top models; they would be young people from the communes. In response to his demand, the administration started the search for potential candidates.

A week later, they already had contacted a total of thirty models. After concluding the first step, the designers focused on convincing the young women to be part of the agency. But logically, they and their families initially refused the offer. They didn't believe their intentions of turning their daughters into famous models for free, considering that in life everything has a price.

Almost all of them assumed that the men were in a mafia or involved in human trafficking, and that their intentions were only to take them out of poverty for a few weeks, and then turn their daughters into sex slaves in other countries. Even with that uncertainty hovering in their minds, ten of the girls would answer yes. In return for their trust, Marlon de la Roca and I, his secret man, became their protectors, and their families would be covered by all benefits. Under Marlon's tutelage, the girls were sent to the best modelling agency in the city, where for three months, they were taught the ropes of being a professional model. After undergoing small cosmetic surgeries, the girls were ready for their international debut.

A few days after finishing his apprenticeship, Sotomayor, currently Marlon de la Roca, together with the girls, launched his summer collection to the world that would be a success. As they completed several fashion shows, the brand that they were represented started to commercialise around the world.

His triumphs aroused the envies of the other twenty girls, who had rejected the initial offer. These girls driven by greed, wanted to recover the lost opportunity. Marlon de la Roca didn't deny them the opportunity to become models but imposed certain conditions on them.

In his new offer, he didn't offer the same benefits; however, they accepted these without objection. As a reward for their generosity, they would act as drug mules for two years and work equally with the other ten girls. However, the other girls shouldn't discover the true objective of their mission under any circumstance.

De la Roca, for his part, would seek to achieve four things for the girls.

The first was to get them, in record time, their American visas and turn them, in a minimum of one year, in famous models. For the second condition, De la Roca would provide the girls financial support for all their expenses, until his demands were met.

The third condition, he promised to them, after the date stipulated in the agreement had passed, was the girls would be exempt from their commitments. Finally, in the case that some of these girls are arrested, he would take care of them and their families until months after they were released. In addition to this, De la Roca would divide thirty percent of their total profit between the girls.

The girls' positive response wouldn't surprise Marlon de la Roca, because he was sure that they would be accepting to anything. Immediately after their agreement, he sent the girls to be trained. There, while they trained their modelling ability like the first girls, they also trained their body parts to transport capsules with pressed cocaine around the world.

With long days consisting of vaginal exercises and hours swallowing whole grapes, they adapted both, their stomachs, and their genitals.

After finishing their lessons, they began modelling along with the other models at photoshoots, and at the same time, initiated the drug trafficking.

In international waters and by cruises, the girls travelled to Miami, their final destination.

Although in their arrivals to these ports, the girls were submitted to rigorous inspections, the police never found anything suspicious in them, and so, their travel would become a piece of cake.

Months after their first deliveries, Marlon de la Roca, for the sake of his security, ordered them to change the routine of their trips. The girls wouldn't travel in a group as before; they would do the trips one by one and by airplane.

The Marlon's decision was more than a strategy, it was a way to provide comfort to the girls as they would reduce the journey from about two days, to just a few hours.

With this, he avoided the night before their deliveries, when the girls would have to swallow the drug and vomit it again in the morning. This news pleased the girls because that would avoid repeating the painful process. Due to that, the twenty girls constantly flew over American territory. However, Sotomayor didn't imagine that with this new change, fate would begin to forge a plot against him.

Sometime later, simultaneously with one of the flights of the young models, in another country thousands of kilometres away, the date of the G7 world meeting was approaching. But on that occasion, the conference wouldn't take place in its usual location. For the first time, it would take place in a neutral country. This obliged all international authorities to tighten security control of airports and maritime terminals all over the world, and above all, on the access border roads to the city of Cairo, the capital where the G7 meeting would be taking place to fight against poverty around the world.

Although this meeting would take place in one of the safest countries in the Middle East, the global security agencies didn't rule out the possibility of being sabotaged by Islamic fundamentalists.

The priority of the Egyptian government was to provide security to all the political delegates who arrived from all around the world, since in the last few hours, more than seven terrorists would attempt to immolate themselves inside aircrafts. So, military forces in several countries, were at maximum alert. Ministers of defence of each country involved ordered that not only would the suspects pass through the airport scanner but also, all passengers, including the crew would also have a strict inspection.

But the security plan imposed by the authorities was not ready to counteract any terrorist action, because according to the terrorist's strategies, they knew the location of where the meeting will take place in advance, as well as the delegations that would be participating. With this knowledge, they would block the actions of their opponents. While the government exercised its control, Al Qaeda members infiltrated the city and took great advantage over their adversary. As they knew, in advance, the place where the G7 meeting would take place, they had started their plan eight months earlier.

One day in Cairo, several groups of Islamic fundamentalists, led by their leader called 'Sahara,' simultaneously took different residences of Egyptian workers and archaeologists contracted by the government. Between them, the Rahyfel brothers would oversee the excavation sponsored by the state. That night the terrorists, undercover, easily took the next group of workers elsewhere, where at the same time, they would be supplanted in Cairo by members of Al Qaeda.

While some fundamentalists initiated the plan in different places, the others, who had interrupted the silence of the dawn in Rahyfel's mansion, took Yasher, their youngest son and nephew, as hostage. Before taking him by force, they warned their parents and families that if they want to see him alive again, they as government contractors must stay on the side lines and not obstruct their project that they will be running simultaneously to their excavation. They promised that if they accept to collaborate, a month after finishing their mission, they will return Yasher.

After the extremists' ultimatum, the Rahyfel brothers agreed to follow the plan, and according to the Al Qaeda members, their movement would supplant the Egyptian workers and together they would start their own excavation parallel to the original. The zone chosen by the extremists coincided with the excavation that these brothers would carry out just three hundred metres from the Marriott Hotel, where according to historians, hundreds of years ago, the effect of a volcano had buried an ancient city.

The evidence found by the archaeologists made the terrorists immune from any suspicion by the authorities and, at the same time, led the archaeologists a possibility to discover the antique city. But the main objective of the members of Al Qaeda wasn't that: their priority was to build a path that would bring them to the temporary residence of the G7 leaders participating in the meeting.

As the weeks passed, the extremists made new progress in the project and at the same time, developed the tunnel with which they would successfully complete their purpose. Six months after the excavation began, the supposed archaeologists had extended the conduit to the hotel parking lots. Once underneath, they looked for the box where all the communication circuits where the parking was and that previously had been assigned to the Pakistan delegation.

Weeks after, the group of the alleged workers was in front of the thick concrete wall, the main objective of their mission and their last barrier to overcome. By the difficulty and strong obstacle, it was necessary to drill a metre more without alerting security.

Hours in their arduous work, they adjusted the entrance and left it ready to go in. After that, one of them would restore the wall, ensuring that the changes would go unnoticed.

While this happened in the hotel basement, other members of Al Qaeda in the streets of the Cairo were following in the footsteps of the Pakistani delegation, a group of ten politicians that had been staying at their embassy for days. Then, after following them and knowing from them the smallest detail, the terrorists forged the plan to execute. With everything ready, they only had to wait for the time to pass. One day before the meeting, from very early in the morning, the delegations from around the world began to arrive.

That morning, the first commission, Pakistan, was ready to go to the meeting. The driver of the Pakistani limousine took the route planned on the map, being escorted by several police officers in cars and motorcycles. But a few kilometres down, the procession ran into a military patrol, who made them divert the route.

Just five minutes later, the delegation's bodyguards would immediately see the terrorists pointing the rifles at their heads, quickly making them understand that they had fallen into a trap. Immediately to their surprise, the leader of the commission was subjected to a surgical procedure, where the fingerprint of his thumb was removed and was implanted to whom would usurp his place. Then, the delegates and their escorts would be stripped of their personal documents and dresses too.

In underwear, handcuffed and with tape covering their mouths, they were forced to climb inside of a big truck and taken to an unknown destination. While the kidnappers were leaving with the Pakistani delegation, a limousine with the same characteristics and similar number of people arrived at the meeting. They used the badges already registered by the country authorities, which along the fingerprint from the leader gave them immunity at the checkpoints. Once in the parking lot, at Marriott Hotel the terrorists started with the second part of their plan.

The first thing that they did when they were in the parking lot was communicate with the men inside of the tunnel, who were waiting in the circuit box. Immediately after their call, both entrances doors were opened simultaneously. One door from the false limousine platform and the other from the circuit box entrance. By this door under the floor, one by one, the ten members of the terrorist cell inside of limousine received a pistol with silencer, ammunition, and some electronic devices. As well as this, three more members would join them to provide support.

Five of them, wearing fine dresses and black sunglasses, left the vehicle and went to the suite designated by the hotel to the Pakistani delegation, where their contacts waiting for them. The rest of them, to avoid any suspicion, would wait hidden inside the vehicle until the rest of delegations arrived; this way, they intended mixing with the delegates in order to go unnoticed.

An hour after the arrival of the first fundamentalists inside the hotel, the other eight companions inside the limousine had achieved their goal. After gathering a total of fifteen terrorists in the suite, five of them were placed strategically throughout the venue to support their exit. The remaining ten in the suite synchronised their clocks and went over mission. In groups of three, the first thing to do was remove their tuxedos and dress in same way as the hotel's waiters. Then, the ten of them planned to attend the hotel's reception and at strategic points, place small smoke explosives which would explode through a remote control at the exact time.

A few minutes after their first manoeuvres, everything was ready. The other nine terrorists inside the suite, upon receiving the signal, went to the elevators to intercept the waiters, to whom they would bribe with a good amount of money. Following that fake waiters, at different time, they returned to the Pakistani suite. There, inside the elegant room, they took the small rolling table, and in one of its compartments, placed some tuxedoes and weapons with a silencer and went out to complete their mission. Synchronised in groups of three, the fake waiters directed their steps towards to their goal in where, without any obstacle, they would arrive at the different suites.

The first group was in charge of killing the USA delegation and to kidnap the ambassador. The second group's task would do same to the UK's delegation.

The last of these groups were assigned to execute the French representatives and take the ambassador captive.

Every group, in front of the victims' doors, rang the bell. Then, one of them in a strong tone, exclaimed the phrase, "Room service!"

Immediately after gaining access to the rooms, each of them sent the signal and the man stationed near the reception activated the explosive. Simultaneously with that and while the hotel fire alarms sounded, several silent shots in the different rooms would end the delegates' lives.

Subsequently, each of the groups took their corresponding hostage and placed them with a security device attached to an explosive charge, which activated with low frequency waves emanated by a GPS.

The digital device, controlled by a frequency emitted by one of terrorist member, had a coverage of three meters, which would be triggered if the hostage escaped. Having already warned their victims of this, the false waiters changed their clothes and together they mixed among the hotel guests before they ran through the corridors in search of emergency exits.

While this was happening, the authorities stationed around the hotel to secure the perimeter and didn't allow anyone to cross its security barricade. At the same time, firefighters, through a megaphone warned all the delegates, to maintain calm. Regardless, the panic due to not knowing what was happening was palpable. The exception would be the terrorists and their victims who in groups of four would walk slowly towards the parking lot.

The first of these groups, without the slightest difficulty, obtained their access to the outside accompanied by Jesse Murray, the financial secretary of the United States. The remaining two groups and the five terrorists, who were watching the exits, would go to the limousine in intervals of five minutes each. Of them would arrive Wilson Rutherford, British minister of agriculture and his French colleague, Jean-Pierre Marat. There, at different periods of time, a total of eighteen men arrived at the Pakistani limousine. As soon as they arrived, they were taken out to the secret tunnel where higher ranked Al Qaeda members waited for them and took the hostages.

Immediately after the deliveries, the groups and their leaders returned to the tunnel, where they placed small explosive that minutes later would be detonated, and so the tunnel became plugged.

Simultaneously with the controlled tunnel explosion, the firefighters, oblivious to what just happened underground, took control of the hotel, and reported that the incident was a sabotage without any importance, and that everything was fine.

After that, the security managers suggested to the guests to go to their suites and wait there until the conference that was to start. Once the time had passed, the delegations one by one arrived at the auditorium. But the host delegate noticed that the seats of the United States, England, France, and Pakistan were absent. Immediately, they postponed the meeting by an hour and ordered the security officers to investigate the delays caused.

Minutes later, the security officers arrived at the corresponding suites and pressed the doorbells repeatedly with no response, and so they proceeded to open the doors by force and found, in each revised suite, an unpleasant surprise, they saw corpses scattered inside the rooms.

Following their discoveries, the news was broadcasted that the summit was cancelled, and for all delegations to return to the embassies of their countries. While this was happening at the Marriott Hotel, the authorities found, on the outskirts of Cairo, the corpses of ten Pakistani diplomats and several Egyptian police officers.

The evidence left behind confirmed to the authorities that this was a plan to carry out a kidnapping. Due to that, the Egyptian Ministry Defence, wanting to safeguard its responsibility in that plot, declared the country in a state of emergency, and made a call to the military reserves, who together with all the active military forces, focused on the search for the three hostages and the kidnappers.

Immediately to this request, the Egyptian authorities began their investigation inside the official Pakistani limousine, in which, after a thorough check-up, they found a false floor, which when they opened it, produced an opening to the metal door underground box, where all the hotel electronic circuits were present. With that discovery, the authorities linked that fact with a supposed underground tunnel, and that hypothesis led them to the excavation that the Rahyfel brothers were making in the area.

Minutes later, agents of the Egyptian Security State had an understanding of the tools used by the terrorists for the kidnapping, which involved alleged accomplices to the two archaeologists and the rest of the workers who continued in the other excavation. The detectives focused on their interrogations, but ultimately, they didn't have evidence to implicate them. However, they found false identification and papers used by the kidnappers. Without further options, the authorities began to work on those clues – an investigation which would be executed by special forces of the three nations involved.

The number of soldiers deployed in Cairo's streets was so overwhelming that it looked more like a foreign invasion than a search. The multinational efforts to achieve their mission were negative.

Two months and nineteen days after their military operation began, the kidnappers communicated with the respective embassies and sent them a video showing members of al Qaeda, pointing their AK47 rifles at the hostages. As well as that, in their ultimatum, they demanded the amount of five hundred million dollars for every hostage; money that must be thrown from a helicopter over a specific point in Afghanistan.

In the recording, the terrorists warned the ambassadors that they had ten days, from that date, to deliver the money. They also informed them that if they didn't comply with their request, it would lead them to behead the hostages.

Immediately after making contact, the negotiation began, and the embassies demanded, as proof, a new video where the three hostages would appear, carrying a dated newspaper in which on its front page, each one of them had to print their signature and fingerprints.

As soon as the demand was received, Al-Qaeda members, somewhere in Cairo, removed the hostages from their cells and gave them a local newspaper where, seconds later, the diplomats recorded their signatures and fingerprints next to the date of that day. After this, the kidnappers began a new recording with the hostages.

Before sending the recording, they did a thorough examination of each signature in order to prevent the prisoners from leaving a hint that would give the authorities a clue of where they were being held.

All the members at the shelter, as well as the three prisoners back in the cells, saw this verification procedure as normal, except for Jesse Murray, who was the only one aware that on his signature, he had attached seven tiny extra words, written in shorthand. Although these signs for him meant the hope of a possible rescue, it also could mean immediate death, or divert the authorities in the wrong direction.

He worried of this because he wasn't sure if the location provided in his hidden message had any relationship with the place of their captivity. He knew that a bullet to the head as an answer any of the terrorists would give him without hesitation, if one of them were to discover his secret message.

After verification of the signature, Jesse Murray was expecting to receive retaliation for his audacity. However, although his secret message went unnoticed, it didn't yet restore his optimism. He was a realistic man and didn't want to deceive himself because he knew that in any case, if his release didn't take place before the arrival of their ransoms, his days were numbered.

Due to his conviction, Jesse Murray kept the pen, and from that moment that he was locked in the cell, on a newspaper given to him to use as toilet paper, he hid one and began to write his thought process towards his death on its blank spaces. His thinking wasn't wrong, since the terrorists had already received the order to kill them minutes after their Afghan allies received the money.

Because of that feeling, every day that he spent in his captivity, he described his feelings in the newspaper. As well as that, he wrote about the torture of being held hostage, and every word emanated from his captors, he wrote down in English as he heard it. Although he didn't know what it meant, it would replace for this word, for one that he thought, was closer to the original.

While that was happening in Jesse's Murray life, there at one of the Cairo borders, the Rahyfel brothers were waiting for the return of their son and nephew, Yasher, as the terrorist group had promised them almost three months ago, although the archaeologists knew the hope of finding him alive was very remote and were anxious.

That morning, the two in the middle of a mountainous landscape, watched how time devoured the hours of the day, until it turned the afternoon into night and the young man didn't appear. The two brothers, without choice, would resign to losing him. Unhappy and with a bowed head, they embraced the truth and immediately, tears began to run down their cheeks. That feeling with the hours passing would leave them with swollen eyes, which reflected the aftermath of betrayal in them. Their ambitions to safeguard their most precious treasure would have led them to betray the country. With their actions, they knew that they had violated all the rules of their professional ethics.

Their feelings at that time showed them that they were guilty because by omitting their forced complicity, they had negotiated the death of many people for nothing, because in the end, they would be left without Yasher and empty hands. Due to their destructive criticism, both contemplated killing themselves as a viable option. However, according to them, they would make their deaths at home, since they were sure that his wife and sister-in-law would not handle Yasher's loss and they would want to die with them.

Determined to a fatal outcome, they headed their vehicles towards the city, arriving at their residence when the dawn was starting to die. When they got off the vehicle, with surprise, they observed all the lights in the mansion were on and through the windows, they saw the silhouettes of three people who were talking when everything at the mansion would typically be silent. That scene returned their facial expressions to their faces, and without fear of being wrong, the two yelled, "Yasher is alive! Yasher is alive!"

Immediately, they went from anguish to euphoria. Exalted to confirm their hypothesis, they went inside the house and from the main floor they quickly reached the second floor. When they saw Yasher safely at home, they couldn't control their emotions and they practically detached the young man from his sister's and mother's side. After hugging him for several minutes, they went down to the main floor to celebrate his return, since he had been the only one of the kidnapped victims who the fundamentalist group had spared.

This was an unusual way that the terrorists had proceeded with Yasher, which ultimately caused such happiness in all of them that they were overwhelmed with relief for have that privilege. So, that early morning, they consumed even the old wine used as an aperitif. That morning, as they were sharing that comforting moment, Yasher described his story.

That day, Yasher said when he woke up on the hard-concrete slab from the room where he was being detained, he didn't feel the chain that typically imprisoned him against the sewage pipe. So, he sensed that something abnormal was happening. He, although fearful, approached the basement door and turned the handle to leave but was disappointed to feel that it still had the bolt placed. However, when he was looking through the small grille from where the terrorists gave the food to him, he noticed that the keys hung from a hook, where he could easily reach them.

Although this was an opportunity for him to take advantage of, he wasted that moment and prudently decided to wait until the afternoon hours passed.

Through the small window at the other side of basement, he could see that midnight arrived and he was yet to receive any food, nor could he hear any noise, which confirmed that he was alone. Without any other option, he cautiously started to walk towards his freedom. Through the enormous residence basement, little by little, he extended his steps until he arrived at the main floor. There, after several minutes of slow movements, he managed to reach the street. Once outside, with great joy and surprise at the same time, he saw that his place of captivity was only a few metres from his mansion.

The Key Message and Lorena's Tragedy

Two days after Yasher's self-liberation in Cairo, a multinational force led by agents of the FBI, M15 and the CIA verified the video and the signatures written by the three diplomats on the blank space of the newspaper. On Jesse Murray's signature, they found small passwords attached, which they immediately recognised as a key message. After expanding it, they extracted, from their deformed letters, seven stenographic signs which would unite in order and form the word 'ramlene,' a word that, at first glance, didn't make sense. Although they looked for the meaning in other languages, they obtained the same result. However, one of the researchers, after writing the word on a blank sheet of paper and reading it from behind, gave him a key Spanish phrase, *en el mar*, which they recognised as Spanish for 'on the sea.'

Minutes after that interpretation, hundreds of officers were deployed over the seaports of Cairo. In a synchronised manner, like piranhas, they made meticulous inspections on every boat that was arriving at the docks. Despite this, the search to find the three diplomats remained unsuccessful.

After exhausting this option, the researchers focused their operation on a remote possibility, a boat cemetery on a beach near the sea. As this place was state property, the site practically remained deserted, and so according to the investigators, it could be an excellent captivity place. After a meticulous analysis, the military ruled out taking over the area by sea, because if they are right, the magnitude of this could give their plan away. Due to that, they opted for airborne forces.

In a matter of minutes, battalions of paratroopers stormed all the ships stranded. Stealthily, they began their search in the command cabins. Half an hour into the mission, one of the commandos located the target and ordered the rescue.

Immediately after giving the order, the snipers with silent shots killed five of the guards and cleared the entrance for the explosives experts to continue their advance to meet the three hostages.

As each second passed, the military security became more extreme because the rescue commands contemplated the possibilities that the custodians were more than just five, and they also were afraid that the ship, any time, would be busted. For that reason, each ship compartment had an exhaustive checking, so that when the militaries came their steps back all the persons involved in that operation would be out unharmed.

After the command checked the ninety percent of the ship, they found the three diplomats in a machine room, and as they had expected, the entrance door had a digital mechanism connected to an explosive charge attached.

While the explosive experts reached their objective and secured the perimeter, two of the terrorists from out of nowhere, returned to replace the guards. When they saw their comrades' dead, the terrorists tried to activate the explosives. However, the explosive experts had quickly deactivated them, and they didn't explode.

Angry by the obstacle, the terrorists tried to achieve their purpose, immolating their bodies. Although the explosion caused great damage to the deteriorated boat, they didn't reach the kidnapped group or the special command, and since seconds before the burst, they moved away and wounded the last two terrorists.

Hours later, after bringing the diplomats through an exhaustive medical check-up, the FBI, M15 and CIA authorities obtained, from the delegates, all the information possible, including the newspaper where Jesse Murray had written about his last days in captivity. When the authorities were analysing part of his notes, the translators deciphered the pronunciations that he had perceived during his kidnaping.

According to the CIA experts, the words of the Islamic fundamentalist referred to a second attack against one of the most representative symbols of the United States; in this case, it could be the Statue of Liberty. That possible attack would take place during the days of Ramadan, a date in which the Islamic group would commemorate the death of their former leader and, at the same time, they wanted to show the 'Yankee empire' that their revenge wasn't over yet. As the investigators hadn't much knowledge about the future attack, the American authorities tried to avoid the terrorists taking them by surprise.

As a security measure, the CIA started an early prevention and USA president declared the country in high alert. Immediately to this order, the CIA considered all access to the patriotic monuments as possible routes of the announced attack. For which, they increased the security measures in all airlines and seaports. In addition, on cruises and airplanes to the public service, they camouflaged their personnel as part of the crew. Under that strict control, the terrorists and the trafficker women, on day of the attack, still boarded the flight without any problem.

Two months earlier to the liberation of the hostages, twenty of the Le Fallèle models, from weeks ago, had ended the agreement with Marlon de la Roca. The international fame reached by these girls allowed to them to work for any agency. However, five of these girls, after having known the management and the cocaine commercialisation, would continue with the traffic at their own risk. The girls, after coming to an agreement, would usurp, from their ex-boss, some clients and started a small cartel named the Divas, which the large dividends left for each trip and would be consolidated their societal.

Due to this status change, Lorena, the most ambitious of the quintet, was thinking of getting the biggest business slice and proclaimed herself as boss of the newest cartel and imposed her own rules. Her rules led to discrepancies and rivalries between the group. With that, three of the former models disassociated and began their independent work. The other two girls, by that misunderstanding, became enemies; Lorena and her friend, Yamile, were hurt for their betrayals and would make a wicked plan. Their plan consisted of informing the DEA authorities the place and date where they would be making their next cocaine delivery.

However, that day in which Lorena and Yamile would try to carry out the plan, a parallel event in the trip would leave that intention unfinished. The airplane where both women transported would be taken over by Al Qaeda terrorists, who would unleash an attack that would finish in them, both plans.

That summer afternoon in which this would take place, the Boeing 747, managed by International Aero Flight Company, departed from Panama City Airport towards the United States. According to the terrorists' plan, when the airplane would be flying over the neighbouring country of El Salvador, they would overtake it. Their mission was to take control of the aircraft and later, when the plane would be flying over US airspace, they would crash it at the port of New York, or more precisely, on the Statue of Liberty. They planned to start this attack at the moment when their watches showed 05:32 pm.

The extremists in advance had managed to introduce two small transformer toys and all the necessary things for their attack in the aircraft. Even though at first sight the toys seemed harmless, their manufacturer had made them in a special design, with which, when several of their pieces were disassembled and reassembled, the toys would be transformed into a powerful weapon.

The sophisticated toy design would make the guns adhered to their mechanisms and not be detected by the airport's anti-terrorist controls. The same way that the bullets and the small explosive charge would pass unnoticed inside the toy's alkaline batteries.

Immediately to the time's confirmation, the terrorists in charge of the attack took their carry-on baggage, where each of them kept the supposed transformer toy. Already with the assembly instructions memorised, they went inside two different bathrooms. There, each one took his toy, and one by one, detached all its vital parts until it converted the robot into a sophisticated gun.

After the initial configuration, they proceeded to remove, from the batteries, the cathodes, and the manganese dioxide, in where they had the bullets camouflaged, and also the ammonia gelatine to make a small device explosive – a process in which the terrorists didn't spend more than fifteen minutes on.

With all their equipment ready, they returned to their seats to wait for the clock to read the programmed time and proceeded to take over the airplane. According to their list, this would be carried out two hours in advance of them arriving, and when the plane would be crossing the airspace of the New York Port they would have total control of the aircraft.

While on the flight this event awaited its fatal outcome, in another part of the aircraft, Lorena and Yamile, who travelled in the second-class section, mentally from different positions, made plans with their luck and, at the same time, focused their wicked thoughts on their revenge. However, when both women poisoned their souls with their resentment, they were abruptly interrupted by the two men shouting. They pointed their pistols on the heads of two flight attendants and took them as hostages. Immediately after this, one of the terrorists very emotionally expressed to all present.

"We are Al Qaeda's members and today we were chosen to die, in the name of Allah."

When their warning was over, the first people who heard the message immediately went to panic and, inside the aircraft, a chain of hysteria began. Some prayed and entrusted their souls to God. Others used their cell phones and sent messages to their family, as if sensing the last goodbye.

The most optimistic thought for a moment to pounce on the terrorists, to try to change their plan. But making that decision was the same as perpetuating the attack, as one of them had, at hand, a supposed explosive device, so they aborted their attempts.

Minutes later, through family calls, the US Department of Defence received the distress text messenger made by some passengers from the Boeing 747.

Moments after their requests, two fighter-bombers went out to intercept the aircraft and divert it from the original route. While these fighter bombers were visualising the airplane, the airport controllers communicated with the captain, who was very worried, and reported that they didn't know about was happening in the passenger sections. According to him, the flight attendants, more than fifteen minutes ago, cut off the communication with the cockpit. As captain, he couldn't call them because their silence meant that something abnormal was happening and he had instructions to wait for their requests. Once the fighter bombers were over the airplane, their pilots ordered the captain to follow their instructions for the landing. Then, they warned him that changing directions without their permission would trigger an immediate attack.

The first order issued by the two fighter-bombers' pilots was to raise the airplane altitude and make a ninety-degree turn to the left. Immediately to the demand, the airplane captain diverted the Boeing from its original route, and so, passengers and infiltrated CIA agents in the airplane, with a new surprise, observed the two Eagle F5s. This meant that if the captain didn't comply with the fighter-bomber's requests, the airplane without doubt would be knocked down.

This unexpected tactic would be counteracted and the astonishment of seeing that two White US citizens were part of the terrorist organisation, since everyone on the aircraft thought that if an attempt of this magnitude would happen again, the executors who would carry it out would be of Islamic origin. Simultaneously with the passenger's reactions, the terrorists, dragging the hostages with them slowly, went towards the flight deck to take control.

When the terrorists arrived, one of them tried to obtain access and observed, with a surprise, where it informed to all passengers that the compartment would be open only a quarter of an hour after the airplane had landed.

The extremists, at that moment, taken by their astonishment, lost control. This circumstance was taken advantage by the alleged flight attendants who, upon seeing this, entered in a struggle with the terrorists to try disarming them. Minutes later, the terrorist who carried the pistol and the small explosive device was knocked out. However, the other, still trying to maintain his dominance, continued to attack.

In the middle of the battle and seconds before to being subdued, the terrorist managed to activate his weapon. The gunshot crashed against the synthetic carpet and bounced on the floor, brushing very close to Lorena's shoulder and embedding into her back seat. Once the mutiny was controlled, the terrorists were chained at their hands and feet in underwear and were locked in one of the bathrooms.

After that, the captain received a report from the flight attendants, and from his cockpit, he issued a statement to all passengers, where he apologised for the panic and thanked God for leaving all unharmed from the attempt. As well as that, he announced that he had received instructions from the Eagle F5s fighter-bombers to make an emergency landing at the closest city in approximately an hour and fifty-five minutes. Immediately after the captain's report, the four CIA agents identified themselves and then announced that, for security reasons, the two passenger sections would be under their surveillance. Also, everyone should remain in their seat; if someone needed to go to bathroom, before entering, they would be inspected and with the exception of their clothes, wouldn't be allowed to bring anything with them.

With that, the aircraft returned to a relative calm, and so the flight attendants took advantage and thought of ways to raise the passenger spirits. To do this, they decided to give all passengers free access to the cognac stock in the airplane.

Lorena, carried away by her nerves, forgot that she couldn't drink any kind of liquor. Not only did she drink one, but continued drinking.

Fifteen minutes later, the silence in the aircraft would be interrupted again. But this time, it wasn't due to a terrorist attempt but was from a sharp cry of pain emanating from the economy section.

The strong moan shocking everyone around would be expressed by a young woman who was traveling with a tourist visa to New York, the same woman who, minutes ago, had been startled by a rebounding bullet from the hands of the frustrated terrorist.

Despite her cries, the nearby CIA agents, who were near her, didn't pay her attention due to their priority to maintain vigilance over the passenger section. That indifference caused the person sitting next to her to press the assistance bell. But in that moment, no flight attendants would appear immediately.

While they waited for the flight attendant to respond to the call's request, the seatmate provided first aid to Lorena. Based on the woman's difficulty to breathe and the pain by her left breast, the passenger confused her symptoms with a premature heart attack. Because of that, he took her by the arms and spread her body on the airplane floor, loosened her belt and unbuttoned her pants. After that, he inclined the Lorena's legs in a vertical line and began to press on her chest.

While the minutes passed, the young woman presented new symptoms. From one moment to another, her face began to change colour and her stomach grew double in size. Because of the strange symptoms developing from the woman's body, the man understood that his initial diagnosis was wrong and stopped his approach. Then, he remembered the liquor that she had consumed minutes before and assumed that she was dealing with alcohol poisoning. Helpless now, he got up with the intention to look for a flight attendant. At that moment, one of them walked towards him. When he saw from afar, he began to shout, "Flight attendant, please come faster."

When she heard his cries, she immediately ran to him seeing his distress. When she was face to face with him, the flight attendant asked, "What is happening? Can I help you?"

"Of course, but help isn't for me, it is for her, she is dying and needs medical assistance."

The flight attendant, surprised, asked, "What's the matter with her?"

The man replied, "Sorry, but I don't know, I am not a doctor! However, I think that she is having a heart attack; also, she can be intoxicated, based on my knowledge," he said, "I provided her with CPR."

The flight attendant was grateful for his help and told him, "Okay sir, thanks for your help."

While the flight attendant tried to find out what was wrong with Lorena. Her partner Yamile, at the other end of the economy section, was between the sword and the abyss. She, in agreement with Lorena, had been prohibited to talk to her friend during the flight because if something did happen, the authorities couldn't find any connection between both. Due to this, she didn't know what to do. She wasn't sure if she should take the risk until the end or throw away her cocaine cases that she carried in her genitals.

The biggest worry for her was knowing that she had just a few minutes to make the decision before the Boeing landed. After thinking about it, again and again, under the watchful CIA agents, she got up and calmly walked down the airplane corridor. Before Yamile went the washroom, the CIA agent ordered her to stop and performed a meticulous inspection, which she would pass without problems.

She hadn't walked two metres towards the bathroom before seeing that the only bathroom available had several people waiting for their turn. That circumstance didn't make things worse for her, in fact it was quite the opposite because being last in line would give more time to decide what she needed to do. Inside the bathroom and without pressure, Yamile extracted the two cases from her genitals and disposed of them in a drawer located next to the toilet. But, in the short time that she would have before the airplane landed, it would be impossible to throw up or defecate the drugs that were inside her stomach.

Simultaneously to this, the flight attendant who was helping Lorena was observing how she continued to swallow in her ailment and looked towards the passengers and exclaimed, "Is anybody in this section a doctor or paramedic or nurse that would be able to help me, please?"

When she observed the helpless faces in the economy cabin filled of anguish, she went to the first-class cabin and asked the passengers the same question:

"Is anybody in this section a doctor or paramedic or nurse that would be able to help me, please?"

Moments later, one of the passengers got up from the seat and together they went to where the young woman was. During that time, the moans that Lorena emanated from her due to her stomach pain became distressing. When the doctor came to help her, he would find the woman in a state of convulsion and with her eyes wide open. Immediately, the doctor took her pulse and then asked:

"What kind of food did you eat during the flight?"

Lorena, suffering in agony, couldn't answer. The answer would be provided by the seatmate who, very worried for her, expressed:

"She drank two cognacs only. However, right after the second drink, she started complaining about the pain."

At that time, the doctor wanted to ask another question, but seeing that Lorena was losing consciousness and emanating white foam from her mouth, he immediately diagnosed that the woman was carrying cocaine capsules inside her stomach and one of them probably had exploded inside of her. With anguish drawn on his face, the doctor looked at the flight attendant instantaneously and said:

"I am sorry, but here is nothing I can do for her, she needs to go to the operating room immediately because she is dying!"

Because of the serious nature of the diagnosis, the crew, after reporting to the Eagles' pilots of the incident, hurried the flight and soon after, the airplane would be landing.

Moments after the plane touched down, the track was surrounded by soldiers, who, for safety measure, thoroughly conducted a search inside the aircraft for explosives, finding in the bathroom, the two full cocaine cases that Yamile abandoned. There on the airport tarmac, while some military personnel detained the terrorists and transferred the woman trafficker to an emergency room, the other soldiers would make sure that all airplane passengers, one by one, went through the scanner.

Yamile would be the first person to pass the test without any problem. Despite this, her joy would be temporary, since the scanner was only detecting explosives and weapons. She wouldn't run with the same luck in front of anti-drug dogs however, which, from the moment that she left the sophisticated machine, would start to harass her, as if they wanted to eat her alive. Immediately after this, Yamile, as a suspect, was arrested and taken to have a body check, where they found the illicit packages inside her stomach. While Yamile would be detained, Lorena would die by an overdose at the airport's emergency room.

Hours after her death, immigration authorities ordered an autopsy on Lorena's body, where they took from her stomach, one hundred cocaine capsules, two of these exploded inside her. In addition, they found two plastic cases with a smaller cocaine amount inside her rectum and its vaginal cavity.

Simultaneously with the DEA surgeons performing, on Lorena's body, the cocaine extraction, the Interpol, in different international airports, would be arresting several women with similar cocaine loads in their stomachs.

After their arrests, they were transferred to the Colombian prosecutor office's hands, where these women would be interrogated.

The authorities didn't obtain any response from the women that would lead them the person for whom they were working. However, the prosecutors in the preliminary investigation concluded that being trafficker mules from different Colombian cities, they had many things in common, by which the prosecutors related all of them in the same case.

For them, the evidences weren't just coincidences. They were all beautiful women, they had been Le Fallèle models and all of them, on that day, were travelling to New York City.

The afternoon of their arrest, all these women had two full cocaine cartridges inside their genitals and one hundred capsules hidden in their stomachs.

But the most surprising thing about these young women were their trips itinerary, since each of them was carrying more than thirty international flights in her passport.

Another thing that caught the authority's attention was that days before each trip abroad, several of these women, together with their former boss, Marlon de la Roca, would visit the Colón's town, a bordering municipality between Panama and Colombia.

The prosecutors, based on the operating mode of their most elusive criminal, focused their research on the famous designer, to whom they linked as being Sotomayor's front man or a new cartel's boss. Under these circumstances, the Colombian prosecutor's office, through Interpol, issued his capture.

Immediately upon request, the Panamanian authorities, to prevent Marlon de la Roca leaving the country, extremely took security controls at airports and border cities. While the militaries would be doing this, the special forces raided the fashion house Le Fallèle and other places, but in these operations carried out by the police, Marlon de la Roca wasn't found, since I, his secret man, minutes later in advance from the airport, had informed him about his trafficker mules' fall.

Sotomayor's New Cartel and Olmeda's Departure

Days after the unsuccessful attempt to capture to Sotomayor in Panama City, people from different Colombian cities arrived at the municipality of El Paso. Due to territorial dispute between Colombia and Brazil, the population didn't have any kind of military presence. The law was established by civil authorities led by the mayor, his inspector and one hundred private security guards.

Despite this, its inhabitants, although they didn't know with certainty to which country they belonged, had pushed El Paso forward; its growing development served as an example for other municipalities.

Among the new residents of El Paso were David Salamanca, Helmer Gutiérrez, Jorge Sotomayor and Dirceu Figuereiro – me.

Parallel to our arrival and with different intentions, Toniño Cerezo and Zeledon Lindarte arrived at the same town. The latter was accompanied by his family his wife, Olmeda, and their children, Henry, and Karen.

Within a few hours of our arrival, with the exception of Zeledon's children and myself, each one of these newcomers started their own marketing research, to take advantage and discover a better way to invest their money.

After several days of research, we all made our own plans.

The first of afore mentioned newcomers established a timber exporting company, whose administrator would be Helmer Gutiérrez.

Toniño, third in the list, would choose to create a cheese cooperative. Independent to them, Jorge Sotomayor, or 'Santos' was inclined towards the poppy plantation. This autonomy shown by these characters was only a façade, since in a neighbouring municipality, the four had created a secret society.

Those who were outside of them were Zeledon and his wife, who, beset by debts in the city, arrived at El Paso, convinced that from there, they would make enough money to pay their arrears.

On the other hand, I, Dirceu Figuereiro, arrived as an emergent man, known by many as 'the Poet' due to my romanticism wherever that I went. My job was to secretly provide maximum security services to Santos.

Two weeks later, the new businesses had already opened their doors to the public. They based their services on the needs of El Paso's people and began to fight for their dreams. In their attempts to achieve their dreams, not only would they benefit, but it would also benefit the municipality and its many people. The arrival of all of us would bring El Paso to a greater economic boom.

David Salamanca and his partner initiated the venture to purchase wood, but as requirement demanded that instead of traditional beams, they would bring rough logs – six meters long by sixteen inches wide. This request was simple comparatively, contributing to the reason why so many sawyers decided to work for them. Those who accepted the proposal received free chainsaws and personal safety equipment. In addition to that, the recent entrepreneurs offered them the task to replant the entire deforested area with new improved mahogany as extra work.

While five of them settled into their new jobs, Jorge Sotomayor offered to employ anyone who wanted to venture into the poppy planting industry.

Immediately after, every unemployed person in the municipality would respond to this offer.

The creation of hundreds of jobs caused a crisis in the community's food supply, which at that time was not suitably self-sufficient. Zeledon observed this dilemma, and although he already had set up his business, he quickly opened a new public establishment with the capacity to supply the entire municipality for a month.

In front of Zeledon's premises, his wife, Olmeda opened a store filled with electronic devices and a spa and massage parlour, which would employ a professional aesthetician.

Because of their futuristic vision, the couple knew that with the lumber company opening and poppy plantations in the area, the economic status of El Paso inhabitants would improve, generating income for workers and stimulating the economy. Naturally, they would want to have access to new technology in the market as well as feminine luxuries.

Eighteen months after the first planting, the new mahogany on the hills had grown two metres and, between their furrows, the poppy began to show its first buds. But this didn't stop the reforestation, because as the sawyers cut down the trees, a new combined plantation was started.

Days after the poppy crops bloomed, Santos and his workers began the incisions into the poppy bulbs.

The first collection was a total success for the cartel; the milky poppy amount obtained was so much, the profit would exceed all predictions. For that reason, the next day, Santos took the initial steps to transform over two hundred and fifty kilograms of the poppy's milky fluid into heroin. Because of Santos' knowledge in this business, months earlier, he had instructed several villagers regarding the chemical process of creating heroin and had built an immensely large laboratory in the middle of the jungle.

The abundance of wood and poppy became a bonanza, and as a result, the money coming from the new businesses expanded throughout the municipality. Some invested in clothes, food or appliances, and others, in worldly vices, which particularly benefited the profits of Zeledon and Olmeda, who had in their premises any item that the inhabitants needed.

The communities of El Paso wanted to take advantage of the economic boom and at the same time, the municipality's progress, a circumstance which turned everyone into custodians of their own interests. For that reason, the poppy cultivation industry became a secret that didn't cross El Paso limits.

After the first twenty-four months, each one of the new entrepreneurs began to collect the large profits from their work. But this poppy bonanza would not only benefit their personal profits, but the town residents would also benefit. Because the cartel's capos, as custom in all of them, he identifies with the poorest and give them part of their gains.

Based on that prosperity and with the sponsorship by the wood company, David Salamanca sought out to build a community centre in the town with a dining room where, daily, the elderly received their food portions. In addition to that, he gave the municipality a dispensary and hired two medical specialists, so that the elderly community were treated without any cost, including the medicine.

As well as this, Santos' generosity had not been limited. Every month in the dispensary, he met with people who couldn't work and gave them the equivalent of a minimum wage. In cases of extreme importance, he paid for them the expensive surgeries and the patients' transfer to other cities.

With those benefits granted, Santos and Salamanca ensured that every person residing in El Paso would be at their command, including the mayor and his inspector.

As the days passed, the illicit income from the heroin trade was increasing. Because of this, Santos was forced to hire security personnel for his safety; in addition, he needed a place where his false company façade would operate and a residence that provided protection to him.

So, due to this, weeks prior, through his sowers, he bought an old house in the centre of El Paso. A house that the restorers, after several improvements, converted into a fortress of modest appearance, since according to Santos, he didn't want to draw attention with extravagances. Simultaneously, the builders gave him the place where he would operate his false company façade.

After receiving these properties, Santos invited several of his sowers and proceeded, without many preambles, to tell them about the purpose of the meeting.

With the employees already all aware, he would choose among them a group of escorts for his personal safety and three key men, as he named them.

The key men would oversee supplying chemicals and foodstuffs among the poppy growers and would be controlling the heroin quality. On top of that, they would have the task of providing protection to Toniño, during the tour with the cheeses, where allegedly the heroin would be undercover.

After selecting the personnel, Santos agreed with them that the organisation was internally constituted as the Poppy Cartel.

In addition, he stipulated that a member could depart from the organisation, only if all those who belonged to it agreed.

Immediately afterwards, everyone, including the boss, signed a pact, committing to be loyal to their cause and agreed that those who betrayed this pact would pay for their disloyalty by death.

One day after the initiation of the Poppy Cartel, the chosen ones travelled to the neighbouring country's capital. There, each one of them acquired a weapon and sophisticated communication devices. In addition to this, they returned to the municipality with a convoy of brand-new cars and two modern twin-engine boats, vehicles that would be used to supply rural provisions and the transport of raw material between El Paso and the riverside paths.

Over the months, the cartel became a brotherhood, but despite that fraternal connection between its members, no one until then, except for me and Toniño, knew the relationship between the wood company and Santos. Everyone in town was convinced that the heroin was taken inside the cheeses.

Due to this reason, each trip taken by Toniño to Bahia occurred suddenly, which was a last-minute security operation where all of Santos' escorts guarded the boat from its departure to its destination. With that strategic approach, he would manage to mislead his bodyguards and the law for several years.

In those days, it wasn't difficult for Santos to maintain the poppy production during its peak and, above all, to protect it from the guerrillas, since his strategy to share part of his profits in El Paso provided incentive for its inhabitants to maintain the secret of its production.

Another circumstance that would assist Sotomayor in his plan was that, as mentioned previously, the municipality was in a territorial dispute between Colombia and Brazil, and both countries expected that an international court would define their nationality. This was advantageous for him, as the two countries didn't have any police authority in the region, despite their administrative presence.

In fact, El Paso border was guarded from neighbouring municipalities with an international army composed by military forces from Brazil and Colombia. These circumstances would provide Santo's immunity from authority and immunity from harassment, from groups outside of the law.

Two months after the beginning of the heroin production in El Paso, Zeledon's children, Henry, and Karen, were infected by a dangerous tropical disease. That scared them too much because years earlier, they had lost a child by similar sickness. Thus, Olmeda was forced to sell the spa to her stylist, Fernanda, and leave the electronics store in her husband's hands.

Afterwards, she and her children would settle in Bahia, a city in the neighbouring country. Nevertheless, every week, Olmeda returned to El Paso with a shipment of food and merchandise to stock her business.

On Saturdays, when she arrived at the town, her face reflected great happiness for two reasons.

The first was the love for her beloved Zeledon, or rather the false love that she feigned in front of her friends and acquaintances.

The other reason was knowing that they had paid sixty percent of their debt, and at that time, the remaining debt was not the priority, since their moneylender was in prison and couldn't pressure them.

Thus, the two were able to invest their profit and the rest of money from their loan in order to build a small shopping centre. With this, not only did they contribute to the municipality's prosperity, but at the same time, they also received a large profit from this capital.

As the months passed in El Paso, the Poppy Cartel grew stronger. With their key men, Zé Maria, Paulo and Manamu, the organisation marched on and although they only exerted control internally, their external dependents became increasingly more efficient and productive. Thus, the work would increase.

That growth led the three men to begin their work very early. Zé Maria, with her twin brother, Manamu, and several security escorts, would cross the river until they reached Toniño's cheese factory. There, after distributing the grocery bundles among their suppliers, they would weight and purchase the poppy milky liquid from the farmers' crops associated with the cartel.

On the other hand, Paulo and his men travelled by land to all the purchasing points located in the municipality's rural region, places in which they carried out a similar operation.

After collection, the three returned the milky liquid to the laboratory, where, after a chemical process, it was taken back to Toniño's factory. There, supposedly, he would put it inside the cheeses, which would be delivered to a specific point soon. However, this was not the case. In fact, the heroin wasn't being transported like this. The drug would still stay in the cheese shop until Toniño transported it to the lumber company through milk containers.

After arriving at the lumber company, the heroin would be pressed and wedged between hundreds of logs that would travel abroad. Before each trip, Helmer Gutiérrez, the person in charge of this process, would take five shorter pieces of timber, make in them two-metre perforations, and insert, in them, a metal valve filled with heroin. Then, under pressure with a wedge from the same wood, the trunk's drain mouth would be sealed. The retouching and final seal on each piece of timber would ensure that the heroin was unnoticed by US anti-drug controls. The arduous work needed throughout this process meant that Toniño, Helmer and the key men were always committed to the organisation twenty-four hours a day, week after week.

This extraordinary work dedication would begin to produce problems in Manamu's relationship, as out of the three key men, he was the only one married. Thus, his absence led Raica, his wife, to make the serious decision to leave the town.

Manamu, although hurt by her departure, didn't have time to search for her. Without any other option, he resigned himself to losing his wife.

The Prosecutor's Harassment
and Ludiela's Capture

While Sotomayor was in El Paso, the Colombian authorities in its capital city advanced their investigation against him. They already knew with certainty that the model company Le Fallèle had been owned by Sotomayor, and that Marlon de la Roca and he were the same person.

With these clues, prosecutors began to tie loose ends and returned to the preliminary investigation to focus on Ludiela. However, a surprise was waiting for them, because when they arrived at the community, they found that the nightclub no longer functioned as a place of night-time entertainment, the local area was under renovations to establish a marketplace, and according to the guards that protected the property, it had been sold by its former owner several weeks ago.

The new discoveries found by the prosecutors increased the suspicion of a direct link between Ludiela and Sotomayor. So, the prosecutor's office issued a search warrant against Ludiela's credit cards, which, due to frequent use, revealed that she was in a hotel in Leticia, a border city in Colombia. Immediately, a covert detective began to follow Ludiela's movements.

In the first twelve hours, the detective would come to know all about Ludiela and several of her eccentricities, including her addiction to casinos, expenses lotions and street gambling. However, although the detective conducted her investigation from a discreet distance, Ludiela had already observed the vehicle and the woman who was following her throughout the night.

Despite this, she didn't pay too much attention. Her concern at that moment was her unsuccessful gambling that night. So, cursing her luck, she decided to walk away.

After returning to the hotel suite, Ludiela peeked out onto the balcony and noticed again the same woman who had been following her hours earlier. When

Ludiela observed that this person was parked near her hotel, Ludiela's suspicions increased, and she sensed that this wasn't merely a coincidence. Intrigued to know the intentions of her follower that morning, she planned a clever trick: to surprise her persecutor flagrantly and confront her.

With everything ready, Ludiela paid the bill for the suite and requested that one of the bellboys go to her suite at eight o'clock, pick up her suitcase and take it to her car's luggage rack. With the bellboy in Ludiela's room, Ludiela had paid him to wear her wig and her sunglasses and drive her car to La Parada, a tourist site located only fifteen minutes outside the city.

Here, Ludiela would be waiting for his arrival. Simultaneously, Ludiela called a taxi to pick her up at the hotel's back alley. With this, Ludiela would bait the detective, hoping that she would fall into her trap.

After accepting Ludiela's plan, the bellboy took the route to La Parada. While he was driving, the detective chased him from a moderate distance, and at the same time, the taxi driver was chasing her.

Twenty minutes later, the first to arrive at the location was the bellboy, followed by the detective, who would be surprised by Ludiela. Ludiela immediately demanded to know the reason why she was being followed. Without any other options, the detective identified herself and improvised; she told Ludiela that the reason for her following was due to suspicions of having links with the illicit emerald trafficking industry. According to Colombian Prosecutor Intelligence section, she was a cartel boss.

This accusation wasn't surprising to Ludiela but produced a smile that ended with an insolent question.

"Do you have any evidence against me? If you don't have anything, you will go into serious trouble by looking in the wrong place."

After warning the detective, Ludiela returned to the taxi, paid for her trip, thanked the bellboy and left in her car. That issue caused the detective to report to Baena what happened.

In response, he ordered her to abort the mission. The detective returned to her workplace and Ludiela continued searching for Sotomayor. Her desire to have sex and get money easily from Sotomayor became her obsession.

Half an hour into her trip and having passed two international military checkpoints, she would reach El Ramal, a point that divided the Pan-American road into four tracks. There, after meditating for a few minutes, Ludiela crossed the bridge and went to El Paso, arriving in town in the early evening. Her extravagant arrival caused a lot of noise, especially with the youngsters, since, for the first time in their lives, they saw a BMW sports car in front of them.

Ludiela, driving at a great speed, ran in circles around the town until finding the Villa de Rancel resort in a central street; the only one hotel that, according to her, had a five-star rating. There, Ludiela booked one room on the third floor for four nights. With the key in her possession, she entered the room, secured her things in the closet, took a hot shower and changed her clothes. Then with a lip liner in her hand, she went out to the balcony to apply her makeup and took note of the whole night-time atmosphere of the town.

Whilst giving herself final touches to her makeup, I, Sotomayor's undercover man, made a call to communicate to Santos of the woman's arrival.

Minutes after my call, the night began and with this so did the fun. So, Ludiela, encouraged by the bustle that came to her from the balcony, went out to enjoy the night.

In her anxiety to distract herself, she went through all the bars, but her need to gamble drowned out the party atmosphere and, within a few hours, she went into a total meltdown.

Her compulsive addiction to gambling made her deviate from her course, and although her weakness was the casino, when she is unable to find one, she searched for any dogfights occurring.

Immediately after Ludiela entered her environment, her mind calmed and she began to spread her bets. As the first fight passed, more and more fans arrived at the dog track. Among these would arrive a very popular character in El Paso, accompanied by very elegant woman, and they both very slowly moved closer to the preferential platform.

Their presence was a novelty for Ludiela, and although this was the first time that she would had ever seen them, she had the feeling of knowing the man for a long time.

With her curiosity peaked, she was informed by the person beside her that they were Santos and Tania.

Santos and his female companion, without any arrogance, made their way through the crowd and situated themselves a few metres from where Ludiela was. She, enraptured, didn't take her eyes off on them; her mind at that moment although was saturated in so much thought, she couldn't come to a definite understanding.

These thoughts kept her elevated on another planet. This distraction prevented her from observing what happened in the official fight, but the winning crowd's celebrations interrupted her concentration.

Due to the screams, she would react and focus her gaze again on the dogs' fight, where, with sadness, she would see her favourite dog wallowing in a pool of blood.

Confirming to her that luck was not on her side, she had lost all her bets. Thus, she went back to the hotel to try to sleep. Although she tried, the image of Santos didn't allow her to sleep.

Ludiela, intrigued to decipher her obsession towards Santos, got out of bed and went out to investigate in the town to discover more about Santos' life.

In her investigation, she discovered the public profession of Santos' and his connection to the wood's exportation for almost a year. However, Ludiela's intuition warned to her that there something he was hiding.

For that reason, as the days passed in El Paso, Ludiela would continue to search for more information, but despite her fixation towards Santos, the version of his story told among El Paso's inhabitants was always the same and she couldn't discover anything new about him. The only positive achievement in her research was that she had more than one casual encounter with Santos; however, the first would be without any result, as Santos' appearance was very far from resembling the man that she was looking for.

But not everything about her search would be in vain, as during her fourth encounter with Santos, in Zeledon's supermarket, Ludiela would eventually realize that it was Sotomayor.

The afternoon that Ludiela had discovered him, she had arrived at Zeledon's supermarket in search of some fruits. This was becoming customary to her recently since the supermarket was the only town's business where the owner accepted credit cards and she could get money advances without queuing.

When her purchase was completed, Ludiela went over to the cash register, ordered an advance of twenty thousand cruzeiros and proceeded to enter the code; however, to her surprise, her credit card was declined.

Distressed by that circumstance, she, with a feigned smile looked the casher and exclaimed:

"Are you sure, sir? Please, try again."

To the consecutive negative responses, Ludiela tried to return the items. At that moment, she heard a man's voice behind her, who, in a thick and coarse tone, said, "Don't worry! Beautiful woman, I will cover your purchase."

Once the order was paid for, the cashier opened the cash register again, counted the amount of money that Ludiela requested and placed the bills on the metal platform. Ludiela with cheeks flushed, turned her body around and found herself face to face with Santos. Ludiela, so astonished by his charity, shyly expressed:

"But sir! That's a lot of money to give to a stranger."

Santos, with a spontaneous smile, answered:

"Take it easy! This is not a gift, just a small loan! And the day that you can pay it, leave the money here with Zeledon or you can bring it to my residence."

That leniency offered and her urgency to pay for the hotel stay made Ludiela accept the conditions of the loan.

They hadn't even spent a few minutes conversing when pink patches started to sprout on Santos' face, accompanied by constant sneezing and strong nasal congestion.

This interrupted the conversation and Ludiela alarmingly asked, "Sir, are you okay?"

Santos, placing a handkerchief on his nose, replied, "Yes, miss, this illness is temporary, I am sure that it will pass soon."

After his response, Ludiela said goodbye and wished him a speedy recovery. Also, while was walking out of the Zeledon' store, she promised him that as soon as possible, she would pay his loan.

After this embarrassing occurrence at the supermarket, Ludiela started her car and drove back to the hotel.

After paying her debt, she would leave the town to nowhere in particular.

As she drove and minutes passed, the music playing on the stereo reminded her of the intimate moments with Sotomayor.

Romantic feelings awoke her need to find him and placate the passion inside her body that demanded sex. In addition, she knew with certainty that by being by his side, her difficult financial situation would be solved.

After driving for an hour and listening to ballads, Ludiela went into melancholy. Drunk on her sadness, she decided to play more cheerful music and, with this, improve the mood.

Without thinking, she took the iPod, changed the artist song, and began listening to reggaeton. While the song was playing, Ludiela sang along. However, when she was repeating the chorus, she focused on the lyrics: *"Today I want to be allergic to your skin, forget your kisses and your body, break your woman charm, and to empty this passion that I carry inside."*

At that moment, as Ludiela repeated the verse, she was reminded of something that happened several months ago. She recalled that, the Angel, (Sotomayor's former pseudonym), years before, was allergic to the same lotion that she had used in Zeledon's supermarket.

The previous occasions when she was next to him and used this kind of lotion, the Angel had presented the same symptoms shown by Santos back in the supermarket.

That, although could be a coincidence, made sense, since she was wearing the same lotion at that moment. Thanks to her intuition, Ludiela suddenly pressed on the brakes, producing a chilling sound on the road. Immediately after, she turned the car around and for five minutes, she drove against traffic until arriving to the entrance that would lead her back to El Paso.

Motivated by her anxiety, the minutes felt long. Thus, she kept her foot pressed on the accelerator, reaching the town in record time.

Back in the town, Ludiela took the terminal way. There, in a public bath, she showered, changed her clothes and reapplied different lotion. Without hesitation, she headed towards the town's centre. Her journey concluded in front of an old house, where after parking her car, she proceeded to enter. However, as Ludiela took her first steps towards the house, a man guarding the gate prevented her from entering. The obstacle made her anger rise as she began to scream at him.

Santos, hearing the commotion from the second floor, ordered the guard to let her pass.

While Ludiela waited in the reception room, Santos dismissed his lover Tania, to whom, weeks ago, after sensing the return of his beloved Ludiela, he had commented the possibility of a sudden separation between them. However, Tania, who, at that moment, was his lover, knowing that Santos would return to Ludiela's arms, forgot the agreement clauses that both had promised to respect until the end. So, as the decisive moment arrived, Tania breached the agreement.

Immediately at Santos' decision, Tania lost her senses and filled with jealousy, she locked herself in his room with him. There, with tears rolling down her cheeks, she warned him that she wouldn't leave the house and that, although she would stay at a distance, she wouldn't give him the pleasure of moving away from her life so easily and would always be very close to him, so that when he needs true love, he would know where to find it.

After drying her tears, Tania left the room and went to the pool as if nothing had happened.

Ten minutes later, Ludiela, a little calmer, ran her eyes over the immense main room. Although surprised, she didn't relax until she focused on Santos' eyes, who from the end of the main floor asked, "The miss came to pay her debt, or does she need something new from me?"

Ludiela, with a small smile, answered, "Yes! I need to talk with you! In private!"

Santos, without hesitation, expressed, "Of course! Let's go up to the second floor."

According to the version that Santos told me later, as the two walked up the stairwell, he was asking to himself, "Could it be possible that Ludiela discovered me? Or does she need more money?"

His incognito disguise would be deciphered as soon as they arrived at the second master bedroom, when Ludiela, with a triumphant tone, exclaimed to him:

"If you thought that I wouldn't recognise you, you were wrong; I know that you are Sotomayor."

Santos, astonishment expressed on his face, said, "Miss, please! Lower your voice and stop speaking incoherently. You are making a mistake!"

Ludiela's response was immediate. With an energetic tone, she insisted:

"No, sir, I'm right. I don't understand why you are trying to pretend that you don't know me. It's best for you to accept that my love and my persistence were more astute than you, and that today, I found you again."

Despite the familiarity that emanated from Ludiela's lips, Santos continued to insist that he did not recognise her, attempting to confuse Ludiela again.

Immediately upon bringing her face to his, Ludiela, like a hungry lioness, jumped on him. She clung to his body and made Santos' limbs fall one by one.

As Ludiela tried to caress him, Santos, knowing his skin's reaction to the products that Ludiela used, attempted to evade it.

This reaction, instead of interrupting the intimacy, caused an opposite effect in Ludiela, who, excitedly, began to caress his neck and whisper in his ear:

"Don't worry honey, take it easy! Before came here I took a shower and changed my lotion. You can be sure that my body that your lips want to taste will not cause you any kind of reaction."

After assuring this to Santos, Ludiela lustfully pushed him against the wall, took off her intimate garments one by one. Santos, aroused by Ludiela's touch, couldn't tame his passion until both achieved orgasm.

Their lustful caressing continued. Ludiela, wanting to reach her climax once more, clung to his lips, and from the corridor, Santos, with Ludiela on his arms, walked to the master bedroom. There, moments before her climax, Ludiela questioned his indifference by pretending he didn't know her.

Then, between heavy breathing, she asked, "I would like to know, do you still love me?"

At that exact moment, Sotomayor, unable to respond, was overcome with the feeling of climaxing again. However, seconds later with his voice tired and emotional, he replied:

"Of course! You will always be a part of my life, because despite my detached response earlier and the fact that I have more than one woman as my lover, I have always loved you.

"For that reason, I didn't want you to find me again because this love could cause to you to have serious legal problems. And as I truly love you, I don't want to involve you anything illegal.

"How you noticed me, I always tried to avoid that misfortune in many ways. Because of this, in my previous goodbyes, I always left you a large amount of money and properties, hoping that you would settle and make your dreams come true, so that you would stop looking for me. But with disappointment, I saw that my generosity is only enlarging your problem. My disapproval is not because you wasted money, since you know that I don't care about that. The really worrying thing for me is that I saw the woman that I love become a compulsive gambler, who was making extreme decisions like selling the apartment and gambling all of the money at the casino."

Suddenly, Ludiela, who was in a submissive position, leaned her legs on Santos's back and managed to ride over his body and take the dominant position.

Embarrassed and without arguments to respond to his concerns, Ludiela went back to caressing, her most seductive weapon.

After successfully silencing Santos' mouth with a very passionate kiss, she made him concentrate on her needs, and they both began a passionate journey all over their bodies. This ended at their genitals, where the two focused all their passion until they reached another orgasm.

At the end of the exciting moment, the fake smile was erased from Ludiela's face and replaced with shame. So, with words shaken by her emotion, she whispered into Sotomayor's ear, "My love, I promise that my behaviour will change."

"Of course, it is going to change!" Santos argued. "Now that my security is less vulnerable, you will be under my supervision. If you prove to me that you can control your gambling addiction for good, not only will I cover your credit cards, but I will also buy you another apartment. As well as that, you will get enough money to set up your own modelling agency, and an extra amount that you are free to use however you wish, if it is not gambled away."

Those conditions proved to Ludiela that Sotomayor's love, although strange, was true love.

The fact that Ludiela could clear up that doubt, didn't manage to control the carnal passion in her, as she lay naked on the bed, still lusting for more sex. However, Santos had to leave to supervise the heroin production. So, the two said goodbye with a passionate kiss, which would leave Ludiela on high erotic voltage, waiting for the night to arrive, to burn next to him all the remaining volts.

Before detaching himself from Ludiela's arms, Santos reminded her of his conditions.

The thought of the tempting offer, instead of encouraging her, left Ludiela thinking, since she didn't know with certainty if she would be able to control her compulsion.

While she was contemplating her decision, Santos took a shower, changed his clothes and went down to the first floor, where he ordered the kitchen chef to give her guest treatment fit for a queen. After his demand, Santos went to the patio and personally decreased the water level of the pool. Santos knew very well that Ludiela, in her eagerness to achieve her goal, would take refuge in swimming, but she was not a very good swimmer as she pretended to be.

He, with the protection and comfort he offered, wanted to make her feel as if she were at a five-star hotel, so that her stay would be pleasant, and she could uphold her promise.

During that day, Santos kept his cell phone off, as he didn't want to press her with his calls. He concentrated his thoughts on the event that was approaching him, of which Santos would arrive home prepared. He knew the sexual task that awaited him, if Ludiela hadn't decided to leave.

After arriving home, although Santos didn't ask for Ludiela, his eyes searched for her, and he confirmed that Ludiela wasn't in any main-floor rooms. He, sensing his abandonment, went up to the second floor and continued the search in his master bedroom. When he didn't see her there, he went to the balcony, hoping to see her in the pool.

Overwhelmed by her absence, Santos dropped his body heavily on the bed and began to think about her.

In that moment, as his mind was saturated with her memories, Ludiela appeared, showing off a new hairstyle and a seductive baby doll dress.

Immediately upon her arrival, she began to strip, leaving her body in a tiny bikini, which Santos would finish undressing with his mouth.

However, Santos' approach to their intimacy tonight changed from his usual routine. It wouldn't be with the same intensity as in the previous months, when, after a passionate night of lovemaking, he would push himself away from her life. Now, with more time to share together, he had the chance to not rush their sexual encounters.

As the days passed in El Paso, the two became the couple of the moment. So, seeing them together at night, visiting different places of entertainment in the town, including the cock fighting and illegal dog fighting, became normal.

Being forced to visit these places seemed greatly ironic to Ludiela, which she credited to Santos' foolishness. He, without obfuscating himself, made her understand that if she wished to have control over her addiction, she couldn't achieve it by running away from the problem; the best way to defeat it was by facing it.

With such a contradictory method, according to Sotomayor, in just one month, he had made excellent progress in Ludiela. However, sometimes she would clarify to him that her recovery was because he was by her side giving her attention daily.

Although that queen-like privilege controlled her compulsion for gambling, it didn't help her to overcome her emotional state, since the monotony of the small province and its inactivity made her extremely bored.

Sotomayor, aware of the dilemma, proposed for her to take a vacation. That proposal was always rejected by Ludiela, who fearfully warned him that this option could be premature, as most likely, if she were away from him, she would fall back to her addiction. Due to her refusal and obvious fear, Sotomayor became speechless.

After a few seconds of reflection, Sotomayor with expectation tenderly whispered in her ear, "Okay my love, tell me. What can I do to help your mood?"

Ludiela, a little annoyed at his ignorance, replied, "The truth? I need a job that keeps my mind busy."

Santos, showing a small smile, promised to help her, because if her desire was to work, he had the solution to her problem.

Immediately after, the two climbed into their truck and ten minutes later arrived at Belo Horizonte Ranch. There, after an economic agreement with its owner, Santos managed to transfer ownership of the property to Ludiela, who from that moment on had the authority to carry out any changes that she wanted or let the ranch continue normally including the horse-breeding centre.

Ludiela was speechless; the idea of dealing with these animals fascinated her. Excited, she wanted to start working immediately, but due to the transfer, she would have to wait until the next morning when the local court validated the sale. With the property in her hands, Ludiela began supervising the ranch, convinced that her new responsibility was going to keep her entertained for a long time.

Although that wouldn't have assured Santos that she would stay, he would do whatever was possible for Ludiela, so that she could achieve her goal.

After the first two days as ranch manager, Ludiela's mood drastically changed. Being close to these noble animals and others that roamed around made her love for them endless. Due to that reason, her interest in other species grew. Thus, after a month, she had the ranch turned into a zoo.

The new hobby of his beloved filled Santos with optimism, but the positive achievements that he observed in her would have an opposite effect on Tania, who saw Ludiela's permanence as an obstacle to which she had to put a stop.

For Tania, it was very painful to see that for Ludiela, due to having Santos submitted to her whims, everything had become very easy.

Due to the rivalry, Tania silently began to search for a strategy that would counteract Ludiela's privileges. However, as the days passed without figuring out any plan on how to hurt her, Tania felt greatly desperate and powerless, but even so, she didn't resign herself to her fate.

In anguish, Tania would spend three months researching Ludiela and with this, she also discovered some negative events of Ludiela's life, such as her adoptive brother Dario's accident.

This was a misfortune that Tania thought to take advantage of considering that her rival's misfortune would give her the opportunity to be alone with Santos. However, Tania would have to wait impatiently for several days more in order to achieve that as Ludiela, due to the stepbrother's frequent bad behaviour, at first didn't give much importance to the news. The reaction that Tania expected would come to her a few weeks after the initial news when Ludiela was remorseful and felt the need to help him.

One day before Ludiela's departure, those who oversaw the heroin control, Zé Maria and Manamu, carrying several heroin samples in their backpacks, surprisingly arrived at the house; their intention was to obtain an approval of the new heroin quality from Santos.

After a tour of the building's main floor, they spoke with the chef, who prepared the house's menu for them. While they ate the delicious food, Manamu noticed that the zipper on his bag was open. Immediately, when both visitors reviewed the bags of samples, they noticed that one of the small heroin packages had disappeared.

Initially, they imagined that the package had fallen out somewhere in the house. Convinced that they would recover it, they got up from their seats and attempted to retrace their steps until the main entrance, but when the search didn't result in anything positive, they concluded that they had lost it elsewhere.

Due to the packet's minimal amount, it didn't worry them much; they had extra packages and the remaining samples would be more than enough to get the final verdict.

They returned to the reception room without worry. When they returned, Santos went down to meet with them. He ordered them to accompany him to the basement, where, after verifying the drug's purity, he gave them his approval.

After the meeting, both left the house to continue their work. Simultaneously, Tania, back at the house, was wondering what to do with the heroin package that she had found; at that time, Tania didn't know if she should return it to Manamu or put it to better use, where she would benefit much more.

After several hours of thinking, Tania concluded that the heroin package would be the solution to her problem; she knew that the sample was enough to get her rival out of her way, forever.

Due to this convenient turn of events and the knowledge that Ludiela would be travelling in the early morning, Tania started her Machiavellian-like plan. That night, she took the drug and left the house with the intention of camouflaging it inside Ludiela's car. However, when discovering the car's locked doors, she realised that carrying out the evil task would be impossible.

Tania, disappointed and full of anger, without further options, returned to her room, where she silently started to plan her next strategy.

While this was happening, Santos called me and ordered me to protect his beloved during her time in the capital.

Hours after Tania's failed attempt, Santos said his farewells to Ludiela with a passionate kiss. In the middle of that intimate moment, Ludiela promised him that she would return Saturday evening. Concurrently, Tania observed from a distance the privilege of her rival, and although it increased her hatred, the situation also produced some happiness.

Particularly because it meant that Ludiela would be away for several days, and Ludiela's absence for Tania meant that she would usurp her place on Santos' bed.

Ludiela's sudden departure caused suspicion for Manamu and Zé Maria, who thought that due to Ludiela's addiction she had found the heroin sample and saved it with the intention of selling in order to use the money at a casino; thus, thinking it was merely lost, Santos would not realise that she had relapsed again into her vice.

Their hypothesis was very far from reality, since Ludiela had managed to maintain control over her compulsion and was not even considering going back.

After some time, the stipulated date of her return arrived and Ludiela returned without any issue. After arriving, she noticed her house on the ranch was normal, and if anything, strange did happen, Ludiela could never find out because everything was status quo, including Santos, who, that night, was having sex with her just like the first time.

Until that moment, Ludiela had everything under control, nothing worried her; she was so entertained by the mare's pregnancy and the new foals that she didn't have time to think about anything else.

Nevertheless, two months later, she would be planning again to travel to the city. Of course, on that occasion, her trip wouldn't be caused by misfortune, it was due to the veterinarian's recommendation who had discovered a terrible sickness on a mare's blood test.

The veterinarian revealed to her that the equine was infected with herpes virus EHV-1, which had mutated and thus, could not be treated through vaccinations. For this reason, the veterinarian advised Ludiela to urgently administer a stronger vaccine by another vet. She, based on the recommendation, went to look for such a treatment from the town's veterinarians, but when they could not administer such a treatment, she returned to the house and spoke with Santos about the urgent issue.

He, worried, recommended for her to take a blood sample from the infected mare and travel to the capital where she could receive a second opinion from other veterinarians.

Agreeing with Santos' recommendation, Ludiela quickly planned her departure at sunrise.

Ludiela's new emergency reached Tania's ears, who, for months, had been planning severe espionage that allowed her to discover even the most intimate moments of Ludiela's routine. Tania knew that for each trip, her rival used a different coloured suitcase and that for very urgent travel, she always departed the next day in the early morning.

Having that knowledge at her disposal, Tania would anticipate Ludiela's plans; she went to a shop in town, purchased a suitcase and a handbag identical to ones used by Ludiela.

That afternoon, after purchasing the necessary items, she went to the saddlery and instructed to the operator to make in each one of these accessories a false compartment which would be unnoticed by the eyes of others.

I, Santos' secret man, despite spying on her from a distance, saw that purchase as something normal. It was strange to me, to see her bring the luggage to the saddlery in order to do some modifications. But even with my insight, I never thought that these modifications to the accessories would trigger a plot against Ludiela's happiness.

When the saddler finished Tania's requests, she returned to the house and, taking advantage of her rival's absence, she wanted to make a profit again. So, from her hiding place, she took out the package of heroin, divided it into two packets and camouflaged each part in each carry-on accessory. At the same time, she went up to the room where Ludiela had her suitcases and carry-on bag and made the exchange.

Several hours after having managed to successfully switch the suitcases, Tania walked around Santos' bedroom. Her intention was to confirm if Ludiela would use the bags in her new trip. However, to be sure, she would have to wait until the next day early morning, since that night Santos and Ludiela were locked in their bedroom and would only leave at dawn.

The confirmation that Ludiela was not carrying Tania's planted baggage with her assured Tania of Ludiela's lucky fate. Although that circumstance ruined her plan at that moment, Tania wouldn't give up, because her obsession to hurt Ludiela would eventually produce the expected result, but while this was given, Tania would have to resign to seeing to Santos from the other side until that time.

Ludiela's trip to the capital would be very positive, since she managed to obtain a vaccine able to counteract the virus in the infected mare.

Days after administering the vaccine, the horse was recuperated, and the fear of abortion no longer presented a threat.

Once the crisis was over, the new foal was born. With its arrival, Ludiela doubled her love for them.

This made Ludiela enthusiastic to improve the life quality of these animals. Particularly because she had always searched for the newest veterinarian advances in order to take good care of them.

That interest would make that her travel back to the capital; however, this time she would travel with the intention of participating as a special guest, at the International Equine Breeder's Seminar.

When Tania found out about the invitation, she became overwhelmed with joy. This joy would be increasingly enthusiastic when she saw that Ludiela that night had utilised the suitcase and carry-on bag where she had camouflaged the heroin packages.

With Tania realising that her rival wouldn't be lucky anymore, she knew her hours of freedom were numbered.

Tania's emotions that night didn't allow her to sleep. Impatient, she would toss and turn in bed while watching with irony as the clock slowly stole the minutes from the hours.

When the clock showed four o'clock in the morning, Tania emitted a strong sigh, and with a leap from her bed, she reached to her window room. Then, very gently, she moved the curtain and from there she saw Santos saying goodbye to his beloved.

When Tania saw this love scene between Santos and Ludiela, it didn't affect her as it once did. In that moment, she was distracted by a feeling of triumph that gave her the strength to wait until Ludiela moved out of Santos' home.

Simultaneously to Ludiela's departure, Tania went out into the streets and, through a public telephone, alerted the police to the illicit packages that Ludiela carried camouflaged in her suitcase and carry-on.

Once the information was in the authority's hands, the operation would be carried out. So, hours later, when Ludiela arrived at the airport in the capital, she ran into a police patrol that immediately stopped her and demanded to search her. Immediately, the commanding sergeant ordered her to take out all her belongings from her luggage. Once the bags were emptied, the sergeant began the search for heroin in the bags with false bottoms installed.

During the search, Ludiela didn't feel any fear, as she assumed that it was a mix-up by the authorities. However, five minutes later, with surprise, she observed the sergeant finding two small heroin packages from her luggage.

That finding left Ludiela stupefied, and with elated eyes, she refused to believe that this was true and asked herself, "How the hell is this drug in there?"

As much as she searched her memory, she couldn't find a reasonable explanation; Sotomayor was the closest person for her to incriminate. Regardless, she was sure that he had retired from drug trafficking, since during her stay in the town, she never heard any rumours that linked him to illicit business.

Ludiela, due to her innocence, claimed to have nothing to do with the substance. She argued to the sergeant that the drug was placed by him to incriminate her. The sergeant, with an ironic smile, sarcastically replied, "That is the typical response from all drug mules captured. They want to pretend that the drug appeared by the grace of the Holy Spirit."

After his satirical response, he ordered to his police officers to arrest Ludiela and take the heroin and her belongings as crime evidence. I, from the distance, observed Ludiela's capture very cautiously. From there, I could see the reason why she was arrested, and in addition to that, when I saw the small suitcase and carry-on where the police found the heroin, I understood why Tania, months before, had acquired something similar to Ludiela's luggage.

In addition, I understood the reason why Tania had ordered the modifications.

After figuring out the facts and deciphering the mystery, I continued with my work. Without thinking twice, I called and told Santos what happened, telling with sincerity who was guilty of the plot against his beloved.

As I concluded my report, Santos was saddened. By his melancholy voice, I assumed that his eyes were clouded with tears reflecting his tragic pain. Even so, he doubted that Tania, despite her rivalry towards Ludiela, could do something so evil, since during the time that she had remained in the house, Tania never showed any resentment towards Ludiela. But even so, he couldn't doubt me, his secret man.

The uncertainty led Santos to investigate Tania's room, but when he didn't find the suitcases that he was looking for, he went to the store referred by me, where one of the employees would confirm Tania's purchase.

After knowing of Tania's betrayal and Ludiela's misfortune, Santos gathered several of his men to whom he ordered to build, at specific points in the jungle, four small lookout points, clarifying that these should be camouflaged among the tree branches and maintain in each, a guard twenty-four hours a day.

With that strategy, Santos sought the tightest possible security by land and, at the same time, would avoid attracting attention in the air, since with Ludiela's fall and the future punishment that he had planned for Tania, the military attack by detectives Baena and Guerrero would be inevitable.

After giving the instructions, Santos returned to the house accompanied by Manamu. There, the two prepared the scene for their act, in which, Tania would be the main character.

With everything ready and without any malice, Santos approached Tania and told her about the problems in Ludiela's life due to her gambling addiction.

Immediately afterwards, he insinuated to her the need for someone to go to the capital to inquire about Ludiela's fate. Due to his persecution, he couldn't do it.

Tania, pretending to have nothing to do with Ludiela's fate, offered herself as a volunteer. Due to her intention to impress him, fifteen minutes later, she had her suitcases ready to travel. Santos, pretending to be grateful for her generosity, would sweetly speak in her ear and passionately touch her inviting her to make love; Santos, leaving Tania even more convinced that her trip is not a dirty trick, carried her in his arms and brought her to his room to make love to her.

While the couple were having sex, Manamu exchanged Tania's suitcases. This procedure would be the same dose that Tania had given to Ludiela. But in this case, it will not be necessary to inform the authorities since the International Port Police would ensure a sad end to her story.

The morning hours before suffering the fatal outcome, Tania, after taking a shower and changing clothes, took the suitcases with the intention of keeping them in her car trunk. However, at the same moment, Santos appeared and insisted that he would do it for her. After arranging the luggage, he bid her farewell with a passionate kiss on the mouth.

Soon after, Tania boarded the ferry without any inconvenience. However, at the end of the tour, each car and its driver would be searched, and Tania, having parked first, would be the last to exit.

Immediately during her turn, a police officer demanded that she get out of her car with her documents in hand. Once her identity was verified, the police officer proceeded to register the luggage, finding at the bottom of the car's trunk one kilogram of heroin packed inside of a black bag. Upon finding the drugs, the police officer shouted, "She is carrying!"

That phrase made Tania instinctually react and, due to her cunning attitude, she ran out on the ferry platform where without much trouble, she threw herself into the water. She knew that on the other riverside, she would be immune to authority, and thus, she aimed to reach the shore. But that day wasn't her lucky day, since at the very moment of her falling into the water, a twin-engine yacht ran over her body, resulting in her body being lost at the bottom of the river for some time. When her body floated to the surface, it was lifeless.

Ludiela's Declaration

Twenty-four hours after Tania's tragic ending, Ludiela continued to deny any link with the drug traffickers. Despite this, the detectives concluded that her trips to El Paso meant that her provider was there. With this circumstantial evidence, Baena and Guerrero suspected that Jorge Sotomayor could be the target, continuing his illicit business in El Paso. Regardless, they knew with certainty that due to the heroin confiscated from Ludiela and the discovery of heroin in Tania's luggage at the border town, Sotomayor had altered the substance's compounds.

Although this was a breakthrough to the investigators, their theory wasn't yet sufficiently concrete as they needed to detain Sotomayor and prove his participation in the ongoing criminal activity in El Paso. Even though the detectives had one of the alleged traffickers in their custody, making progress remained very difficult, since just like the previous four mules, the detained wasn't willing to speak. Similarly, the El Paso inhabitants remained in total secrecy regarding the illicit business taking place there.

Thus, the detective's office still hadn't received substantial leads about the New Poppy Cartel. The detectives could only use their hypothesis in order to convince Brazil's counterparts to give them legal right to invade the town.

A week later, the two countries, based on the amount of heroin seized, agreed to heighten the inspection of all products from the El Paso area. However, until both governments received stronger evidence from the detectives, they refused military deployment in the area, because Brazil could take it as a violation of sovereignty and provoke international conflict.

As their plan was to find enough evidence to allow a raid, each country involved sent helicopters to fly over the region.

After taking satellite photographs, the pilots were perplexed to discover that through the entire jungle perimeter, there was not one single sign of deforestation.

During the inspection, the pilots were in disbelief as their eyes looked over the thousands of new trees but didn't spot any sign of poppy crops anywhere.

The lack of findings in the area didn't discourage the authorities; in fact, quite the opposite, it exalted their spirits, and the requisitions of the region's exports became more constant and rigorous, as all their suspicions now fell on the wood and cheese exports. Thus, all shipments of these products would be subjected to even more detailed checks.

As the authorities increased the inspections, the hope of finding strong evidence eventually faded, as Santos still managed to keep the mouths of El Paso's people closed.

Knowing that the mayor had given land to all that did not have their own home, Sotomayor assisted with the construction costs of their homes. This incentivised the inhabitants to maintain the secret of Sotomayor's business from the authorities. After several months without a positive result, Baena and Guerrero were forced to seek a better strategy.

Considering this reality, the two went back to the drawing board and focused again on the five women accused of drug trafficking. They reviewed their family links, discovering that four of these women all had relatives that were living in the neighbouring municipality, except for Ludiela, who, despite having a foster brother, appeared in the file as an only child with deceased parents.

In realising this, the detectives deduced that Ludiela had the ideal profile to insist and propose to her a new deal.

With hope that she would eventually break, they began to put all their effort into convincing Ludiela to testify against Jorge Sotomayor when the time came.

For that reason, the prosecutors released the other four detainees, as they knew it would be impossible to change the women's minds, since these women had a secret deal with Sotomayor, in which if they maintained their silence during their time in prison, each woman and their families would be rewarded. That agreement would make it impossible for these women to agree to any negotiation with the detective's office. But with Ludiela, in Baena's eyes, the negotiations would be easier for them as she had nothing to lose and much to gain. Thus, after arriving the next morning, Ludiela was surprised when one of the guards informed her that she had a visitor.

Ludiela's confusion wasn't for nothing. She knew that, aside from her foster brother, she had no one in her life. Regardless, she was sure that although he knew that she was in prison, her bastard foster brother would never visit her.

Ludiela, wondering who the mysterious character could be, followed the guard's steps.

Ten minutes later, the two arrived at the director's office, where a man with a face covered by a balaclava was waiting for her. Immediately, upon seeing him, Ludiela knew that it was one of the so-called 'faceless prosecutors.

Moments after her arrival, he introduced himself as Detective Baena. After his introduction, the man went straight to the matter explaining the reason of his visit. He proposed to her the benefits that she would receive if she agreed to testify against Sotomayor.

Ludiela's response was immediate, and with the same unbreakable determination seen months ago; she would make it clear to the detective that she wasn't willing to talk much less with a person hiding his face behind a mask.

It hadn't been three hours since the detective's departure before Ludiela was requested again at the prison interview room. However, on that occasion, it wouldn't be at the detective's request, but rather the request of a prestigious lawyer, who, supposedly had been sent by Dario, her foster brother. After the introductions between the two and Ludiela discovering the person interested in her freedom, she refused to believe that the sudden interest from her bastard brother was true.

Moments after the introduction, Ludiela's lawyer immediately discussed the benefits if she were to accept the detective's offer.

As the two argued, he explained to her that her ability to testify against Sotomayor was the most viable option for her to avoid punishment, to which he even recommended her complete transparency regarding Santos. If she were to do that, she could live a comfortable life as a recluse in the Witnesses Protection Program.

Immediately after the proposal, Ludiela gave a resounding no, even refusing his services. In response to her headstrong refusals, the lawyer attempted to calm her, clarifying that if she thinks it through carefully, she will understand why it is logical.

The lawyer then took, from his suitcase, a fine women's perfume and placed it in Ludiela's hands.

When seeing the gift, she instantly realised that the lawyer's visit was not because of her stepbrother, confirming her prior suspicions formed when her attorney informed her that he didn't use a certain lotion in her foster brother's presence because he was allergic.

Immediately, Ludiela would realise the plan by Santos, which signified his approval for her to accept the detective's offer.

With his task accomplished, the lawyer never returned to visit, since accepting her resignation from the case was part of the plan. With that very contradictory decision, Sotomayor would prove to Ludiela again that his love for her, although strange, was true love. But to Sotomayor, with this trick, he made it clear to his persecutors that even if they were close to him, they would never find him.

A week after his last visit, Baena returned to the prison again in order to interview Ludiela for the second time, and this time, Baena would no longer hide his face so that hopefully Ludiela would have a change in attitude about him. This would inspire much confidence in her. Noticing the peak in confidence, Baena offered once more the original deal discussed days prior where both benefits.

After several hours of conversation and modifying certain aspects of the deal, the two reached an agreement in which Ludiela, days before her testimony, would be removed from prison and placed in a Witness Protection Program in another country. There, she would receive another identity and for five years, she would be protected by the government with all the rights as a citizen. After that time, she would be free to continue there or return to her country of origin.

The detective, without having any idea that the decision taken by Ludiela had been at Sotomayor's permission, took extreme security measures and stipulated that the inmate's departure would be carried out with much secrecy which, according to Baena, would prevent the information alerting Sotomayor.

Due to that possibility, the authorities, along with the prison director, created a plan which would proceed in two days, with the knowledge that a woman named Jasmine would be arriving to the prison who, due to her large criminal record, would cause a commotion. The day before her arrival, a rumour about her aggressive nature even started to worry the prison inmates.

That morning of Baena's plan, after receiving the order, one of the guards led Jasmine, an undercover detective, whom the authorities planted as a dangerous criminal into the third courtyard.

With her strong voice, Jasmine stepped into the prison courtyard and began her performance. She immediately observed Ludiela as the only brunette woman among the prisoners and looked at her with malice. This malice increased when the guard informed her that she and Ludiela would share the same jail cell.

Jasmine, rumoured to be racist often, immediately announced that she hated black people. As the words emanated from the mouth of the new arrival, the inmates immediately reacted with aggression, especially Ludiela who quickly turned to face Jasmine, ready to respond to her absurd announcement. As soon as she was face to face with Jasmine, the guard promptly stopped the attack.

The two stood in silence, impatiently waiting until the guard left. Then, Jasmine returned to Ludiela and, with a defiant tone, she said, "Hey, black woman! Do not be offended by my words. It is best for you to get used to them because while you are here, you will be my slave."

The comments boiled Ludiela's blood and she immediately responded by closing the distance between them even more, to which Jasmine answered with initiating a physical fight. But once again, they were quickly separated by guard who took them both to a solitary confinement cell.

With that, the first stage of the plan was complete. Their performance would continue the next day, after their release from their temporary cells.

That afternoon, only minutes after returning to the courtyard, the two women initiated Plan B. The undercover inmate, in order to provoke more confrontation, approached Ludiela, slapping her. In response to the sudden development, Ludiela took a fake knife from her waist and stabbed Jasmine several times. To all those present, Jasmine's body was bathed in blood and all the witnesses assumed that Jasmine would be taken to an emergency hospital, while Ludiela would be transferred to a higher security prison. However, this was a ruse. After their performance, each one of women would appear at the detective's office. There, the presumed wounded prisoner handed in her work report and Ludiela started her work as agreed under the detective's command, disclosing Sotomayor's participation in previous cartels, his physical appearance, his former aliases, his address in El Paso and the address of his new wood exporting business.

In her report, Ludiela didn't mention anything about Sotomayor's heroin trafficking, as she was still unaware of Sotomayor's link with the Poppy Cartel.

Hours after the completion of her written testimony, Ludiela would be taken by the detective out of the country. Under the Witness Protection Program, she would be living in Panama City.

Baena, counting on the validity of Ludiela's testimony and after reaching an agreement with the Brazilian authorities, would order to deploy a military operation in the area that would be referred to as 'hot dog.'

Baena's Onslaught

Although the evidence against Sotomayor's was stacked against him, it seemed a higher power was once again helping him.

Unintentionally, the day of Baena's assault against Sotomayor coincided with the day of the completion of Zeledon's small commercial centre. Thus, on this day, engineers and builders had been completing the finishing touches to the building.

As they were finalising the construction, the construction supervisor thanked the workers for their arduous work with an incredibly special gift that he was sure that everyone would enjoy. That morning, he brought two boxes of cold beers, and within a couple of hours the boxes were empty, and the builders continued with their work.

Arriving in the afternoon, each builder had their fortnight cancelled before going home. Among them, Sertino, the construction officer, who intended to continue with his drinks, wanted to leave through the building's back door. As he walked towards the back, he stopped in his tracks as he observed his wife, Roberta, so he quickly retreated to hide in a room which stored empty paper cement bags.

Sertino, knowing that his wife was looking for him, stretched out on the floor and covered his body with the empty bags, staying there for a few minutes, so that his wife would assume that he was gone.

But as Sertino was an assiduous drinker and insomniac, he quickly fell asleep. As well as this, as everyone in the building had assumed he left initially; they were sure that he was drinking beers somewhere in the town. After hearing this, his wife Roberta continued in her search.

Several hours after Sertino's supposed departure, the engineer and supervisor accompanied Zeledon to the establishment. After verifying that everything was as stipulated on the contract, they proceeded to handover the keys and leave the building without having any idea that Sertino was sleeping inside.

At the same time at numerous points of the jungle, the silence of the night was interrupted by the noise of four motorcycles, driven by Santos' men coming to relieve their colleagues of their security services.

That night, each one of these lookouts would monitor the area, strategically camouflaged from the tops of the trees. Equipped with night visors and communication devices, these men possessed constant visual domain of the perimeter twenty-four hours a day.

Thus, early that morning, Sotomayor's multiple cell phones rang simultaneously.

These calls would come from multiple different parts of the jungle, communicating to him the eventuality that would come.

The warning from the forest lookouts somewhat alarmed Santos but the report that caused him the most concern was received from his most diligent escort, who immediately informed him that upstream, a police national coast guard had immobilised many armed men on lifeboats that were, without a doubt, heading to El Paso.

Moments after their reports, Santos informed Helmer Gutiérrez, David Salamanca and Toniño Cerezo about the situation that was approaching them. He also warned that they only had a few hours to erase the evidence.

Concurrently from the other end of the river, a concerned Manamu turned on his motorcycle and back to town, arriving at Santos' mansion, before his boss met with the rest of his escorts.

Seconds after Manamu's arrival, Santos proceeded to talk at length, deciding that no one, no exception, could attempt to leave the municipality and that, for their safety, everyone must remain within the town perimeter. Then, Santos ordered each of his men to be dispersed secretly throughout El Paso, so they could contain all information.

Following this, Santos met with his three key men, Manamu, Zé Maria and Paulo, to whom he ordered that the money and processed heroin should be placed in a secure place – the most viable option being Zeledon's new building. So, as time was pressing, the three men took the heroin and divided it into several bags. Then, with the money safely hidden, they repeated the same procedure with the heroin, but beforehand, they weighed each package and calculated that in each sack there was an average of 1.5 billion cruzeiros. After this, the three of them put the sacks on the truck and went to Zeledon's home, who would be surprised by their demand so early in the morning. He, without other options, would accede to their request. So, without any objection, he gave them the keys to his newly constructed building, which he had planned to inaugurate that weekend.

With the keys in their possession, Santos' men went directly to Zeledon's new building. As the three were unlocking the main entrance door and turning on the building's lights, Sertino, who was still sleeping inside, suddenly woke up. He was considerably confused, as he thought he had left the building immediately. As he pulled himself up from the floor, he heard Santos' men entering the building.

The construction officer, astonished, glanced at his watch and realised that it was already 1:50 am. Overwhelmed by his suspicion and fear, Sertino spread out on the floor again and sheltered his body with the empty cement bags.

Soon after, Sertino observed as the three men proceeded to hide something inside the building's electrical room. Then, listening to their conversation, he discovered that only five people knew the reason the men were there – to hide drugs and money.

Once the task had been completed, the three men left the building and returned to Santos' home. There, they gave him the keys to Zeledon's building and information regarding the heroin and money's hiding spot.

At the same time, Sertino investigated the contents of one of the sacks. Realising that it was money, he became persuaded by temptation and began to deliberate whether to take the money. He didn't know what to do, whether to seize the opportunity or go home empty-handed. Time passed; he became convinced that not taking a portion of the money would be stupid on his part, considering no one knew that he was there.

After deliberating over it, Sertino took all the money from one sack, filled it with paper bags and closed it again. He then divided the money into four empty cement paper bags; then, patiently, he placed each full bag into another paper bag. Looking like regular-filled concrete bags, he put them on a wheelbarrow, opened the building's back door and left.

As he walked home, Sertino realised that arriving home sober at such an early would be very suspicious to his wife; thus, he planned to act as if he were drunk.

Before going home, Sertino took the back alley to reach the patio-door where he would leave the money-filled cement bags in view.

After entering his house, he convinced his wife of his whereabouts and lay down next to her, waiting for her to fall asleep again.

Minutes later, he got up again and went to the chicken coop. There, without anyone seeing, he dug a hole and buried the money. At the same time, he promised that himself he wouldn't use the money until he was sure that his actions would not cause consequences.

While that happened, Santos' men were scattered all around different parts of town.

Santos himself took refuge in the Fernanda's house for protection, the stylist intended on transforming him into a double of her father, Ulises.

During his transformation, Fernanda ensured that her father, who was beside her, promised to them that while the military occupied the town, he would remain hidden in her residence.

As this was being carried out, hundreds of men from the military, with detectives Baena and Guerrero in charge, invaded the town. So, as the locals began their daily work, they were surprised to find their town cordoned off by special forces.

Immediately, with a Sotomayor's photograph at hand, the military placed checkpoints at the main roads connecting to the town and began the search. They demanded the passport of any passer-by who had any resemblance to Sotomayor.

Immediately after they successfully identified a person, they would take their fingerprint and enter it into a database, which showed them the identity and the criminal record from anyone.

Eventually, a man using the alias José Lemus would fall victim to the first raid. His real name was Gustavo Espino, who, for five years, had an arrest warrant for the alleged murder of his wife.

Gustavo, confused by that false accusation, resisted his arrest; he alleged that his wife had died of cancer and provided her death certificate as evidence.

Soon after his illegal detainment, Baena was informed of the situation. Upon hearing the name of the detainee, he ordered to the men remove his handcuffs and take him to the school. There, Baena would explain to Gustavo the reason for their decision to escort him, revealing to him that the accusations made were intended to protect him.

They knew that he was innocent and to prove it, Baena used his computer to clear his file and exonerate him.

With this, he was free to leave, but, due to the misfortune of having witnessed a massacre several years ago, he would be obliged to testify for the case that had been closed while they waited for him to appear.

Gustavo, surprised by this, paled in his face for a moment, the panic of that night became evident. Baena, seeing in him such a state, took him by the shoulders and spoke.

"Don't be afraid, for now, just I want to hear what happened that night. You will not be forced to testify with what you say in front of the judge. It all depends on what you have seen or heard to consider you as a key witness. So, all I want is to hear the truth." Gustavo, with a calmer tone, began to narrate what happened.

The Sunday of the homicide, he was in the ceiling that divided the main floor from the attic, he said.

Focused on his work waiting for unwanted raccoons living in the house, he suddenly heard a peculiar noise coming from the terrace door entrance. That sound, so silent, seemed strange to him and he initially thought that it was the two animals on their way to their burrow. So, looking at the time on his cell and confirming that was 9:45 pm, he ruled out that it was caused by any furtive guests due to the time, and the rodents do have a habit of returning to their burrow. Passing midnight, he continued.

Moments later, before the tragic moment occurred, he heard three pairs of footsteps going into different rooms of the mansion. Seconds later, he heard the four bodies one by one fall heavily against the floor. He then heard a call, where the gunman named Vadinho, confirmed to his boss that the traitors and their two bodyguards were dead.

Twenty minutes later, he heard another call being made, in which the assassin reaffirmed to their boss that everything was under control.

Gustavo paused the narration to take a deep breath and proceeded to clarify that, apparently, the person on the other end of the line must not have been sure that as killers had not completed job, so Vadinho reassured him.

"Sure, Mr Moreira, the politician couple will not be an obstacle to your future negotiations! They have closed their mouths forever."

After that, the mansion would echo noises throughout for several minutes, where all objects and furniture were thrown around the house.

After making the scene look like a robbery, the assassin then clarified to his boss that they would ensure that the police found a scapegoat to blame.

Before the call ended, the killer repeated the last name that Gustavo could never forget – Mr Moreira before leaving the mansion. With this, Gustavo finished his narration, confirming that it all that happened in that building, and although he couldn't see anyone, he clearly heard the incriminating conversation.

After hearing the statement, Baena concluded that Gustavo didn't have enough evidence to reopen the case. Even more so, he already knew that knowing the name Mr Moreira didn't help him at all, since in Brazil, there are millions of people with the same last name. And even if this Mr Moreira was the politician Tancredo Moreira, it didn't matter much, as when they first investigated him as a suspect, they did not have sufficient evidence to detain him, and so, if they attempted to send him to jail, it all would be in vain.

Thus, Baena was forced to dismiss Gustavo as a credible witness.

His version could eventually be important if the detective's office found stronger evidence, so Gustavo didn't leave completely free; he was committed to collaborate with the detective's office when necessary.

The detective then demanded, from the witness, his address in El Paso and his contact number. After this, Gustavo left, and the detective's men continued with their task to analyse the locals.

After the first day of the raids, there had been no positive result regarding Sotomayor's capture. The detective ordered to flood the entire city with pamphlets, offering a reward of five hundred million pesos to Sotomayor's potential whistle-blower. Unbeknownst to Baena, he was providing incorrect descriptions of Sotomayor, since he had his body transformed into an old man, unrecognisable to the sight of others. For this reason, Sotomayor walked around the town without the slightest concern; the only people who knew of his disguise were the stylist Fernanda, his father Ulises, Manamu and myself, his most loyal servants, and none of us would dare betray him, even if the price on his head doubled.

The second day of the military invasion would pass in El Paso without any positive news. Although the priority for Baena was to find Sotomayor, he also had to find where to accommodate all the personnel under his command. Luckily, they had arrived during the student vacation, so the schools and colleges were at their disposal; thus, half of their men were dedicated to adapting the rooms to what they required. These circumstances ensured that the harassment against Sotomayor wasn't so persistent. Nevertheless, Santos was aware that this harassment would increase, and although he felt safe there, he wanted to have another option of refuge in case that things in town became even more complicated. And so, he ordered Manamu to travel to the neighbouring country and find him a new shelter in the capital city's suburbs as an alternative.

As Manamu returned, Santos continued to be disguised as Fernanda's father and he even settled in his residence a few metres from his house. This strategy ensured he would remain informed about all detectives' advances. However, he was curious as to how safe he was, so that afternoon along with Fernanda, he walked around the town and even shared with other elders a lunch at the community hall where, that day, Baena and Guerrero were offering an enticing reward and would invite those present to betray Sotomayor and reveal any information about him.

After they listened to Baena's talk, Santos and Fernanda said goodbye and travelled home. With this, the two confirmed that no one doubted that this new character was really Ulises.

On the other hand, Baena and Guerrero still didn't give up on their efforts and continued across town and in the industrial area in search of information.

In their initial investigations, they discovered that Santos' house and the warehouses, where the wood was supposedly stored, appeared as rental premises. Something similar happened with the ranch. Although it appeared under Ludiela's name, it had been acquired by a mortgage, thus the bank was its real owner.

The evidence obtained until that moment hadn't been useful at all, they needed more compelling evidence. Thinking they could find that information in the only civil authorities of El Paso, each of the detectives simultaneously questioned the mayor and his inspector, who simply insisted that they knew Santos only as a wood exporter.

These testimonies, although like the previous ones from El Paso locals, still didn't leave them convinced. Both continued in their search of the truth of Santos.

Baena and Guerrero, with a hundred men, arrived at the lumber company. There, they carried out the most rigorous search of the entire operation, where one by one, the trunks and wood strips were meticulously inspected. But when they didn't find even any kind of superficial evidence, the detectives made several symmetrical cuts on the wood trunks, looking for a possible hidden insert. After completing their hard work, they still failed to find evidence. Thus, they proceeded to the lumber offices to take their statements.

In their investigation, during Baena's interview to Helmer Gutiérrez about Santos, his answers corresponded with the responses of the rest of his employees. The employees insisted that Santos was only an independent wood exporter. As well as that, Helmer proved that the lumber company had no link to himself. Running out of options, Baena and Guerrero left the wood factory and headed towards Toniño's cheese factory. There, chemists thoroughly examined the processed milk and every piece of cheese.

As well as this, detectives with drug sniffing dogs walked around the building from top to bottom. Despite this, they still could not find anything illicit.

This became increasingly frustrating for the two detectives and gave Santos a sense of strength and security. For that reason, when Manamu returned from Teresopolis with the news of preparing the new shelter, Santos decided against moving to another place, since in El Paso although the military harassment continued, there had yet to be any negative impact on his life.

Assessing that everything seemed under control, Manamu told Santos that during the search for a shelter, he had met with his ex-wife Raica, and after a long talk, they reconciled. Due to this, he needed to spend a few weeks with her in the capital to try to convince her to return.

There was a prolonged silence and the atmosphere in room became tense after Santos heard this, but after a few moments deep in thought, Santos gave Manamu all clear. Relieved, Manamu, only a few hours later, would return to Rio de Janeiro.

As Manamu arrived back in Rio de Janeiro, fate would begin to create an ironically tragic end in Manamu's demise.

His fatal end would begin at a local airport when he would be buying flowers for his beloved Raica. As he was paying for them, the florist didn't have the correct change to return. Due to this, Manamu decided to use the rest of the money in a lottery ticket, as the ticket's grand prize was billions of cruzeiros.

When Manamu looked at the ticket, he was surprised to notice that the ticket's number was quite close to his ID number; the difference being just two zeros in the middle and double five at the end.

During his first day together with Raica, despite Manamu trying to his best to rekindle their relationship, she was hesitant. However, Manamu persisted and continued the second day with the same perseverance. After many days, Manamu successfully changed the decision of his beloved Raica to stand by their separation.

One evening after a romantic dinner, Manamu saw the first positive signs from his efforts. Raica, flattered by his attention, suggested to continue their celebration in her apartment; so, they went to a liquor store and bought a couple of bottles of champagne.

Seconds after paying with his card, Manamu focused on the TV in front of him which was broadcasting a local football match. As he watched the replay of the goal in slow motion, in the lower part screen, the lottery's winning number from the previous night appeared.

As the little notice ran along the bottom, Manamu didn't initially catch the full number; however, he noticed that the last four digits coincided with the ticket that he had in his possession. So, he waited for number to appear again in which he realised that it was his number; without a doubt, his ticket was the winner.

In that moment of overwhelming emotion, Manamu couldn't contain himself and very excitedly expressed, "Hallelujah! I won! Those are my numbers. The celebration from Manamu was ignored by the people present, including his wife Raica, who thought that his euphoria was due to the positive date with her or because the soccer match was over and he like the score."

Afterwards, Manamu and Raica went to her apartment where they both got drunk and made love until their bodies were satiated all their passion.

After expending all their energy, Raica would be overcome by sleep first, so naturally, she was the first to wake up. When Manamu woke up, Raica already had come to a decision. She explained that although she was in love with him, she couldn't return to the town again even if it meant losing him. Raica believed if he truly loved her as he said, he should stay by her side here.

Even though Manamu tried to convince Raica with his love to return with him to El Paso, they could not reach a unanimous agreement; thus, they ended up talking about another topic.

As a second option, Manamu promised to her that he wouldn't leave her alone during the night. But Raica continued to insist that she could never come back.

With Manamu becoming desperate, he decided to play his last card and told Raica about the death pact that he had signed with the Poppy Cartel.

During this conversation, he still failed to mention to her the stroke of luck received as he won the lottery. That night, Manamu still had not received a positive answer from her, despite spending the night making love.

The next morning, Manamu returned to the lottery agency and presented the winning ticket in front of manager.

After signing and going through the protocol procedures, the manager gave him a check for the stipulated amount.

However, despite his fortune, Manamu wasn't completely happy, since Raica, the woman that he loved completely, had him pressured in a tricky situation. Thus, he needed to make an immediate decision between losing her forever or deserting the mafia.

Manamu's situation at the time was quite difficult because he couldn't undo the loyalty pact signed with the organisation without facing a trial that could possibly lead to his death.

So, the most viable solution for Manamu would be to propose to Raica to flee together to a place where nobody knew them. However, aware of the danger they would face, he spoke with his beloved about the consequences that their escape would bring. She, after listening to Manamu, accepted the risk without caring about the price that she may have to pay, since her dream was to be with him forever.

With their decision made, Manamu recommended to her that both could not have contact with friends or family for some time. He then erased all information from their cell phones and abandoned them on a bench in the park.

That morning, before leaving the capital, Manamu returned to the place where he had bought the lottery ticket. As the young employee was already informed that the winning number had been sold at that location, she had hoped that the lucky one would share with her a fraction of their winnings. So, when the cashier saw him arrive, she immediately imagined that he had been the winner. She would confirm her prediction when Manamu approached to give to her a check for a considerable amount of money.

The young woman couldn't control her emotions; excited, she hugged him and wept on his shoulder. Manamu then continued to other places where he donated smaller amounts to charity organisations.

Finished with his donations, Manamu returned to the apartment to deliberate with his wife as to where they would live. However, finding the perfect place for their possible refuge seemed harder than expected and took a long day of work, which ended after hours of contrasting opinions and hesitation. Once they reached an agreement, Raica and Manamu, for their safety, would settle in Porto Velho, Brazil, a city located at the other end of the country.

Two days after their arrival, Manamu pretended to be Raica's financial representative and secretly, under her name, bought some stores in the centre of Porto Velho. However, worried about possible consequence from the cartel onslaught due to his lack of security, he decided by prevention to move to a small village on the outskirts of the city and hired half a dozen bodyguards.

Simultaneously, things for Detective Baena were beginning to get complicated because time passed and neither he nor his men had discovered anything that would lead them to the capture of Sotomayor. Even worse, the agreement that he signed with the Brazilian authorities reminded him that had less than a week to leave El Paso, so in pursuit of the seemingly impossible, he demanded that their men to redouble their search efforts.

On the other hand, the detectives, hoping that someone would betray Sotomayor, toured the entire municipality door to door and attempted to entice people with the reward.

Their ingenious plan would lead them to the parks and town's homeless cafeterias, where the detectives were sure that they would find more than one unemployed person desperate for money who could be a future informant.

Santos was still closely observing Baena, and the strategies used by the detectives in order to get information. Using this knowledge, through Fernanda, he contacted the cartel members and ordered them to continue with the monthly assistance to the disabled persons and continue with the purchase of heroin, so that all those who were unemployed, due to the military raids would return to the jungle to continue harvesting the poppy buds like usual. Also, by Santos' recommendation, Fernanda informed them that in order to avoid possible capture of any indirect cartel member, the milky-looking poppy liquid would be transported from the jungle in new milk containers with a hidden double bottom that were available at the community hall. In addition to this, she informed the key men that after the heroin's process, they would have to bring the heroin to Toniño's cheese factory.

When the message was transmitted, Fernanda withdrew, and so the key men would enforce Santos' demands.

While the men were taking care of this matter, Santos contacted his partners, David Salamanca and Helmer Gutiérrez, to whom he demanded that they don't stop the wood shipments abroad for any reason. Then, he recommended to Toniño to continue making the weekly cheese delivery, but on that occasion, he wouldn't be escorted by the usual personnel. On this occasion, his safety should be in charge by the lazy people who roamed the parks and town's cafeterias, who had already been contacted by his key men.

The next day, when the detectives returned to the numerous establishments to continue their harassment, both the parks and coffee shops in El Paso would be empty. This circumstance made Baena, and Guerrero understand that the secrecy of their inhabitants about Sotomayor was unbreakable. Thus, even before the stipulated date, they withdrew the military from the town. With their departure, they added further failure to their long lists of attempts to capture him.

While this was happening in El Paso, far away in Panama in one of the shelters for witness protection, Ludiela felt a sense of unwanted nostalgia. Although her new residence had all the comforts of a home, it was still a maximum-security area. Her custody would be controlled by federal agents, who, in order to control the slightest leak of information, had restricted outgoing and incoming calls to this zone. Her inability to communicate with the outside world always kept Ludiela worried about Santos. She wished with all her heart that Sotomayor had dodged the onslaught of detectives and military; she didn't want to feel guilty that because of his intention to protect her, his life ended in a tragedy. But even with that feeling running through her mind and body, Ludiela couldn't call him. Even the telephones in her residence were merely just extensions to communicate among the residents.

The fact that she was yet to hear any news of Sotomayor's situation in El Paso kept Ludiela awake at night, ears and eyes glued to the radio and television. Logically, she knew that if the military were to capture Sotomayor or even something worse, it would be broadcasted on the news immediately.

After weeks of not hearing any news from reporters, she concluded that nothing bad had happened to him. This would somewhat comfort Ludiela's soul during the day, but at nightfall, she would lose control again and fall back into sadness.

However, her worry would be fleeting, and it wouldn't be long until her former joyous self-returned. Her grief would be alleviated by Baena, who at the end of the military operation in El Paso, would travel to Panama. Speaking to Ludiela, he confirmed to her that Sotomayor was still at large.

While the detective visited Ludiela's shelter, the Congressman Tancredo Moreira, found out about the peculiar mobilisation of troops in the border area of Brazil and Colombia and that caused him to become curious about the situation.

The politician, peaked by his curiosity, began to investigate what had motivated that military deployment. However, due to the secrecy revolved around the operation, he was unable to find out about the case details; the only information that he managed to obtain was the name of the two detectives in charge.

The fact that the detectives were a part of the anti-drug agency made Tancredo suspect that the operation was related to drug trafficking.

The politician, after analysing the area, considered that it would be favourable for Sotomayor, the person who has become his biggest nightmare. If his hypothesis was true as he thought, his assassins would be tasked to end Sotomayor, a happy conclusion to his frustrating years-long persecution by Sotomayor. Therefore, he urgently needed to be sure if the military deployment on the border had been in search of his enemy, Sotomayor.

Immediately, Tancredo thought about bribing the detectives in order to obtain the precise details of the case from them. But when he saw their resumes, he understood that it would be very difficult due to their history of being incorruptible. He knew that he could be successful with at least one of them because everyone, as humans, has a weak point. And this he would find in Detective Guerrero, whose weakness for women would make him the most vulnerable of two detectives. Thus, Tancredo focused all his attention on this detective.

As he didn't want to delay, that same afternoon, he would take advantage of his power to use a woman named Maica to meet with the victim. This expert in seduction, a beautiful and charming woman, would easily enter to his life, and days later, would serve as a connection between the politician and Detective Guerrero.

The Thief's Discovery and the Cartel's Fall

Twenty-four hours after the military left in El Paso, all danger at the time seemed to have passed. The cartel members, including the chief, entered a period of waiting, forcing Santos' personal escorts to remain vigilant in their positions.

The same happened with the key men, Zé Maria, and Paulo, who were hundreds of kilometres from El Paso and, having confirmed the coast guard's departure from the border, would not return to the town the same day. The two remained vigilant, waiting for Sotomayor's order.

On the other hand, I, the secret man, after making sure that the Colombian troops disembarked to Colombian territory and returned to their respective bases, would strategically allow a day to pass before establishing communication with my boss, who impatiently waited in Fernanda's bedroom for my statement.

Minutes after receiving my message, Santos, through Fernanda, called all his escorts in El Paso, to whom, as a priority, she explained that it is time to restore order in the house.

The fact that there was no danger to avoid implied to those present in the building that Santos would arrive there that morning. However, after that day passed and Santos didn't return or communicate at all, they became extremely alert and called for an extensive search door to door. The first person to be visited would be Fernanda, who, upon seeing the heated spirits in front of her, calmed them. Then, she with a relieving tone said to them, "Do not worry about Santos." She knew with certainty where he was and that he was fine.

The next morning, Ulises, Fernanda's father, left town and Santos appeared as if by magic. Immediately upon his arrival, his personal escorts would be reported and everything for the time being would return to normal.

When the afternoon arrived, the payments for the poppy liquid recommenced, but due to the immense production, the funds to pay for the substance ran low. The unforeseen circumstances led Santos to suspend payments for the moment and order his key men to pick up the heroin stored in

Zeledon's new building and take it to Toniño's cheese shop. In passing, he recommended handing over the keys to Zeledon and bringing the money with them, to process the purchase.

Immediately, Zé Maria and Paulo took the keys and left to complete the task.

Ten minutes later, once inside Zeledon's building, they activated the lights and proceeded to collect the money. Taking the two by great surprise, they observed that one of the bags, instead of money, was full of garbage and paper bags. They immediately called and told Santos what happened, so that he would apply the appropriate measures to follow.

The unexpected obstacle failed to alter Santos' mood, who serenely ordered them to remain on task and return to the house with the rest of the money.

While they returned, Santos took advantage of the minutes alone and drew up a list of suspects. Among them, the work engineer, the supervisor, Fernanda, Ulises, Zeledon, Manamu, Zé Maria and Paulo, the only people who had had a direct or indirect contact with the building's keys. Logically, according to Santos, one of them would be the culprit.

Based on his investigation, Santos would secretly draw his own conclusions.

Hours later, when the key men returned, they brought the fear evident on their faces due to their expectations of being interrogated by Santos. However, with surprise, the two observed that upon arriving home, the atmosphere was normal, as if nothing had happened. Santos, in total relaxation, received the remaining money and didn't mention the situation; he only recommended to each to continue their daily routine.

After the first day of his preliminary investigation, Santos already had several of the possible culprits removed from his list of suspects including, Fernanda, Ulises, Zé Maria, Paulo, and the supervisor, although the supervisor interestingly left the town the night of the robbery, which could indicate him as the main suspect. But Santos, knowing that his departure was due to his intention to murder his wife's lover, was enough evidence to declare the supervisor free of guilt.

Concluding the preliminary stage, Santos told me what happened so that my people and I could make a follow-up to Zeledon and the work's engineer to investigate their finances, and at the same time, I would be tasked to investigate the reason why Manamu had not complied with the agreement and not yet returned.

Although the investigation of the three began simultaneously, my detectives would demand several months to complete it, since finding the whereabouts of Manamu and his wife Raica would be difficult for them. Their frustrated searches in Brasília and Teresópolis would take them across the whole country, until finally finding them in a small village of Porto Velho.

While my men were tracing Manamu's finances, I was investigating the engineer and Zeledon. I discovered that the former, in the last few weeks, had consigned large sums of money. However, in the end I was also able to verify that this money was due to fraudulent contracts, thus he would be removed from the suspect list.

In the investigation of Zeledon, I also investigated the bank account of his wife Olmeda and ensured I personally investigated her as well.

In my investigation, I would be very disappointed to unintentionally discover that Zeledon was being betrayed by his wife who was a secret sex worker. She, monthly, was giving a sum of money to her young lover to keep him tied to her sexual desires.

Apart from Olmeda's deceitful secret life, I didn't find anything that revealed both as the thieves. However, due to having sold the warehouse and placing his new building for sale, I still couldn't completely rule out Zeledon as a suspect.

As the weeks passed, on the other side of the country, my men discovered that Manamu, through his wife Raica, had bought a couple of hotels and apartments in the tourist area of Porto Velho, and that their invested capital amounted to more than 1.3 billion cruzeiros.

With that information and his non-compliance with the cartel's agreement, Santos had no doubt about Manamu's guilt. Regardless, he wanted to be one hundred percent sure before issuing a verdict; thus, he ordered me to personally confirm the story told by my men.

Two days later, I, with copies of the notarial register, would confirm to Santos the purchases made under Raica's name. Thus, Zeledon would be free of all suspicion as our focus turned to Manamu.

With the evidence verified, Santos gathered all the cartel members to make a public announcement about Manamu. Then, he reminded them about the agreements they all made years ago, where all those present had committed themselves to be loyal to its cause and whoever betrayed it would pay for his deceit with his death. That meant that Manamu must die under those rules.

However, Santos, with sadness evident on his face, clarified that this sentence was not his personal verdict since it was ruled in advance by all the signatories, including the future victim.

Knowing the inevitable future of his twin brother was a hard blow for Zé Maria, and although for a moment he wanted to appeal the verdict, he didn't do it, since he knew it was in vain to intercede on his brother's behalf. So, he accepted it with resignation and didn't revolt against anyone; he was aware that a deal between the cartel men must be respected. Thus, he only asked Santos to warn those in charge of Manamu's fatal outcome that they should not take any retaliation against his sister-in-law Raica.

Zé Maria, impotent in the face of that obstacle, would leave his twin brother at the will of his fate, but he didn't lose hope that Manamu could repel the attacks and remain unharmed.

Almost as though Zé Maria's thought was captured from a distance telepathically by his twin brother at that moment, Manamu had the feeling that he would be killed. The imminent danger alerted his mind, so he, based on that feeling, ordered his men to be alert to a possible attack.

Not even a few minutes passed before Manamu, when leaving to take his private car, was surprised by several projectiles impacting the rear-view mirror of his car. Immediately in response, three of his men responded by chasing down the hitmen.

While the three bodyguards tried to catch up to the hired killers, Manamu, Raica and the rest of their guards left the village and sought refuge in another town.

A week after their escapes, the cartel hitmen located them again and repeated their attempt to kill him, but on that occasion, they would alter their original plan; this time, they would use a sniper as a second option.

The day of the second ambush, two of the cartel assassins harassed Manamu's bodyguards and provoked a distraction that confused Manamu, as his bodyguards were focused on repelling this attack. With that strategy, the hitmen successfully revealed Manamu's rear guard, allowing a hitman posted the roof to shoot Manamu two times in his chest.

The shooting alarmed the local police, who immediately responded to the scene. As they arrived, the authorities found the place calm, surrounded by an unsettling silence, but seconds after, they were interrupted by Raica's cry over her husband's dead body.

After securing the perimeter, the police cordoned off the area, and a forensic doctor proceeded with the removal the body, which would remain consigned in the morgue while he filled out a report of his death.

The news of the attempted kidnapping and subsequent murder of Manamu was announced on television throughout in El Paso. Immediately after Zé Maria saw the name of the village where his twin brother was killed, he travelled there.

When Zé Maria arrived, he looked for Raica and together they claimed Manamu's body. With him, they returned to El Paso, where they gave him a Christian burial.

After the funeral and receiving the condolences of family and friends, Raica would return to Rio de Janeiro, but before her departure, she ensured that Zé Maria would visit her.

With Manamu's death, the cartel was left with a large gap within the cartel members, which Santos had to fill immediately. So, he and all the organisation's members, that same day after Manamu's funeral, would begin the search for a possible candidate.

Choosing a new key man with the efficiency of the late Manamu would not be easy for the cartel members. However, among the many who presented themselves, one stood out: a former federal agent from Panama, descended from Brazilian parents and based in El Paso, called João, would be most favoured. This person, according to the cartel members, was the one who came closest to Manamu's qualities.

After making the decision, Santos and their men explained to their new key man the agreement and emphasised the death sentence for those who betray the organisation. João, after listening to the conditions, exercised his oath of loyalty and signed the contract that accredited him as the new key man.

With João's arrival, the administrative problem in the cartel was solved. Even so, Santos still lamented for his late friend Manamu and entered a depressive episode. But not only did his mourning for Manamu hurt his heart, there was a reason more powerful. This was his love for Ludiela, who he hadn't seen for a long time.

Little by little, the absence of his beloved was taking away the meaning to his life. Sometimes, even thinking of memories with her made Santos lose control, his eyes filling with tears.

As the days passed in El Paso, João, through their colleagues, would come to know the main cause of his boss' melancholy.

Finding out about Santos' pain enabled to the new member to seek a close friendship with him and, as a friend, offer him a possible solution. In their conversations, João spoke about his knowledge of the witness protection shelter in Panama, which João compared to a five-star hotel within a residential complex but without alcoholic beverages, Internet nor a telephone signal.

In contrast to these prohibitions, those living there had access to other premises, where the government was responsible for covering all the expenses.

After Santos' new key person continued, telling him that having been a member of the Panamanian Secret Service allowed him to have many contacts and thus, he knew everything related to the program. João, due to his ease of access to the federal program, offered to Santos a link to contact Ludiela. That offer and the possibility that she had been taken to one of these places comforted Santos' soul; however, due to the excess of work, that option could be possible only in the future, when the heroin's processing was complete, Santos said.

As time was passing in Sotomayor's life, from a border city in Colombia, his destiny began to forge a new surprise, and the link would be Maica, the attractive woman sent by Tancredo Moreira to seek a connection with Detective Guerrero. She, from the moment that they were introduced, began to get exactly what she wanted. Within a few days, Maica was engulfing him in her seductive game until she became his secret lover. Then, in one of his furtive encounters in a private Amazonia club, with much cunning, she would introduce the politician into the detective's life. The influence of his new friendship and the silent pressure exerted by his lover made the prosecutor quickly enter a friendship in confidence with the politician.

After the first two weeks, Guerrero had visited Maica more than once. Although their dating was carried out in different cities and with much secrecy, Tancredo, as by chance, was always there. That coincidence ensured the three always ended up sharing the same table in hotels and entertainment establishments; their 'casual' meetings strengthened the friendship between the politician and prosecutor and led them to mutually share secrets.

One night, when the three of them were having drinks, Tancredo, taking advantage of their relationship, offered to Detective Guerrero a strange and enticing proposal. He offered him one hundred million cruzeiros if he told him in detail the reason why he and Detective Baena raided the border region. Guerrero considered the proposal, because to him, it wasn't information of maximum security, but rather that it was merely political strategy, and although he saw a bit of malice in Tancredo's intentions, he didn't consider the offer as a bribe. He knew that revealing the information wouldn't put anyone's life at risk and, thus, by accepting the deal, he wasn't betraying the institution.

After analysing the situation, Guerrero accepted the deal, but before he revealed the information, he insisted on one condition to Tancredo. This condition was that he would only discuss what happened at the border at the resort where they were staying and only when the money was deposited in his safe deposit box inside his room. Immediately at the detective's request, Tancredo communicated with men from tables nearby that were carrying out surveillance and ordered them to bring the money to Suite 104.

Already in the privacy of a hotel room and being paid the stipulated amount, the detective revealed that the military deployment was with the consent of the Brazilian authorities. In the joint operation, regular troops and agents from the detective's office participated, and although their operation covered the whole border area, their specific interest was El Paso, where an unknown drug trafficker named Sotomayor was sheltering. However, because of his cunning ability to hide, it was impossible for them to capture him. The operation, despite being quite frustrating for their careers, said Detective Guerrero, hadn't been completely useless because in one of the raids, they found a man with the alias José Lemus, whose real name was Gustavo Espino, a secret witness of a massacre that took place several years ago in the mansion of the Duarte family. "With this, we have the possibility of reopening the case, finding the culprit and having compensation for the military deployment." Nevertheless, this person, due to not having any arrest warrant against him, was released in El Paso, willing to cooperate as soon as the detective's office would require it.

Hearing that caused thick saliva to pass through Tancredo's throat, creating uncomfortable hoarseness, followed by a cold sweat that overcame his entire body. Tancredo, completely ignorant of the existence of this new obstacle, knew he would have to eliminate this threat.

The candid speech by Guerrero filled Tancredo with optimism, and during his drunkenness, he ordered four of his most professional assassins to search for Sotomayor, his most elusive enemy. Then, he entrusted Vadinho to look for José Lemus, his other hidden enemy and kill him.

The politician needed to act quickly, since he didn't want to give Sotomayor or the supposed witness time to move away from El Paso.

The onslaught by Tancredo's assassins would occur just two months after the death of Manamu and on a day that any stranger in the town was presumed suspicious.

With the new demise approaching Sotomayor, the cartel would interrupt its habitual routine and all its members would be alert to their highest capacity.

We, due to our preventative measures, immediately suspected the arrival of five men with an ominous, professional appearance, who claimed to be selling life insurance. Their arrival caused suspicion, particularly from myself, from the moment they made individual reservations in different hotels despite the first hotel having vacancies for all of them.

Other things that caused suspicion was the fact that two of their chosen rooms were overlooking Santos' house, and their stay in the town would only be for three days even though each of these men had brought such large suitcases for such a short visit.

Hours later, as the afternoon arrived, four of these foreigners, by telephone, agreed to meet outside of El Paso where they would seemingly plan an appropriate route and from there, they would begin their objective to kill Sotomayor.

On the other hand, Vadinho, after walking for a couple of hours around the town and asking questions to passers-by, had located the house where José Lemus was supposedly living. Already knowing his address, he decided to wait for nightfall to commit the crime, but unbeknownst to him, three days ago his target had quietly abandoned his residence. No one knew of his departure except for the owner and Ernesto, the beneficiary of his belongings.

When the time for the murder arrived, Vadinho slyly approached the house where he planned to carry out his task. As he arrived, he found a man who was moving out the furniture and furnishings of the house. This left Vadinho no doubt that it was José Lemus.

Vadinho based on that presumption, when he saw the alleged Jose going down the stairs with a heavy object on his shoulder, without analysing him, he approached his back and shot him at point-blank range to his head. The bullet pierced his ear, killing him instantly as he fell down the stairs. Vadinho's strategic approach to the kill ensured that the heavy object fell precisely on the wound, looking like it killed him. Especially considering the silenced weapon used, this ensured the death was initially confused with an accident. For Vadinho, José Lemus had lost his life. As none of his neighbours heard the rumble of the bullet or saw the bullet embedded in the wall, there was initially no cause for alarm. Only minutes later the neighbours would they realize that the man was dead. When they saw him, everyone assumed that the wound on his face, although it showed a perforation between the skin and the bone, was caused by the fall, and so it would be stipulated as such in the initial police report.

As this fatal episode occurred, the other four assassins had ended the telephone conversation in their respective hotels. Then, each of them took their portfolio and went down to reception, waiting for the taxi that would take them to the planned meeting place.

While the taxi arrived, they could see that armed men were guarding Santos' house in the front and in the back alley. That anomaly, although intrigued them somewhat, didn't interrupt their plans at that time.

After the meeting, the assassins divided into two groups, each of which was given a route and began a tour of commercial establishments in El Paso, looking for potential customers for their life insurance.

Everywhere that they went, they offered their merchandise, and after a long talk with the interested party, they showed a photograph of Sotomayor. A photo that both parties would pass it off as a photograph of Aurelio, a missing workmate and someone who had long been sought by the zone.

None of the residents confirmed that they saw this man in town, nor did anyone say that the photo seemed similar to the reward pamphlets placed by the detectives months ago. Even less could they link the photo with Santos, since the picture was too far from reality of Santos' appearance.

As they toured the city, the hitmen listened to the report of a dead man found in the house of José Lemus. The inaccurate news made by many of the locals made the killer think that the deceased was José. With this, Vadinho was convinced that he had executed an excellent job and, thus, the hitman wouldn't verify his death.

Hours into the frustrating search for Sotomayor, the five assassins, including Vadinho, returned to their respective hotels where they analysed other possibilities. Being optimists, they focused all their attention on Santos' home, since they knew from experience that the physical appearance of Sotomayor had always confused them. For that reason, they couldn't rule out Santos.

Even with their change of strategy, the hired assassins, at that time, couldn't manage to find out much about Santos, but the little information they had would be enough to discover that their lumber company was a front for laundering illicit money.

That first positive step encouraged them to continue their investigation. Then, from their hotel rooms, the five of them took videos and photographs of Santos and sent them to a computer expert from the capital.

This person would process, through software, a photograph of Sotomayor from years ago; this would design a depiction of the possible current Sotomayor.

After creating this virtual image, the specialist created Santos' green eyes, his bushy beard, extended his hair, created a bulging stomach, his hat and dressed him in a tuxedo, resulting in a perfect double of Santos. Without a doubt, for the computer expert, Santos and Sotomayor were the same person.

Confirming his identity, the assassins sent by Tancredo began a follow-up mission for three days, in which they learned that Santos, every day in the morning, went outside El Paso to monitor the mahogany crops. They also verified that he and his escorts, during the daytime, always took the same route towards the small hill called La Ye, an intersection where they would deviate from their route to enter the jungle.

The killers, based on Santos' routine, discarded their original plan and decided that the attack would take place at dawn the next day, just outside El Paso. Convinced that at that time he wouldn't escape, they called their boss and assured him that after so many years of persecution, Sotomayor was unknowingly counting down his final hours.

As the five foreigners finished their investigation, I recognised one of them. This was the supposed peasant who years ago, in Ipiranga, who had led me and Vinicio into a death trap. At that moment, I realised that his goal was to end Sotomayor's life.

Immediately after my realisation, I alerted Santos to the danger, but also recommended to him that when sending his bodyguards to investigate the situation, he warns them to act with great caution, as these people were professional murderers. In addition to my advice, I encouraged him to carry out the search between 6 am and 7:30 am. This was the hour of least risk for his investigation because, in that space of time, the assassins would be in the outside of town, planning the finishing touches.

Santos, following my instructions, made a call to João, his most experienced key man, who, in command of a dozen security escorts, took all precautions and went out to complete the mission.

Upon arriving at the hotels, his men were divided into groups of three: two of each group, would distract to receptionist, while a third bodyguard registered the corresponding room.

Without any obstacle, the five in charge of checking the rooms, including João, completed their objective, finding that the hitmen's inspections' suitcases contained Sauer pistols and powerful Barrett rifles, each one equipped with mufflers and laser sights.

Once they had confirmed the foreigners' intentions, the escorts left the hotels and returned to the house, where Santos was informed of the presence of the weapons. With this, Santos decided that the assassins should die. But their deaths would not be executed by their escorts or happen inside the town, as he didn't want to bring El Paso into panic. He also didn't want to draw the attention of the authorities of both countries, as the mafia men on the border would be responsible for their murders.

While on the other side of Brazil, Tancredo's men prepared for the ambush, João and his partners, based on the continuous exits and long-range rifles that the killers had planned to use for the future attack, deduced that their plan was to ambush Santos in the outskirts of El Paso, as he was going to inspect the mahogany crops. João's experience in the protection of witnesses made him realise that the strategic point for a possible attack was La Ye, and so, in advance, they would secure its perimeter.

After the analysis, João deployed his men to the back of the hill and ordered them to be ready for a surprise operation.

In groups of two in two and keeping no more than ten metres of distance between each other, João's men camouflaged themselves in the undergrowth, waiting for Tancredo's thugs to arrive to take their positions.

At 7:45 am, in two taxis Tancredo's hitmen would arrive to La Ye. There, after taking out their suitcases, they went to the small mountain to prepare the ambush. However, the moment they began to place the rifles, they were surprised by a dozen men from all angles, who in a matter of seconds subjected them to their will.

After their capture, the five were handcuffed and taken to the middle of the jungle, where, one by one, they would be interrogated and threatened with losing their tongues. Their confessions, except for the supposed death of José Lemus, were recorded on a digital camera. After the investigation, João's escorts would discover their participation in numerous murders, including the death of Vinicio,

Falcão and his men, and the place where they were buried. They also discovered that all of the hitmen were registered under false names and that the five belonged to the armed wing of Los Cariocas, a cartel run underground by a top politician named Tancredo Moreira, the intellectual mind behind the crimes and the person, who, for years, had been practicing a death chase against Sotomayor.

The information obtained from the assassins was transmitted directly to Santos, who ordered their men to keep them there until midnight, where they would be transported and abandoned on the riverbank.

After the mission, the escorts planned to return to the house. While they were leaving, the hitmen freed themselves from their handcuffs and, for a moment, thought of returning to take revenge, but analysed that to do so unarmed, without communication and without vehicles, would be a meeting with death.

Without further options, the best thing for them to do was to flee, so they waited for the fishermen to transport them by canoe to the Bahia Dock.

That morning, when arriving at the fluvial port, their arrival alarmed the police, who upon finding them without documents subjected them to a thorough interrogation, in which, they claimed to be personal escorts of Senator Tancredo Moreira.

The five declared that their unpleasant situation was due to sexual harassment, in which a group of women, who they contacted in a nightclub to have sex, had supplied them with Burundanga, a strong sleeping powder which allows others to take advantage of you against your will. Then, they stole all their belongings from them.

The police, after hearing their story, took the phone number and verified their statements.

Ten minutes after the call, all five would be released. From there, they went out in search of a taxi to transport them to the capital. However, when they reached the main street, several bursts of rifles were shot, suddenly ending their lives.

The statements of hours before, expressed by the alleged escorts before the police, were in vain because Sotomayor's hitmen killed them as a precaution and, his knowledge of them being involved in different crimes. The police couldn't know.

The news of the murder of five of his men, although altered Tancredo Moreira's spirit would prevent him from insisting on a new attack. He knew that any reprisal of an attack on Sotomayor would be useless, and he wouldn't want to divert attention from his political campaign due to more killed security escorts. Although Sotomayor was his priority, the circumstances forced him to give him a truce. Despite the five murders, although they were a hard blow for Tancredo, were not in vain because according to him, they had managed to eliminate José Lemus, one of his potential threats. But Tancredo was wrong, because that person he believed was dead, merely few days before the arrival of his assassins and weeks after having divulged the secret to Detective Baena, went into panic and became carried away by his delirium of persecution and from that moment, started to run away again.

Hours after the politician's hitmen were killed, Sotomayor, via mobile phone, invited me to the mansion and personally thanked me for saving his life. In his talk, he confessed that for the first time in so many years, he was worried, because his most dangerous enemy had been a few metres away from him and that meant that his persecutor, little by little, was gaining an advantage.

He knew that in the next attack, his enemy could have better luck, and so he contemplated the possibility of surrendering to the detective's office or to settle in another city with a new alias.

In response, I optimistically told him that if he continued to reside in El Paso and maintained his leadership in the organisation, nothing would happen. The town's inhabitants and security would be a barrier of protection against the possible murderers. Nobody, no matter how professional they are, would try to kill him inside the town. They knew that by attempting such a thing, they would be lynched. With my perspective, I made him understand that his weak point was outside of El Paso's perimeter, so all that he had to do was change his routine and leave that responsibility in the hands of his key men. Then, I ensured him not to worry; the assassins were dead and, with that, the next ones who wanted to hurt him would think twice before trying.

At that moment, Santos wanted to continue with the conversation, but it was interrupted by an incoming call. Thus, he said his goodbyes to me and concentrated on the important call from Toniño, who warned him that the boats would be sailing in three days and the trips delivering wood were incomplete. They needed one hundred trunks more, including five with less than six meters containing, in one of them, the twenty kilos of heroin remaining. So, Santos immediately spoke with Helmer Gutiérrez and Toniño at the same time and demanded, from his sawyers, to hurry the cutting process.

The short time left for the shipment led them to cut all the trunks of the same size, including trees that at that moment were the appropriate size, yet too green and, thus, not yet suitable for the process. When the date arrived, the deficit was supposedly covered, and the trip started.

With the departure of the ships, I would return to my usual job as a secret man always alert regarding Santos' safety. My job was to analyse every new person arriving in the town. Due to this, that day I entered Zeledon's super store, greeted those present and continued with my objective. With my arrival, I interrupted, for a few seconds, the business that Zeledon was proposing to a merchant. After the momentary interruption, both returned to their original talk, with one party asking and the other offering. Zeledon, at that moment, pointed out that his inventory, the commercial bonus and the groceries, amounted to more than three hundred million cruzeiros. However, since his priority was to sell, he would leave everything for two hundred and eighty million.

The merchant, locked in his proposal, asserted that if he lowered the price by twenty percent, he would take his offer.

After many moments of not reaching an agreement, the merchant decided to leave. But he wouldn't do it without making a final proposal, in which he offered two hundred and fifty million.

With that amount, although it was quite equivalent to its original price, Zeledon didn't allow himself to be easily seduced and so, he told him that he would think about it.

Once the negotiation ended, I took the grocery basket and arrived at Zeledon's desk. Since he was no longer busy, his attitude became more professional and we both initiated a pleasant conversation, and so I took the opportunity to ask him, "What is the reason why you are thinking about selling the supermarket?"

Zeledon, with a nostalgic tone, told me that the main reason was that he loved his wife and missed his children too much, as he could only see them a few times. His children were always reproaching him for his abandonment. Their sadness was eating away his soul; he knew that they needed a father and husband to lead a normal life. In addition to that, as he had a debt to cover, it had forced him to sell the grocery store and his other property. With that decision, he had planned to kill two birds with one stone, repay the debt and return to his family's side, Zeledon concluded. As I listened to his explanation, I thought for a moment of revealing to him the truth and talking with him about the bad behaviour of his wife Olmeda, but for the sake of their children, I kept silent. So, anxious to be soon with them, I offered to lend him the money without any interest, an offer that Zeledon rejected. He explained that by accepting it, it would tie him even more to El Paso's people, and what he least wanted was to have a need to stay. Thus, I didn't insist on my offer. I was prudent, and indirectly, I supported him in his decision. I knew from my own life experiences that it is useless to possess material things if the soul is not strengthened.

The Drug's Confiscation and the Discovery

Weeks after my conversation with Zeledon at his superstore, two details would cause me to feel a mixture of euphoria and concern. To my surprise, I learned that after Ernesto's autopsy results, the coroner ruled that the cause of his death was a broken neck. However, he had found a bullet wound on his left ear. Thus, someone had shot to kill.

"But who and why?" were the questions everyone asked.

Finding out that my compadre José and his family mysteriously had disappeared from El Paso made me assume that the death was destined for him. However, due to his luck and the misfortune of Ernesto, the night that the killer would commit the attack against José, the murderer confused his victim.

The other news of Zeledon selling his supermarket would be more comforting. This caused me great joy, because this would allow him to reunite with his loved ones and fill him with happiness. However, Zeledon knew that leaving his friends and the people who offered him support in the past would cause him sadness as well. Due to this, he wanted to distract himself with liquor, so he went to the 'Perródromo,' a place where the dogs fight to their death. Zeledon knew that, at that time of the day so early in the morning, the place would be empty.

Nevertheless, on his arrival, he would meet Santos, who arrived with a similar intention, to drink to forget his memories. Although Santos' sadness stemmed from losing his love. It had proven very difficult for him to tear this feeling from his heart. Regardless of his attempts, the whiskey was ineffective, even causing the opposite effect. So, during his drunkenness, Santos cried for Ludiela, with Zeledon consoling him. Santos' escorts, seeing that both Santos and Zeledon were drunk, took Santos' keys and didn't allow them to drive. One of the security guards transported Zeledon to a hotel and the others took care of taking Santos back home. There, they loaded him into the car and then escorted him to his room.

Minutes later, Santos got up from his bed, intending to continue drowning his grief with liquor. When he reached the stairs, he mis-stepped and fell down the stairs. The accident, although not serious, caused a backache that worsened when trying to walk. The escorts, seeing Santos' alarming condition, wanted to take him immediately to the clinic, but Santos, even in his inebriated state, thought that the town doctor could discover his disguise, so he ordered his men to take him to Fernanda's home. There, after examining Santos and listening his story, she knew that his pain was caused by a swelling between his lungs and rib cage.

Regardless, Fernanda decided to wait until Santos became sober. However, due to his audible suffering, she ordered the escorts to leave her alone with the patient and immediately she started a remedial body massage and applied a suction pad.

After several minutes, an exhausted Santos was eventually relieved of the pain and immediately fell asleep and didn't wake up until the next day Thus, his men guarded Fernanda's house until Santos recovered.

Hours earlier, while Santos and Zeledon were still drowning their sorrows, three ships loaded with wood from El Paso arrived at the port of San Francisco. There, after passing all the customs security controls, they docked at the port.

Then, the workers began to unload the trunks that matched the size required. One by one, they stacked them on the trailers of several trucks, where, as each one was filled its capacity, they would go to the sawmill to deliver.

The trunks that were not the required measurement were rejected. Among these was a six-metre-long trunk that the cutters of El Paso, in their eagerness to comply with the quota, had cut too green. This was taken by mistake and sent with the selected trunks to the pencil factory. This trunk, due to the elevated temperatures during its travel across the ocean, had unintentionally dilated.

The truck driver knew by routine that from the pile of trunks, he only had to transport the rejected trunks to the furniture store where he was working.

After several waiting hours, the driver of the old truck had filled his quota. Regardless, he knew to keep waiting; he couldn't leave without checking the progress of unloading of boats, so he was always the last driver to leave. However, that afternoon, due to an error in the cutters, his quarterly delivery would be changed, since back at the logging company in El Paso, Helmer, a month earlier, had wedged twenty kilos of heroin in one of the six-metre-thick trunks that were going to the milling machine.

That day at the sawmill, as the trucks arrived, their workers ensured that each trunk passed through the mechanical brushes.

After that procedure, a dozen saws would convert the trunks into small pieces that, later, would be turned into pencils.

Three hours later as the workers were about to complete the first trip, they, after bringing the final piece of timber to the machine, heard a strange noise. They quickly discovered that this strange noise was accompanied by sparks of fire and a white powdery cloud that would slowly spread throughout the premises. Immediately in response, the machine automatically turned off and its alarm began to sound.

The machine operator, concerned, approached the machine. The first thing he saw were the disks of the saws embedded in a metal case which continued to emanate dust. Immediately, he reported the situation to the manager and his boss, who telephoned the authorities.

When the police arrived, they were accompanied by DEA agents, who upon examining the substance, verified that it was heroin.

This discovery meant that all workers and company executives became suspects, and so, each one had their cell phone confiscated and were barred from having contact with the outside.

After a few minutes of investigation, the DEA cordoned off the area and ordered to arrest the driver and apprehend his old truck, which was still parked on the loading dock.

In their search, they found four additional trunks where Helmer Gutierrez had planted the remaining eighty kilos of heroin.

The detainment of the driver, although completely innocent, would be the starting link for the DEA, starting at a furniture store in the city of San Francisco and eventually start to disassemble the cartel in El Paso.

In their first attack, the authorities successfully detained seventeen members of the cartel and apprehended information that could lead them to the supposed cartel leader.

The DEA, to prevent the information leak, contacted agents in Brazil. That same afternoon, the authorities, together with the SIB and detectives Baena and Guerrero, initiated an operation called 'Speedy González' which, soon after, resulted in the detainment of the Poppy Cartel's treasurer in Bahia.

At the end of this second blow to the cartel, the three combined forces continued with their plan. Their next objective would be the capture of David

Salamanca, Toniño Cerezo and Helmer Gutiérrez in El Paso. And although Santos or Sotomayor was not listed as a member of the network on the San Francisco list, they included him in pursuit. The detectives knew, from experience, that his disguises aliases had been the strategy which he had always confused them with, and they had no doubt that Santos was the capo. For that reason, the military tactic to be used in El Paso would be a quick and silent invasion, executed by a paratrooper commando that would ambush four key areas: the logging company, the cheese factory, Santos' supposed residence and Salamanca's apartment. Their mission was to detain the suspects and leave with them by helicopter to the DEA's base in Panama.

That morning at two O eight '0208', according to military time, as the militaries synchronised their clocks and boarded two C-17s, they soon arrived in international airspace. They referred to the coordinates and, simultaneously, the four units ventured to their separate objectives.

Ten minutes later, a silent invasion seized El Paso. In a matter of seconds, each unit secured the perimeter and started the countdown. As the clock marked 14:50, the authorities disrupted the town's calmness as they raided numerous establishments.

The chaos of the authorities surrounding Santos' house ordering those insides to open the door startled the residents of the central district awake.

After identifying themselves as Interpol, the sergeant demanded that the house's occupants come out with their hands on their heads. As the authorities did not receive an immediate response, they threw tear gas canisters through the windows and destroyed their doors to continue their search. They would be surprised to see that the house was empty and that, seemingly, Santos had escaped.

But the reason for not finding Santos and his escorts was pure coincidence, as the previous day, Santos had been drinking and was recovering at Fernanda's home, from where he was observing the entire operation against him.

While the first command unit failed in its attempt to capture Santos, the other three groups detained the rest of the cartel with ease.

Fifteen minutes later, two Apache helicopters arrived in El Paso, withdrew the troops, and took the detainees Jorge Salamanca, Helmer Gutierrez and Toniño Cerezo to the United States, as per the extradition order.

As Santos heard the helicopters land, he glanced at the clock, which showed 15:20 military hours.

Soon after, Santos heard the helicopters leaving, hinting that the military invasion had concluded. Cautiously, Santos sent his key men to investigate the situation and ordered his escorts to check if there were any soldiers still in the town.

Several hours later, they returned to Fernanda's home to confirm to him the capture of his partners and cartel members, as well as the troops' evacuation.

Knowing the fate of his three colleagues further increased the sadness in Santos, who was already struggling due to Ludiela's absence. This crumbled all his remaining strength. Thus, he arranged that the ownership of the ranch title deeds be passed onto me. Then, Santos reunited with his men and, before giving them the sad news, he gave each of them a large sum of money. With this, he relinquished them of their commitments and ended the Poppy Cartel. Despite this, everyone wanted to follow him. However, he opposed to this, clarifying that he was going to surrender to the authorities. As per his request, only João and I would continue to accompany him.

Two days after the military assault in El Paso, Zeledon the legal documents for the shopping centre left in the hands of his former employee, along with signed authorisation, so that he can process any future purchase of the building without Zeledon.

After this, Zeledon started his vehicle and took a final tour of the town, where he would say goodbye to his friends before driving toward the capital.

That afternoon, by coincidence, Zeledon and Zé Maria boarded the same ferry. However, upon arriving in Bahia, they both took a different route. Zeledon set off on his car towards the north, and Zé Maria travelled south.

Zé Maria, taking advantage of his freedom, decided to fulfil his promise to Raica.

The reunion of both Zeledon and Zé Maria with their loved ones would fill them with joy. Zeledon would reunite his family and Zé Maria would fill the void left by his deceased twin brother left in Raica's life.

With Zé Maria's arrival, little by little, he began to supplant the role of Manamu which Zé Maria would enjoy. So, in his eagerness to assist Raica, their relationship changed. She still held on to the memories of her late husband, and so her attitude changed as she lived with Zé Maria. She began to live in a kind of fantasy, where Zé Maria would become an indispensable part, in order for her to continue living.

Raica's desire to keep him by her side meant that she spent most of her time beside him. Every day, they were seen in luxurious restaurants, cinemas, and nightclubs. Because of that close friendship, the two would end up having sex and Raica became pregnant. That unexpected circumstance made them both think that their relationship should end, but the life that was beginning inside of Raica instead of separating them, only reaffirmed their true love.

One afternoon after visiting the Raica's doctor, she, encouraged by her whims, asked that Zé Maria drive their car to the shopping mall to buy a dessert that was being advertised in an ice cream parlour.

Immediately as Zé Maria arrived, the storeowner was filled with happiness. She, in a muffled voice, said to herself, "It's him, he's alive! He is not dead like the news announced."

The woman excitedly called over the waiter and ordered her to give the two arrivals a royal treatment.

The attention they received surprised Raica and Zé Maria. This surprise increased when Zé Maria attempted to pay the bill, but the waiter told them that their meal was free, courtesy of management.

Zé Maria, at that time, thought that this privilege was a marketing tactic. Intrigued by their strategy, he approached the young woman and asked.

"Excuse me, miss. Do you regularly serve the customers like this??"

The waiter, with a small smile, answered.

"No, sir! If we did this regularly, the business would go bankrupt. This was by the owner's request."

"Then I would like to know who is the owner?" Zé Maria asked.

The employee answered, "The owner is the young woman in front of the cash register."

Raica, looking into the eyes of her lover, asked suspiciously, "Do you know her?"

He responded, "No, my love! This is the first time I've seen her in my life." The two walked from their table to the owner; Zé Maria, still with doubts, turned to the woman at the cashier desk.

"Excuse me, ma'am? I tried to pay our bill, but the waiter said that all was paid. Ma'am, are you sure that we do not owe anything?"

"Don't worry, your dessert and many more were paid in advance, months ago!" she responded.

"In advance? And who made that payment for me?" Zé Maria asked.

Immediately, the young woman replied, "You!"

"Me?" he replied with surprise.

"Yes!" said the woman, "And thanks to your generosity, I managed to buy this place. I bought it with the gift that you gave me for having sold to you the winning lottery ticket."

At that moment, they were both speechless; with surprise drawn on their faces, both Raica and Zé Maria looked at each other without knowing what to say.

Seconds later, Zé Maria broke the awkward silence and said, "The truth is, I always try to keep that a secret, thus I pretended to not remember it, but to pretend in front of you was a mistake on my part. Thanks for reminding me."

Then, pretending be the lucky winner, he said goodbye to the young woman with a big hug, to which she responded by praising God and expressing her relief that he is alive and not dead as the news said.

Minutes later, when Raica and Zé Maria arrived at their apartment, both knew that Manamu, the twin brother and ex-husband, was innocent. He had been killed by mistake.

The two, based on the young woman's story, agreed that the execution of Manamu couldn't be left unpunished. Zé Maria's duty as a brother was to find the true culprit of the robbery and kill him. After the agreement, Zé Maria promised Raica that he would return to El Paso to begin his investigation, since he had an idea of who could have been responsible.

Concurrently, Zeledon, who had settled in the capital, had received, from Teresópolis, several calls from the loan shark, who, now released from prison, demanded him to pay the outstanding owed amount.

In response to his demand, Zeledon asked for a few more weeks while the sale of the shopping mall processed. However, with the loan shark's threatening persistence, Zeledon handed over the profit of his two previous sales to him, remaining only the loan's interest. Regardless, the loan shark wasn't satisfied and gave Zeledon a deadline of the end of the month to pay the remaining amount. Due to the short time, Zeledon knew that this would be impossible. So, afraid of a possible attack, he decided to leave with his family to another city in Brazil.

The morning of their departure, while they waited in the terminal for the bus to leave, Olmeda would be taken by surprise as she left the cafeteria when she saw a man with a couple of teenagers, who closely resembled Zeledon and their children. The resemblance was so uncanny, that she thought he was Zeledon's double.

Minutes later, surprised at what happened, she told Zeledon that when walking down the terminal corridor, she saw a person so identical to him that she was confused. The most peculiar part was that this man possibly even had the same name, because when she called out Zeledon, he turned his head toward her.

A day after Zeledon and his family's departure and that strange coincidence, Zé Maria said goodbye to Raica, but before leaving the city, he made a call to Zeledon's cell phone from a public phone, the person Zé Maria assumed as the only possible culprit.

Based on his assumption, Zé Maria threatened him, "Enjoy the money while you can!"

As the call had been made from Teresópolis, Zeledon assumed that it was made by the loan shark. However, as he tried to respond, the call had already dropped.

Hours later, Zé Maria was back in El Paso. He discovered that Zeledon had sold the supermarket and that he resided in the capital looking for a client to sell his small shopping centre, and that his intention was to settle in the city. Knowing that, Zé Maria's suspicions increased and that same afternoon, he planned to take his revenge.

In his plan, he contacted a person in Bahia to pose as a potential client and speak with Zeledon. The undercover buyer stated to the intermediary that he was interested in buying the shopping mall, but demanded that to carry out the sale, the owner must be present. When Zeledon heard that proposition from the potential buyer, despite knowing that he didn't need to be there, he knew it was suspicious. Thus, he didn't travel to El Paso as he thought it was a trick being played by his moneylender who wanted him to pay the interest that he still owed with his death.

On the other hand, Zé Maria's anxiety to find the culprit that caused the death of Manamu led him to announce a death, in which Zeledon was the victim.

The information about Zé Maria's plans reached my ears, so knowing the innocence of my friend, I made an anonymous phone call to Zeledon from Bahia and warned him that someone in El Paso planned to kill him.

The fact that Zeledon never returned to El Paso confirmed to Zé Maria that he was the culprit. So, personally, he initiated a hunt against him.

For three months, he looked for him everywhere. When he failed to find him, he hired a group of assassins to whom he provided a recent photograph and all the information about Zeledon so that they could look for him.

After making a deal with the hitmen, Zé Maria returned to El Paso. He knew that Zeledon would be in contact with his former employee and that could lead him to his hiding place.

Thus, he deceptively convinced Zeledon's former employee that he needed to urgently find Zeledon. He told him that although he had called him several times, he didn't answer his phone. So, he needed to know if he had changed his number, and he only needed the telephone number that Zeledon had made his last call.

That lie presented to Zé Maria his first success. The person put in charge of selling Zeledon's property, without having any idea of the malicious intentions of Zé Maria, searched among his answered calls and gave him the telephone number that Zeledon had communicated from last.

Although the calls were made from a public telephone, it would be a great tip for the hitmen. With this information, after tracing the call, they confirmed the location of the public telephone. There, they began their search. The hitmen, wearing district uniforms and wearing social worker badges, asked, among pedestrians, about the new arrivals to the neighbourhood. With his photograph in hand, they focused their questions on Zeledon.

Several blocks down, one of the passers-by remarked to them, that he had seen a person terribly similar to the one in the photograph who had the same name at the apartments. As well as that, he and his children had arrived in the neighbourhood a few weeks earlier, the man assured.

In response to this, the hitmen waited until they saw him arrive. When comparing the photo with the man's face, they had no doubt that it was him.

Despite this, although everything coincided with photo and the information that they about him, it was not the man that they were looking for.

This Zeledon that the hitmen had now targeted was a man under the pressures of a divorce and custody battles.

This individual, desperate and determined not to lose the custody of his children, was willing to defend this with his life.

So, when seeing the social workers from a distance, he thought that they were here for his children. With no other options, he took his gun and immediately shot at them. The instant that he reached the street, his shots took the hitmen by surprise, as they initially assumed achieving their goal would be simple.

Although in the exchange of bullets the man was slightly wounded, he sheltered behind a garbage container and kept them at a distance until the local police arrived. Their arrival immediately made the undercover hitmen escape.

After his wound healed, the man, through radio and television news, took advantage of his misfortune. He confirmed to news reporters that he was attacked by professional assassins and blamed his ex-wife as the culprit behind the attack.

What this other Zeledon believed was a dirty trick from his ex-wife was in fact only a coincidence that almost ended his life.

Although this event had nothing to do with the divorce process, it would eventually help him in court, as the judge ordered to stop the custody process against him and, for the time, allow him to be with his children for protection.

Hours later, the hitmen heard the televised report of the shooting and naturally realised that they had made a mistake. Despite this, they wouldn't stop their search for the true Zeledon. They planned to follow his footsteps, but this time, they assured themselves that they wouldn't make the same mistake.

In another city hundreds of kilometres away, the Zeledon that they were looking for was also watching the news. When listening to the news report, he wasn't paying much attention, but when he saw that the person who they tried to kill had the same name and an uncanny physical resemblance to him, he instantly became alarmed. His alarm increased when he discovered that the attack occurred in the same city of his former residence. This made that him increasingly worried, as Zeledon knew that this attack was intended to be against him. The coincidence with this doppelganger warned him that the hitmen were closely tracing his footsteps.

Overcome with fear, Zeledon recommended to his family that, as a precaution, they should again relocate to another city. Immediately, he told them to pack while he was buying the tickets.

That morning before leaving, Zeledon called his former employee in charge of the sale in El Paso. The man very happily notified him that the shopping centre had been sold. In response, Zeledon gave him the mobile phone number and the bank account detail to deposit one hundred million cruzeiros to the loan shark. Then, he requested that once the transaction was completed, he should confirm to the man that the money had been deposited.

After this, the person in charge of the sale called Zeledon again to confirm. Zeledon, grateful for his help, ordered him to take a commission of five million and deposit the rest of the money in Olmeda's account.

With his debt paid off, Zeledon thought that his persecution would stop. However, that wasn't the case; his attack was coming from a person that he least expected.

While Zeledon assumed that the problem was solved, back in El Paso, Zé Maria, through Zeledon's former employee, discovered Zeledon's new telephone number. That day, Zé Maria immediately sent the telephone number to the hitmen, who due to the area code, would know immediately that Zeledon was in Tenerife City.

For them, finding his residence and the room number was simple, so after nightfall, the hitmen planned to enter the residence, execute Zeledon and leave. So, five minutes before seven, the four entered the hostel by force. After tying up everyone present, they locked them in the kitchen and secured the doors with padlocks. One of the hitmen, with a gun in his hand, remained outside to provide surveillance, while the others performed the task at hand.

Successfully eliminating the first obstacle, the hitmen went to Room 125. However, the room was already occupied by different people. The killers focused on the three occupants. Immediately, they took the picture of Zeledon and demanded the older man to show his identification card. When they confirmed that he wasn't the person that they were looking for, they asked.

"Where is Zeledon?"

The occupant's response was immediate. With a trembling voice, the man replied, "Man! We are new in the city and we don't know anyone with that name. However, this morning when we arrived, we observed a couple, and two children left this room."

The hitmen, overwhelmed with anger, exclaimed, "They escaped from us again!"

Minutes after the hitmen left the hostel, the police arrived. Upon hearing the report of what happened, they immediately began their investigation. With intention to alert the true Zeledon that the hitmen are looking for him, the police ordered that the report be broadcast on a regional newscast.

Hours later, the information reached Zeledon's ears. He didn't understand why the hitmen continued with their hunt for him when he had already paid the total of his debt. The continued danger forced him to take more radical measures and so, in search of protection, he took refuge in Brasilia City.

As Zeledon arrived in the capital, thousands of kilometres away, his partners, Salamanca, Cerezo and Gutiérrez, were sentenced by a Californian judge to ten years imprisonment, without the right to parole. Despite this, they never linked Sotomayor with the Poppy Cartel, and thus, the United States never put an extradition order out on him.

After hearing the verdict and sentencing against his former partners, Sotomayor's sadness increased. Thus, he planned to go through João to get in touch with Ludiela.

João's arrival to Panama would surprise Sotomayor a surprise that was not included in the original plan, since João, thinking of making things easy for Sotomayor, asked his boss if he could return to his previous job as a SIP (Panama Intelligence) agent.

His excellent resume and achievements would present opportunities for him again and, a few days later, he would be reinstated to the organisation. With João reinstated in his former employment, the first thing he did was inquire about Sotomayor's file. As there was the possibility that Panama was the only country that would request his extradition, João decided to continue working in the agency. He knew that being close to his former boss, he could be extremely useful in the case that Sotomayor reached an agreement with the detectives.

Days later, João finished his main investigative task. Having all the tools necessary at his disposal, he focused on the search for Ludiela.

A few weeks later, he discovered that she was in a resort, the 'Twenty-seven' as the prison was known by in the military. He also discovered that her inmate's name appeared in the archives as Number 403. As well as this, João was able to find out the area code and the access digits where Ludiela's mail arrived.

It was easy for João to investigate Ludiela without suspicion. Amongst Ludiela's mail, he camouflaged a letter that Santos had written in advance.

In this letter, Santos explained to his beloved Ludiela the memories that he was reminiscing, his attempted murder by his most dangerous enemy and his desire to surrender to the detective's office. Once the first paragraph was finished, in an extra note, Sotomayor asked her, 'My love! If you agree with my decision, please, provide to Detective Baena this mobile phone number.'

Ludiela, after reading the letter again and again, analysed the two options. After some time, she reached the conclusion that it was best that Sotomayor lose his freedom for a few years instead of his life.

For that reason, when Baena came to visit her, she showed him the telephone number where he could contact Sotomayor. That news and the fact the letter had arrived at the resort surprised Baena because, to obtain access to the mailbox, this person must have circumvented all security measures and that itself warranted investigation. However, the prosecutor set aside this concern for now and would give priority to Sotomayor's request.

The day of contact, Sotomayor was in a hotel in El Paso, watching from the window of his room how the moon at sunset seemed as it was painted in a vibrant red colour. Amazed by the natural beauty, he reminisced once again. Through his mind, he travelled beside his beloved.

Seconds later, his longing moments of nostalgia would be interrupted by the ringing of his cell phone. The man at the other end of the line identified himself as Detective Baena, who after a spontaneous greeting, expressed:

"In so many years of searching for you, I never thought that one day I would hear from you that you wanted to surrender yourself. Your decision has surprised me. I imagine that something immensely powerful forces you to do it."

Sotomayor, grateful, thanked him for being willing to listen to him, but before discussing the proposal, he warned that this conversation should be completely confidential. Since, if the information were to be revealed, his life and the lives of other people, including the detective's life, would be in imminent danger.

"My life?" the prosecutor asked, surprised.

"Yes sir!" Sotomayor answered.

As Baena was silenced due to his surprise, Sotomayor warned him, "The secret that I am about to tell you, is a secret a very powerful man is willing to silence with your life."

The detective, somewhat sceptical, asked, "And who is that powerful person?"

"Tancredo Moreira," answered Sotomayor.

The detective, immediately astonished, clarified, "Tancredo Moreira? The Brazilian politician?"

"Yes, sir, the same one that was involved in a drug trafficking investigation, years ago, but fortunately for him, nobody could prove anything," Sotomayor replied.

The prosecutor, shocked by Sotomayor's revelation, exclaimed:

"This is quite a development. The new attorney general of Brazil would love to hear this, considering he is carrying out an investigation towards various government officials and politicians linked to money laundering and drug trafficking. This information would be crucial."

At that moment, hearing the politician's last name suddenly caused Baena to realise the possibility that this person was the same Mr Moreira that Gustavo had talked about months before.

According to the story from the rodent exterminator, he was hidden in the mansion ceiling the day in which Moreira's hitmen killed Melquiades, his wife and their escorts.

Baena, with surprise still evident in his voice, continued asking questions:

"Do you have conclusive proof?"

"Of course! I have two videos; in one, Tancredo Moreira is receiving money from drug trafficking and congratulating his men for the murder of Falcão and their escorts.

"The other video, it appears his assassins are confessing their participation in multiple murders, including the death of Vinicio Braga, an agent of the Brazilian Secret Service. However, for my protection, I didn't bring the SIM cards containing the videos. They are being kept in a security box in a neighbouring country, under a poet's name. The person who, from the moment of my surrender, will have access to the bank's name, the safe box combination, and a signed letter where I leave authorisation for him to pick up these belongings if something unexpected were to happen to me," Sotomayor replied.

Hearing this left Baena speechless for a few seconds but after the short silence, he returned to the conversation subject, continuing the questions, "Would you be willing to testify and provide this evidence against Tancredo?"

"Yes sir, but only if you and I reach an agreement," Sotomayor answered.

Detective Baena, who still wasn't sure of Sotomayor's intention, asked him.

"So, that means that you are determined to be a part of the trial?"

"Of course! But there are some terms that we need to agree on," Sotomayor responded.

"Terms, such as?" Baena asked.

Sotomayor exhaled deeply and with a determined tone, he replied, "Well, firstly the day of my surrender, Ludiela must be free, and her drug trafficking charges must be dropped.

"My second term is, in the case that I have an extradition order pending in the United States, the detective's office must transfer that order to a Panamanian Court, so that I can be tried there.

"Finally, my surrender should be carried out discreetly and in a place that provides me with the greatest security possible."

After listening to Sotomayor's demands, the detective analysed that they were simple in comparison to the benefits that he and his Brazilian counterparts would obtain if Sotomayor testified provided evidence against the politician. However, at the end of Sotomayor's requests, Baena informed him that the decision to grant him these requests was not simply in his hands; he must talk to his superiors, Interpol, the SIP and the DEA about his criminal record and the possibility of reaching an agreement.

Nevertheless, the detective knew that these requests would take time. For this reason, Baena asked Sotomayor to give him at least five days to make the arrangements before speaking again.

Before ending the call, Baena recommended to him that, for his safety, he must again hide behind new character and stay away from his old house.

Following Baena's recommendation, Santos went to Fernanda's house. There, for the second time, he would usurp the personality of Ulysses, Fernanda's father.

Hours after the conversation with Sotomayor, Baena sought to communicate with Gustavo Espino. However, the operator informed him that the number had been cancelled weeks ago. The detective, worried as he hadn't heard news about him for months, ordered the regional officer of the Amazon to send one of his men to El Paso to confirm if he was still at the address stipulated in the message.

The response received from his subordinate was that José Lemus, or Gustavo Espino, as was his real name, had not been seen in the town for weeks; he and his family had disappeared as if by magic, and his friends had no idea why or where they were. His departure was a complete enigma; no one could confirm to the detective's office whether they were alive or dead. But Baena had the suspicion that his sudden departure was somehow linked to the death of his friend Ernesto, because during the days that Gustavo and his family disappeared, Ernesto, his best friend, was found murdered in front of the residence where José lived, and according to the police report, his death occurred when Ernesto was moving the furniture and appliances that, before leaving the town, Gustavo had given him. Therefore, Baena assumed that Ernesto's murder had been a case of mistaken identity, and with no doubt, this death was planned for Gustavo.

Baena, filled with uncertainty, thought that the most logical thing was that considering Tancredo was an expert in eliminating 'obstacles,' somehow, he had learned of the existence of this witness and took charge of silencing him.

At that moment, Baena questioned himself for not realising the truth in time that Mr Moreira was a corrupt politician as Gustavo had mentioned during his questioning.

This made Baena feel as though he was a failure. However, both he and Tancredo in their own way had been deceived because the supposedly dead Gustavo and his children were in the capital, sheltered by a Mennonite church. Their situation was already known by the pastor, who gave them the hope that they could help them leave the country legally.

After Baena realised the possible misfortune of Gustavo and his family, he notified his colleague Guerrero of the mysterious disappearance of his witness and their children, as well as informing him of the talks with Sotomayor, in favour of a possible surrender.

Until that moment, Guerrero understood the magnitude of the mistake he had made months ago when he gave the information to the politician in exchange for money. But the most worrying thing for him was that Tancredo had the situation in his hands. He couldn't call him and tell him that he was a corrupt murderer and trafficker – that would alert him that they discovered his secret, and with no doubt, he would escape from Brazil. Much less, could they threaten him with an arrest since he had no authority as a prosecutor across the borderlines.

Guerrero also knew that if he did such a thing, Tancredo would attempt to blackmail him, so Guerrero began to ignore the situation and from that moment, he didn't respond to any of Tancredo's calls.

His sudden change in his behaviour led the politician to think that something the detective had some enormously powerful evidence against him.

Intrigued to know what had happened, Tancredo communicated with Maica, whose new task would be to extract, from Guerrero, any information that Tancredo wanted to know.

That afternoon, Maica picked up the detective at the airport and together they went to the hotel suite, where, after taking a shower, the two went out to a private club to spend the night. Guerrero, although overwhelmed by having betrayed his colleagues, was equally as amicable towards Maica as their previous meetings.

Moments after their arrival to the restaurant, they were greeted with a romantic dinner, which they enjoyed with plenty of drinks, kissing and caressing, which awakened, in Guerrero, his desire to make love to her. That passion and the atmosphere made Guerrero even only temporarily forget the worry that was weighing on his conscience. At the end of the night, they returned to the hotel. Back in their room, he wanted to continue the intimate mood. However, when Maica took him in her arms, the moment didn't feel the same as their previous encounters.

Guerrero, stressed and strained by the situation, dropped heavily on the bed. Despite this, Maica didn't object to his behaviour and proceeded to do her job. She, beside the morbid-looking detective, began to remove from her body, one by one, all her clothes. Then, like a feline, she launched herself on her prey and began an erotic massage all over Guerrero's body.

After several minutes without Guerrero achieving an erection, Maica asked surprisingly, "What is wrong, my love?"

He lamented, "The truth is that, for days, a moral dilemma is causing in me intense regret and that problem has remained so rooted in my mind that today, even my passion for your body cannot awaken my sexual desire."

Maica, wanting to know in detail what had happened, cunningly put aside the caresses and held him in her arms. Then, with a concerned tone, she whispered in his ear, "My love! Forgive me for having pressured to you to have sex with me, when right now, what you need from me is understanding."

Guerrero, breaking the current mood, let Maica know that next weekend they couldn't meet, although jokingly he clarified that the reason for cancelling their meeting wasn't due to his current impotence, but due to a possible important mission that he and his colleague would be executing in Bahia, next Sunday.

Maica, with a slight smile, pushed him against the head of the bed, and with a passionate kiss, she silenced Guerrero's mouth, expressing, "Honey! You don't have to explain anything, and much less, you are obliged to meet with me. I know that your work is more important than pleasure. Although only due to my curiosity, I wanted to know what is the problem that is worrying you so deeply."

Guerrero, consoled by the understanding attitude of his lover, decided to reveal his secret. However, he intended to hide the identity of those involved, so that to him, Maica couldn't discover that he was talking about the politician Tancredo.

Thus, Guerrero, satisfied that he could keep the issue confidential, said:

"The problem began months ago, although it was just five days ago that I discovered the magnitude of my error. Because who I thought was an honest man and my friend, turned out to be a person of the worst kind, involved in murders, drug trafficking and corruption. But the most difficult part of the case is that the criminal that I am talking about is not located in my jurisdiction, and with the trap that this person set for me, he has turned me from prosecutor to traitor, and now, I have my hands tied."

Maica, pretending that she didn't know about who Guerrero was talking about, tenderly exclaimed, "My love! Why don't you provide the proof that you mentioned me to the authorities in his country?"

"The reason," the prosecutor explained, "is that I still don't have that evidence. It was deposited in a safe deposit box in a bank in Brazil, and only the person known as 'the Poet' has access to the information. This person will only bring these to the authorities, when a witness named Ludiela, living in a penitentiary in Panama, confirms to him that she is free."

Maica, showing fake surprise on her face, asked, "So, what are you going to do?"

"I will face the storm and, if necessary, I will pay for my mistake, because now I don't care if I must sink with the ship," Guerrero optimistically replied to her.

Maica, still naked in bed, hugged him again and assured him that she supports his decision.

After her encouragement, both took a shower, changed clothes and went to the airport. There, they said their goodbyes and took different flights.

Maica, upon arriving at her destination, informed Tancredo of the information from Guerrero, who promptly sent his hitmen to the three different locations mentioned by Guerrero.

Tancredo, entertained by his Machiavellian mind, planned that the detectives, as well as Sotomayor, Ludiela and shall be eliminated simultaneously.

With that, Tancredo aimed to have none of those involved in a possible trial against him alive, thus killing all evidence against him would die with us.

A week after their last conversation, Sotomayor and Baena communicated again. Baena informed Sotomayor that the United States had no extradition order against him, and that his previous partners appeared as the capos of the different cartels that he had created during his years as a drug trafficker. Additionally, all had already been sentenced without linking him to his crimes.

In addition, Baena confirmed him that Panama was the only country in which Interpol had ordered extradition; he was designated as Jorge Sotomayor, alias 'Marlon de la Roca.' Finally, Baena ensured him, that the first of the terms of his surrender would be fulfilled as stipulated.

Regarding the second point, he had consulted with his superior and the authorities of other countries, and he confirmed that his surrender would be completely secure and secret. Only detective Guerrero would accompany him.

However, he admitted that with his third point, there was legal issue. This was because all the homicides and the events that he had mentioned in his statement were very serious and dangerous, by which to achieve a sentence to Tancredo Moreira as the mastermind of murders and being anonymous boss of an unknown cartel, it was necessary to prepare for his testimony behind his back. Thus, they would need to take him discreetly, since Tancredo was a high-level politician from Brazil, and as Sotomayor is an essential witness, he must present his testimony and evidence in a Brazilian court. Nevertheless, for that to happen, the general prosecutor of Brazil would have to negotiate his extradition with Panama. "If they accept the agreement," Baena said, "you would be extradited to Brazil and there, a court will try you for drug trafficking, with the benefit that by providing evidence against the politician, you will receive a lenient deal. After completing the third part of your prison sentence, you will be free."

Baena paused to give Sotomayor time to make the decision. After a few seconds, Sotomayor interrupted the silence, "I accept the deal."

Once they reached an agreement, Baena recommended him to appoint a person that he trusted completely, so that they could serve as an observer and verify that both of their commitments were totally legal. Sotomayor, although had many trustworthy friends, recommended the first person that he thought of – Ludiela. He knew that this was the only way for both of them to have contact. He did not care if it only was only by telephone.

Baena paused in thought for a few seconds before accepting Ludiela as their intermediary, with one condition: Sotomayor must reveal the place of residence and the original name of the person who can access the two SIM cards.

Sotomayor didn't object to Baena's request and told him, "That's no problem, his name is Dirceu Figuereiro and currently he lives in El Paso."

After hearing this vital information, Baena said goodbye with the promise that in two days, the negotiation with Panama authorities would be complete.

At the same time, Ludiela, who was beside the detective, unintentionally, heard the deal between both Baena and Sotomayor. She was astonished when hearing the prosecutor confirmed that, by telephone, she would be in contact with Sotomayor to settle the final details of his surrender.

Two hours later, Ludiela communicated with Sotomayor. Overwhelmed by emotion, tears ran down their cheeks and they simultaneously emanated the phrase, "I love you." Through the telephone with love and passion from a distance, both expressed their true feelings.

After the couple reconnected and reflected on their time apart, both determined which location offered the most protection for his surrender: the airport, sewage plant or football stadium. Sotomayor, after going over his options, told her that if Baena successfully manages to negotiate with Panama regarding his extradition to Brazil, he would be willing to appear at the stadium at the date and time determined by the detective.

After stating his decision, Ludiela wanted to continue the conversation, but at that moment, a voice over the phone warned her that there was only one minute left.

Ludiela said goodbye to Sotomayor, reminding him again that she loves him. Then, she assured him that there was no need for anxiety or sadness, as she would be in contact again soon.

Hours before to the stipulated time, detectives Baena and Guerrero obtained the approval from the Panamanian government, immediately notifying Sotomayor of the good news. And so, they began to plan their secret operation. There, they also agreed that on the weekend, they would travel to Bahia to coordinate the final details.

Two days before the detectives' arrival to Bahia, Sotomayor, and me, made our own plan and start travelling from El Paso to meeting point in Brasilia. But beforehand, Sotomayor, without me noticing, left, with Fernanda, an envelope which contained a bank's name, a signed authorisation to claim the deposit under my name and the security box combination code.

As she received it, Sotomayor advised that if something happened with him, that envelope should be escorted by her to the Poet personally.

Hours after our departure from El Paso, Tancredo's hitmen, who had arrived at the various cities to search the information that would lead them to their victims, were already working on a plan.

Those who were in Panama City had already located Ludiela and they were waiting for her to make an attack.

The other group in Bahia, from the moment that Baena and Guerrero arrived, began to follow their steps through the city. As they followed, they were in contact with the third group of hitmen who were in El Paso looking for me. Two of them had already found out who the Poet was and where they could locate me. However, although they knew my original name, no matter how much they searched for me in El Paso, the hitmen would never find me, since I was already in a shelter with Sotomayor somewhere in Brasilia. From here, Sotomayor would contact to Baena and tell him that we had arrived at the city.

While we waited for a safe opportunity, Baena and Guerrero arrived at a private flight company and hired the pilot and a helicopter for a flight to Brasilia, agreeing with the pilot that next Tuesday in the morning, he would have to pick up three passengers on the stadium grounds. They, from the stadium, would call to confirm the precise time.

With the reservation made, Baena, through Ludiela, told Sotomayor that as was agreed, his surrender would be carried out next Tuesday at nine in the morning.

Then, he reminded Sotomayor of the meeting point and also requested that they arrive one hour early at the football stadium's washrooms.

Baena informed him that, for the protection of everyone, including him and Guerrero, they would be there early, and upon his arrival, they would have the main stadium door open for them to enter. Finally, Baena advised that, for greater security, Sotomayor must dress in the same way as the maintenance employees, with blue denim pants, a white cap, shirt and black sports shoes. After his arrival, he would have to cross the dressing rooms and go to the middle of the field, where the three would finally meet and be picked up by a private helicopter to be transported to a military base on the outskirts of Brasilia. After this, he would remain in SIB custody for a few weeks while the trial against the politician was being prepared.

"Upon the culmination of Tancredo's trial," Baena said, "they will continue with your case and you will return to the court, not as a witness, but as an accused, where, as agreed with the Brazilian prosecutors, your sentence will be in the SIB's guard rooms, with the possibility that in a few months, you will be released." In addition to this, they guaranteed that when his sentence was completed, he wouldn't be left at the mercy of his enemies, since they knew of the danger of the politician. So, for security purposes, they would process a visa to get him out of the country. Sotomayor said goodbye to Ludiela and expressed once more how much he missed her.

Optimistically, she wished him the best of luck and told him that she predicted that he would soon be by her side.

During this conversation, one of the hitmen, paid by Tancredo in Brasilia, arrived at the private flight company. With his manipulative tricks, he managed to get the information from the manager, who gave him the possible location of where the pilot would pick up the crew.

As the hours passed, their fatal outcome approached.

Sotomayor, worried about his beloved Ludiela, communicated with João in Panama. After thanking him for everything that he had done, Sotomayor commented about the agreement that he made with the detective and asked him to please protect to Ludiela during her release.

João, upon hearing Sotomayor's surrender, immediately warned him to take all possible precautions.

Second, he demanded that Sotomayor not worry about his beloved Ludiela, since she would be guarded heavily from the resort to the airport.

Once Sotomayor was reassured by João, they said their farewells. João promised him that he would visit him in prison.

The day of Sotomayor's surrender, the first people to arrive at the stadium were the two detectives. Then, the maintenance personnel arrived and, minutes later, Sotomayor, hidden as Ulises, and I entered through the main entrance. But, when I arrived at the stadium washroom, I would walk towards the 'sun tribune,' and Sotomayor would remain in the dressing room, waiting for me to give him the signal to go to the centre of the field.

Once at the sun tribune, I observed the maintenance staff on the stands and didn't find any reason for suspicion; I knew in advance that they would be there, since that Tuesday, early in the morning, there was a football cup final, and so, the maintenance personnel were preparing to clean.

Each one of the employees, carrying their cleaning tools, assigned themselves a row of the bleachers and began cleaning up and down.

Simultaneously, Ludiela, in Panama City, left the resort and went towards the airport escorted by a dozen guards, by which made her feel safe.

Back in Brasilia, I was calculating her departure time, and soon I gave the signal to Sotomayor, who at twenty minutes to nine, went to meet with Baena and Guerrero. Seeing him from a distance, the detectives immediately communicated with the helicopter pilot to give him the coordinates. As Sotomayor walked towards the detectives, Ludiela called me to tell me that she was close to the airport.

Exactly seven minutes later, she called me again. The instant that she was talking to me, I heard the rumble of bombs and machine-gun blasts through my mobile phone. Instantly, I realised that someone had set a trap for her. Immediately, I tried to warn to Sotomayor and the detectives, but it was too late. The supposed maintenance workers had already taken out their hidden weapons and unloaded these against Sotomayor and the detectives. I would be attacked too, although because of my long distance from the attack, it would be impossible for them to successfully kill me. Conveniently, I was only a few metres from the emergency exit, and I easily managed to reach the street and lose myself among the pedestrians.

When the pilot arrived with his helicopter to pick up his crew, from the air he spotted three corpses lying on the grass and immediately notified the authorities.

Moments later, the police would be there. They, after cordoning off the area, began their initial examination of the scene. In their investigation, the authorities would find the real workers inside an abandoned trailer, who they found gagged, tied down by their hands and feet, and to a wire that was to the safety ring of a grenade.

The Deaths of Maica and Sertino
and My Asylum in Canada

After the attack carried out by Tancredo's men, my escape immediately started and the days after, I monitored the news of radio and television from my shelter in order to keep updated with the investigation of the deaths of the detectives and Sotomayor in Brasilia.

At the same time, back in Panama City, special forces searched for the perpetrators of the attack which took the lives of Ludiela and several of her security escorts.

Because it was considered a terrorist attack, journalists had quickly spread the news. Gustavo, upon hearing of the violent death of the detectives, felt a great fear in him. Something told him that, just like the massacre in the mansion and the death of Ernesto, the same person was involved. If the assassins had been successful in silencing Baena and Guerrero, there was no doubt that he and his children would be the next victims.

Gustavo, overwhelmed and without other alternatives, took refuge in the Mennonite temple. The church's pastor searched through his ministry for somebody in another country that could obtain visas for them. The pastor would have to be successful before his transfer to another province. However, when he heard of the events related to Gustavo's persecution, he promised not to leave the country until he saw them on an Air Canada plane.

In Brasilia, when Maica learned about Guerrero's death, she couldn't hold her tears back. That news, although should not have affected her, split her soul into a thousand pieces.

The mistake of falling in love produced in her a mixed feeling between love and guilt, which made her feel like Judas after sending Jesus Christ to Calvary.

Thus, she wanted to wash her hands of her guilt and blame the politician, and so she began to reproach him for not having clarified that his plans were to end the detective's life.

The politician would take that pressure from Maica as a threat and decided to eliminate her, but her death would not be carried out in a conventional manner. The hitmen decided to use another method and that same afternoon, in a fatal traffic accident, Maica would be killed.

Days after the killing of Sotomayor and the detectives, Interpol gathered evidence and linked Maica's accident to Sotomayor's surrender and the condemning evidence against the politician.

Although both district attorney offices were aware of the agreement reached by the agents of both countries, they were unaware of the agreement that detectives Baena and Guerrero had made with Sotomayor.

With the main witness, Sotomayor already eliminated by Tancredo, I would become his priority target. So, Interpol decided to focus on finding and protecting Dirceu Figuereiro, the only surviving person who could provide evidence and, according to them, the only one who could ensure that Tancredo's crimes wouldn't go unpunished.

The desire of the federals to find me led them to offer a high reward for any person who provided them any information that would lead to my capture.

However, as their search didn't produce any results, they tried to find the incriminating evidence against Tancredo in Brazil's banks and border cities' banks as well.

Due to this, the Ministry of Internal Affairs ordered to all bank CEOs that accounts under the name of Dirceu Figuereiro, Ludiela Cochaeira or Jorge Sotomayor must be reported to Interpol.

Even with that measure in place, they failed to find the evidence. According to the managers, to obtain access to the bank's security box, it was not necessary for the account to be in the name of that specific person; anyone who had the name of the bank, the combination and the key, could have access. That obstacle and the confirmation that none of us appeared as the account holder would frustrate the Interpol agents.

As some were certain that I was alive, I became the most wanted man in Brazil. Both my friends and political assassins focused on the search for me.

On the other hand, this would not be the same for the agents, as they gave up their search and presumed I was dead. With this, the case against Tancredo would be frozen, waiting for my seemingly impossible return.

I, after discovering the fate of both Sotomayor and the detectives, could not trust anyone and decided to flee to another country. While I worked to obtain false documentation to leave the country, I kept disguised, and for my security, I didn't stay for more than two days in each town.

One afternoon, my need to find the person who was processing my fake passport led me to explore the beaches of Rio de Janeiro.

While walking through the hotel zone, I observed with surprise that Sertino, the bricklayer from El Paso, was leaving a five-star resort, accompanied by a beautiful, young woman. The two, holding hands, approached one of the hotel's bellboys and ordered him to pick up his car from the parking lot.

Sertino's extravagance seemed very strange to me; I didn't understand how a simple bricklayer could afford such a luxury.

After seeing that, I continued my original search, but as time passed, my intrigue increased. For a moment, I focused on Sertino's past. I remembered that this man had worked on the construction of Zeledon's property, where someone had stolen a full sack of money that belonged to the Poppy Cartel.

Although it could be just a coincidence, his behaviour was also quite suspicious. Thus, as Zeledon's friend and knowing that his persecution was unjust, I decided that Zé Maria should know about Sertino. So, I put aside my immediate plans, and, from a phone booth on the beach, I made a call to Zé Maria.

That afternoon, when he heard my fake voice, he asked me with surprise, "Who is the hell talking?"

In a strange voice, I answered, "I am a friend who wants to warn you about your mistake. You are looking in the wrong place and blaming an innocent man. Therefore, I recommend stop the persecution against Zeledon and divert your attention to Sertino who, at this moment, is giving himself a great life on the beaches of Rio de Janeiro."

After revealing the information, I hung up the phone and continued with my search.

Minutes after notifying Zé Maria of my suspicions, I found the counterfeiter. From this man, I would receive documents that would allow me to bypass the border authorities of some countries.

With another identity and great effort, I managed to get to Mexico; from there, I passed through security to the United States and settled in the Bronx, New York, but even there, I didn't feel safe. The reason for this was that, as an illegal settler unable to speak English, I could only connect with Latinos in places of dubious reputation and possibly even indirectly linked to drug trafficking. Any of these people could be a contact of Tancredo. These were disadvantages that could give Tancredo the ability to locate me. Not wanting to take such a risk, I moved to a town close Canada, where after a few days, I would cross the border and ask for refuge.

The same afternoon of my request, authorities led me to a small room. There, three immigration officers, through a translator, listened in detail of my persecution. After the interview, they looked through my criminal record, confirming that in the past I had been a member of the SIB, and that position left no doubt of my truth. Subsequently to the interrogation, one of the officers took a photograph of me and said, "Welcome to Canada."

Immediately after I received the permanent immigrant status, I was taken to a guesthouse, where, with the help of the provincial government, I began a new life.

During my stay in my new shelter, a commissioner from El Paso travelled to Brasilia and claimed the body of Sotomayor. Similarly, João did the same with Ludiela's body in Panama City. There, João, after completing the legal medical procedures, transported Ludiela's body to El Paso. Here, in the middle of a tremendous funeral accompanied by hundreds of people, they were given a Christian burial.

At the request of most of the settlers, the two bodies were buried in the same tomb.

While the funeral of Ludiela and Sotomayor was carried out, I, in Toronto, Canada, was going through my own obstacles. The same could be said for my compadre, Gustavo, his girlfriend, and their children, Raúl and Juliana, who, only days before, had found a family from Toronto to sponsor them.

Because of this, their immigration process had been less complicated and faster than mine. The influence of the shepherd was essential to this process.

From the group of acquaintances that sought asylum in Canada, Gustavo would seem to be the most favoured by luck. This was contrary to Zeledon, who, before obtaining his visa, lived a true odyssey.

Six months of running away from town to town with his family would eventually cause his economic status to enter a major crisis.

Their constant travelling and the living costs of his family ensured that the money deposited into Olmeda's account decreased every day. These desperate circumstances meant that two weeks after their stay in Brasilia, their funds were exhausted, and they were forced to leave the comfort of the hotel room to settle in a shelter in the suburbs. But the discomfort and despair of having to spend the nights fighting against fleas pushed Zeledon to go to an NGO in search of financial help. With his arrival at an international organisation, their difficult financial situation improved.

Soon after, Zeledon would find out about the humanitarian program for refugees in Canada.

Immediately after obtaining the address, he went to the Canadian embassy's headquarters in Brasilia, where through the commissioner, he received information and directions to apply for asylum.

Based on the advice, as required by the program, Zeledon quickly arrived at the embassy and, in front of a representative of the state, read his statement.

In this statement, he explained in detail that he was being subjected to forced displacement by a group outside of the law. He also showed them recordings of threats received via telephone and the denunciations made to the authorities during attempts to assassinate him. Although he had proof of his persecution, he couldn't give names, as he didn't know with certainty who was persecuting him and their motive.

After giving his statement, Zeledon proceeded to comply with all the demands of the embassy. His second objective would be the state attorney's office, where he and Olmeda requested to obtain their criminal records. Then, following the order of the list, they arrived at the Brazilian Intelligence Service. In this office, it wouldn't be necessary for him to file a complaint since the authorities already knew in advance of the attacks against him.

Finally, with all the paperwork in order, they would go to the Ministry of Internal Affairs, where both gave evidence of their persecution.

Once the secondary procedures were completed, Zeledon returned to the embassy again and received a pre-form. After filling it out, he delivered the form and hoped to receive news in a week. If he achieved refugee status, the original form would arrive to him by mail.

A day after the deadline, he received the documents, and the embassy requested his family's passports in order to begin processing their visas.

One month later, the immigration authorities would notify him that for their departure, he and his entire family would have to undergo routine medical examinations required by the Ministry of Health of Canada.

After their examinations, the four were called to the embassy again, where an immigration officer called them to his office and welcomed them to Canada. There, he gave them the documents that accredited them as permanent immigrants.

Zeledon, for the moment, managed presumed his chaotic adventure was over. I say for the moment because the true unfortunate chaos of his life had not yet begun. Fate had prepared a great surprise that Zeledon would begin to see only weeks after being in Toronto.

While the first symptoms of disillusionment approached Zeledon's life, Zé Maria in El Paso ordered his assassins to stop hunting Zeledon and begin an investigation into a new suspect.

As the days passed, Zé Maria, through his hitmen, would discover in detail everything related to the good life that Sertino was enjoying at Rio de Janeiro's beaches.

He already knew that Sertino, a month ago, had abandoned his wife and children and suddenly gave to himself a millionaire's life with a young girl, who, seduced by his numerous gifts and a promise of marriage, had become his lover.

In addition to that information, Zé Maria learned that in the last week, Sertino had deposited a generous sum of money into his account, a part of which he had invested into the purchase of a car, a house, and a small commercial store.

After the investigation, Zé Maria travelled to Rio and rented an apartment in the outskirts. After relocating there, Zé Maria ordered his hitmen to kidnap to Sertino and take him to the agreed upon place. After completing their task, Zé Maria paid the thugs their fees and ended his business with them.

As the interrogation began, Sertino quickly discovered the reason for his kidnapping and the reality that he is the culprit of Manamu's death.

Sertino fearfully promised to return the purchased goods and the rest of the money if Zé Maria spared his life. Zé Maria, for the moment, refrained from immediately taking out his revenge by killing Sertino and dedicated himself to making the transfers of Sertino's properties into his wife's name.

After days of paperwork and bureaucratic procedures, Zé Maria managed, with the help of bribes, to pass ownership of Sertino's properties to Roberta and her children, who he had.

As well as this, Sertino gave checks to Zé Maria for the rest of the money that remained in his account.

After a week of his captivity, Sertino's last hours of life were upon him. As planned by Zé Maria, his death would take place that night. However, that afternoon, Zé Maria received a call from Raica, who informed him that she had given birth and that they were parents of a beautiful baby.

That news filled Zé Maria with happiness, who, thinking about his son's future, forgave Sertino and released him. Immediately after, the bricklayer made the decision to move away as far as possible, as he didn't want to give Zé Maria the opportunity to regret his decision.

During Sertino's kidnapping, the relatives of his young lover looked for Sertino to ensure he fulfilled the promise to take her to the altar. When they found him and saw that his intentions were to leave the city, they thought that he was evading his commitment and that his purpose was to only have sex with their sister and abandon her. Their conclusion led them to take revenge on him, giving him several bullet wounds that caused his death.

After hearing of Sertino's demise, Zé Maria indirectly took revenge on the real culprit and with this, he felt that Manamu's soul finally would rest in peace.

One month after Sertino's murder, Roberta, would be surprised by a notary official. There, they read the will made by her late husband and informed her that she would be unexpectedly receiving ownership of several properties.

Zeledon's Arrival to Canada

Forty-five days after his initial request for refuge, Zeledon and his family would obtain their visas to Canada. The morning of their departure at the International Brasilia Airport, their goodbyes would differ from all the other passengers. None of their relatives would know about their departure, so no one would be crying for them, giving them farewell hugs or taking photos and videos. Even less was anyone watching from the windows of the airport's second floor to watch their plane depart.

Zeledon, even while knowing that he was about to arrive to a strange nation without money or friends, was not sad. On the contrary, he felt great happiness because with this opportunity he had safeguarded his most important treasures, his wife, and children. He could never think that with his arrival in Canada, his life would be about to fall apart.

After twelve hours of travel, the four arrived at Quebec City. They were immediately greeted by a breathtakingly cold that was burning their bones, and a language that they didn't understand even a hello.

There, in a five-star hotel, they would spend their first night in their new country. In the morning, an immigration officer led them to the airport and from there, they took a flight to Toronto and eventually arrived at the reception house where they would stay as guests for two weeks.

On the day of their arrival, Zeledon would meet Claudia, a Brazilian woman and friend of the people who came with them. As they exchanged glances, the two felt as if they already had met before. However, both at that time deduced that despite the feeling in their souls it was already too late; Zeledon loved his wife and Claudia was looking for a man without compromises.

As they first arrived at the government residence, Zeledon and his family received the keys to their rooms. After arranging their bags, they attended their first meeting, where the consul in charge warned them that most of the people in the humanitarian program faced great challenges upon arriving to Canada.

Days later and finally settled; they had been informed of the benefits granted by the government and dispelled the myths told by those in Brasilia, who thought that all immigrants get easy money and government aid included a free car and house. Comments all false of course – the only truth was that the country was full of opportunities for hard workers.

Although it offered many benefits, it was not easy to adapt to the climate and culture, much less if you came without speaking English, since as a refugee you had to start from scratch and survive a prudent time of two years with the help of the government. For that reason, learning the language, adapting to the climate and its culture were the priorities of survival.

The psychological pressure that this would produce in many immigrants due to fear of their own impotence. Possibly, the sudden change would fill some of them with insecurity, and several would suffer from homesickness, which would be caused by missing their country, friends, and family.

Regardless, even with these obstacles in place, many here managed to succeed in their dream, although these dreams, in a minority of them, would vanish shortly after their arrival.

The day after that strenuous talk, Zeledon and Olmeda received the first financial assistance from the government – a small amount of money to buy a long-distance SIM card to communicate with their family and friends.

After that comforting moment, they were taken, with the assistance of the administrator, to a bank to open a family account. There, the government deposited $700 for each of them. Afterwards, as they walked around the reception area, they had their first contact with snow.

Back at their temporary residence, they continued with medical examinations, mental health meetings and talked about renting an apartment and searching for a volunteer sponsor who would guide them on all the basics of their new life for the next few months.

Fifteen days after their arrival to Canada, Zeledon and his family received the key to their temporary home. With this, they received furniture, kitchen equipment and a notice stating that the government would cover their essential expenses for two years, so that the spouses can start their first English classes next week.

As the date arrived, Zeledon and Olmeda were introduced before their new classmates. Due to their limited English knowledge, their introduction would be very brief, but six months later during a conversational class, each one of them could easily describe their personal traits and express all kinds of questions and answers. During the class, one of the blunter classmates asked a question to each of them.

A Chinese classmate, intrigued by the stereotypes of Latin men, asked, "Zeledon! Before you met Olmeda, did you have clandestine meetings with other women?"

Zeledon answered, "Yes, I did."

The man then asked the same question to Olmeda. She, without hesitation, answered that she had had several lovers.

All present, including Zeledon, were surprised to hear that. Olmeda, observing the reaction from everyone, let out laughter, declaring that it was only a joke, which all would believe. But truthfully, this wasn't a lie.

As time passed and the new immigrants advanced in their English classes, the teachers and old students warned them that family rules in Canada were very different from how they are used to in their countries.

For example, the teacher told them that it is inappropriate to aggressively call their children, much less reprimand them physically, because according to laws, doing such a thing could be considered child abuse and would risk going to jail or something worse: the government could keep the custody of the children and deport the father.

As well as this, counsellors instructed the women about expectations in the home. Also, they clarified that if their companions liked to go out alone for a drink, women could also do the same without domestic consequence. Thus, it is expected that while women socialised with friends, the husbands should be at home to care for the children.

In addition to this, they were taught that men couldn't submit women to their whims and much less to demand sex without consent, because in this country, it is considered as sexual harassment with severe consequences.

With these new freedoms that women didn't have in their home countries, immigrant women in Canada were finally considered equal to men in the eyes of the law.

Although the constitution gives the same rights for both spouses, women have extra assistance by the government. The teacher informed the class of the government's assistance towards women and children, the elderly, animal welfare and minority groups such as the LGBT.

Zeledon, upon hearing these comments by the teacher, didn't feel attacked. He never had verbally abused verbally his wife and children, much less physically. However, hearing this left him worried; he knew that with these cultural differences, he would lose authority in his home.

While to Zeledon, these warnings left him confused, Olmeda was excited. For her, Canada was the perfect place where she would be given the freedom to show her true personality.

Olmeda knew that here in Canada, her plan could culminate without any difficulty.

After several weeks had elapsed, and since Olmeda didn't have any 'friends with benefits' in Toronto like those she had in São Paulo, her sexual activity with Zeledon doubled. Her sexual needs seemed insatiable, and even started to explore the use of erotic toys to increase pleasure.

Regardless of this, Olmeda wanted more and more every day. Although this did not bother Zeledon at all, he was confused, because never had his wife had expressed such a desire to make his sexual fantasies come true, much less had she performed so actively in bed.

After the first three months in Toronto, Zeledon thought that his partner's sexual appetite would eventually decrease; however, that was not the case. Olmeda would always find a reason to have sex with him, and that fascinated him. His desire for her began to be uncontrollable.

But Zeledon didn't know that this was his wife's plan, where the primary goal was to convert him into a sexual addict.

Zeledon, with the intention of lowering the accelerator to the carnal needs of his wife, got a part-time job. After finishing his English classes, he went straight to his job. Due to that, he would often return to the apartment late at night. Zeledon believed that the couple spending all afternoon together, without other responsibilities, was causing the hyperactive sexual appetite in Olmeda.

That assumption by Zeledon would be a big mistake. Instead of serving as therapy to decrease her desire, it only made it an even bigger problem, since Olmeda was finally free to do all that, she wanted while he worked.

The only concern for her was Henry, her son, but she would solve this problem by leaving him in the company of Karen, their eldest daughter.

For this reason, when Zeledon would return, he almost never found her at home. The few times that he saw her, he found her chatting on the internet, where Olmeda and her chatting partner conversed in a very loving way. Only increasing suspicion in him, Olmeda would immediately disconnect from the conversation when Zeledon returned.

Zeledon initially didn't give much importance to Olmeda's behaviour. In fact, he saw it as her right to privacy and didn't object; his intrigue at the time was focused on her constant departures while he was working.

Thus, one-night Zeledon, driven by his curiosity, called her mobile phone with the intention of asking where she was, but Olmeda did not respond. Only through text message did she respond with the same explanation as days before – that she was at her neighbour's apartment doing English homework with Zuly, her classmate.

When Olmeda returned, Zeledon complained that she had been abandoning her children and he didn't understand why. Despite having computers and internet at home, she always went to her neighbour to do her classwork.

After the reproach, Zeledon demanded a more convincing explanation. Olmeda shamelessly hugged him and silenced him with erotic caresses. With Zeledon under control, calmness swept over them, their arguments ultimately ending in a night of sex.

From the moment that Olmeda began this strange activity, Zeledon thought about leaving his job and devoting himself to finding out the truth. But resigning due to this wouldn't be necessary, since, after his first month of work, he would receive a notification from the school, warning him that if he worked more than twenty hours a week, he would lose government aid.

Zeledon had no choice but to resign.

The afternoon that Zeledon resigned, he returned home early. With great caution, he opened the door and entered without anyone noticing his arrival. Upon entering, he observed through the window that his children were playing at the building's courtyard and that his wife had left her private messenger open and went to washroom.

Zeledon, curious, wanted to know what his wife had been writing. To his surprise, he found the messages sent by the person who Olmeda was chatting to seconds earlier.

In these messages, the contact expressed to her how he has missed her passion and the moments of pleasure that they had together; also, he wrote that his greatest desire was to take her back in his arms.

In one of the messages, the man reminded her of the promise made by her the night before her departure to Canada. In her reply, Olmeda told him that he must be patient, that soon both would fulfil their dreams and that passion that both lived in the past.

As Zeledon read the last of the messages sent by Olmeda's lover, Olmeda who was in the bathroom returned and surprised him, although the most that was surprised was her.

Zeledon, enraged by the shocking content of the messages immediately lost his peaceful composure that had characterised him during his years as Olmeda's husband.

In that instant, his face was transformed by anger and his voice began to tremble. Then, in an emphatic tone, he asked, "Can you explain to me what these messages mean?"

Olmeda, wanting to fix everything with sex as always, approached Zeledon and tried to manipulate him with her caresses. Zeledon, facing her, pushed her furiously against the computer cabinet. She, surprised by his behaviour, started to cry. Then, using her cunning strategy to calm him, answered.

"But my love! They were just joking from a friend."

Zeledon, with a sarcastic smile, replied:

"A friend? As an older woman you must feel ashamed to be reciprocating erotic messages with a young man who might as well be your son. Or after many years, have you become a paedophile?"

Zeledon took the car keys and, in an attempt to control his rage, drove away aimlessly.

Karen and Henry, when hearing their mother's screams, came running to the apartment. Upon entering, they found the monitor, keyboard and mouse lying on the floor. Wanting to find out what happened, they harassed Olmeda with their questions; however, she wouldn't say anything against Zeledon. She could only tell them that it was an accident.

In that moment, Olmeda decided to start her plan that she had designed back in Brazil.

As the night fell, Zeledon came back to the apartment in a very different mood. Without saying word, he ate his dinner, took a shower and went to bed.

Once the new day arrived, the two returned to school together as if nothing had happened.

That morning, Olmeda would act in front of the organisation's psychologist in a way contrary to her true feelings. She described herself as an abused woman living with a macho man who is always demanding sex. That addiction in

Zeledon would lead him to demanded sex from her again and again, abusing her sexually without her consent.

After the first three hours of classes, Zeledon would be taken to the principal, who notified him that due to his violent behaviour at home, he would be transferred to another school.

Immediately afterwards, the principal handed him a newsletter and a small card which showed the phone number and address of the new school and the time that he should be present next morning.

That afternoon when he arrived at the apartment, Zeledon knew that the cause of his transfer was Olmeda. Even so, he didn't comment about the subject, he didn't want to give her the pleasure of boasting about her victory, nor the opportunity for his wife to put into practice the advice of her psychologist. And even less did he want to give a reason for their children to see him as violent father and call the police.

Hours later, a poised Zeledon finished his dinner and after watching a movie, went to their bedroom, took a pillow and a blanket and that night slept on the sofa.

The next day, Zeledon got up at the usual time and went out to find the location of his new school.

Upon his arrival, the new teachers introduced him to his classmates, and he started his first day of classes.

I knew that Zeledon was living in Canada; however, I did not know in which city he settled. Surprised, that morning from my classroom on the fourth floor, I saw him in the distance.

After the morning, his break commenced. Zeledon went down to the cafeteria and ordered the dish of his liking. Excited, I took the stairwells towards the cafeteria area.

I sat waiting for an opportunity to greet my old friend. When I saw him arrive, I didn't interrupt him, I waited until he returned to one of the tables. In the moment that Zeledon sat down to taste his food, I approached him very carefully and greeted him in a surprised manner, "Hello, my friend!"

Zeledon, surprised, turned his head. When seeing who was speaking to him, he exclaimed, "The poet!"

Immediately, Zeledon stood up, hugged me, and asked, "It cannot be! What are you doing here?"

"Studying English," I replied.

"Yes, but what brought you to these lands?" Zeledon asked.

"A problem similar to yours," I answered.

Zeledon, with surprise drawn on his face, continued to ask questions.

"But who could pursue you? You didn't have problems with anyone!"

At that moment, I looked at the clock and responded, "Well, that's a long story and at this moment, our time is limited."

After his response, the school siren rang, and so I returned to class. Both still in the cafeteria, we said goodbye with a strong handshake and promised to wait for each other at the exit in order to catch up with each other.

When our English classes finished up, we met again. Zeledon asked me to follow him to parking lot to pick up his car, and from there, he drove to a Chinese restaurant at downtown where we ordered a special dish.

While we waited for the waiter to come back with the food, I divulged to Zeledon about the secret of my work that nobody in El Paso knew about: Sotomayor's, or Santos,' secret man, and his involvement with the Poppy Cartel.

I would also tell him about Santos' persecution and his subsequent murder, ordered by influential Brazilian politician, Tancredo Moreira. A politician, who, years before, was a drug trafficker and ordered the murders of Falcão and his bodyguards.

I would explain to him that when Santos was killed, Moreira started to hunt me down too because Sotomayor had a video of evidence against the politician that he deposited into a bank deposit box under my name days before his murder. However, the politician would eventually find this out through his contacts, which eventually forced me to flee to the United States and, weeks later, to seek refuge in Canada.

In addition, I confirmed to Zeledon that the culprit of his persecution was Zé Maria and clarified to him his motive.

After he listened my story, I could see in Zeledon how his eyes reflected the sadness hidden in his soul. I was sure that this nostalgia wasn't merely for the death of his friend Santos. Although the news had impacted him, I was sure that this pain was for something more.

Curious to know the cause of his feeling, I sensitively asked, "Zeledon, are you okay?"

With a little melancholy, he answered, "The truth is that I don't know. I am not sure how to explain my situation, and I don't know if it is bad or good. Although for many it may be good, because here in this country, I have health, safety and I am learning English which without doubt will open doors to my future."

He continued, "However, for me, the circumstance of losing the respect of my wife and children is very worrying."

At that moment, I wanted to tell him once and for all the truth about his wife, that for a long time he had lost the respect of his wife. That she, in São Paulo, had more than one lover. I wanted to tell him that, one night, while I was following Olmeda, I saw her leave a motel in the company of a young man who could well be her son. Even repeating the same act of adultery a few days later, but on that occasion, her lover would be military border officer. I thought of telling him that his wife was a complete nymphomaniac, but I couldn't. I knew how much he loved her, and I didn't want to increase his pain.

However, with the intention of preparing him for the event that was approaching him, I commented, "Zeledon, some Latin men in the school are commenting that many of the Latin couples that arrive to Canada, regardless of the economic status that they had in their country, end up separating. According to the men, the reason for this is that the women let themselves be influenced by Canadian culture and believe that they are the priority, and thus, they think they have the freedom to play the man's role. Many of these women forget their principles and good habits and fall into debauchery that they didn't have in their home countries."

Zeledon, afflicted, told me, "Poet, your comment is too late, already I am living through that agony."

With dinner already on the table, I paused the conversation. After a few seconds, as we were enjoying the food, Zeledon began to tell me in detail of all the latest events in his life, telling me even his most complicated intimate details.

Minutes after recollecting our past, Zeledon invited me to his home or, rather, to the little that was left of it. I, knowing that I had an English test to study for, declined his offer. Although truthfully, the reason I didn't want to accompany him was because I didn't want to see the hypocritical face of his wife Olmeda.

Thus, Zeledon gave me a ride to train station. There, he gave me his e-mail and his cell phone number. With a handshake and a strong hug, we said goodbye and agreed to meet in the school cafeteria the next day during the break.

That night, when Zeledon arrived at his apartment, his watch showed 10:45 pm. His children, who were still awake, were surprised when they saw him arrive so late.

"Dad, where you have been the entire night?"

Without much hesitation, he replied to them, "Children, I was talking with a friend from El Paso, with whom after several months unexpectedly, I met with at school again."

At that moment, Zeledon's eyes around the apartment, looking for Olmeda. When he didn't find her on the main floor, he didn't ask for her or call her mobile phone as he usually did. Instead, he just lay back on the sofa without caring about her absence. After a few seconds, his daughter informed him that food was ready. Zeledon, when turning his head, concentrated his vision on the note attached to the refrigerator door. Olmeda had written to let everyone know where she would be. *'I'm in front of Apartment 101, helping my classmate Zuly who has just moved to the building.'*

For a few moments, Zeledon ignored the message, but carried by his curiosity, he wanted to know if this was true. So, he went out to search for her. When he arrived at the location mentioned in the note, he found a woman of humble appearance, accompanied by her two little children.

Zeledon, after greeting her, thought to ask about Olmeda. This wouldn't be necessary, however, because just as he arrived, she appeared with the neighbour's husband, carrying a piece of heavy furniture. Immediately as they saw Zeledon, they stopped and said hello.

Evandro and Zuly, their new neighbours, very kindly invited them to share some delicious pizza to thank Olmeda for her help.

Zeledon, although a little embarrassed, accepted the invitation as courtesy and in this process, helped them to accommodate the mattresses and assemble their beds.

Once Olmeda and Zeledon saw that their help was no longer necessary, they said their goodbyes and returned to their apartment.

In Evandro's mind, the new neighbours seemed like excellent people, and he didn't see Olmeda as a woman who could be harmful to his wife. In fact, he believed all the opposite – that her influence would be greatly beneficial to her.

On the other hand, as Zeledon observed Zuly's respectful, kind qualities, he thought that she could serve as an example to his wife.

As the days passed, the friendship between the two women grew stronger. Both always were close, at school and out. Their friendship became inseparable; when Zuly wasn't at Zeledon's home, Olmeda was at Evandro's house, needing to do something urgently with Zuly.

With some excuse, these women always went out together. For both women, even their young children, weren't an impediment to their plans, since they would leave Karen to take care of their children.

In one of their many supposed urgencies, Olmeda invited to her friend out to Tim Horton's with the intention to introduce Zuly to her Mexican friends, Enrique, and Vicente.

When Zuly met them, she was delighted and asked for their phone numbers and e-mails. From that moment, her calls, and messages from Vicente would be constant.

Olmeda, with the story that she was waiting for Zuly at school, would make plans to meet with them again. There, she began to teach her new friend of all her bad influences.

One afternoon after leaving school, Olmeda proposed that the three go to the cinema together. Zuly initially resisted, but Olmeda convinced her.

Days later, Olmeda began her manipulation; without objections, Zuly would accompany to her to share cocktails or dinner with them.

One Friday, the two women called their husbands as planned and informed them that they would arrive a little late, since they were going window-shopping downtown.

Neither Zeledon nor Evandro saw this as out of the ordinary, because in Canada, it was a custom among immigrant women to tour shopping centres.

After a week of nights out, and coming home late, the two women would give free rein to their debauchery.

One night, taking advantage of the eve of a feminist event, both women would tell their husbands that next Sunday, the school was going to be celebrating International Women's Day in a Canadian nightclub. This was an event in which all women were invited and, of course, they as classmates couldn't miss it. Evandro and Zeledon, who had already heard about the event at school, wouldn't object to their plans.

When the date arrived, both men waited to meet their wives. However, Olmeda, with the approval of Zuly, would change the original plan. That night, they met with their friends and went out to have fun in a more romantic place. There, after dancing, drinking and being intimate, they would end in a motel room.

From the moment that Olmeda began to betray Zeledon in Toronto, she would increase his moments of pleasure; she would seduce him to have sex daily until her period arrived. This kept him entertained and managed to reduce the suspicion caused by the messages found on Olmeda's computer weeks ago.

Olmeda's strategy of turning to Zeledon into a sex-addicted man had given her excellent results, since Zeledon didn't object to her constants departures if they were regularly intimate.

A week after the last clandestine encounter between the two couples, the two Mexicans stopping going to school.

Both women, worried, asked the school director of the reason why their friends were absent. There, they learned that their classmates were only international students that had ended their study period; thus, they had returned to Mexico.

However, that story was very far from reality, as in fact, they would continue residing in Toronto as illegals.

Olmeda, desperate to hear from Enrique, called him and sent him text messages. As did Zuly with her friend Vicente. However, both had suspended their telephone services.

So, the two women tried to use instant messenger and e-mail with their questions. Despite this, they wouldn't get any response for some time. Their lovers wouldn't contact them until they were sure that immigration was not looking for them.

A month after their disappearance, Olmeda would receive a surprise text message from her lover Enrique, who was feeling anguished for not responding for some time and wrote, 'Honey, I need to talk to you, please connect to the internet.'

As soon she read it, she wanted to answer him immediately, but connecting to the internet from her apartment would be impossible as Zeledon was present. Thus, Olmeda went to Zuly's house.

That day, the two communicated again and set a date for their next meeting. The relief to know that Enrique was in Toronto made Olmeda forget for a moment that she was in someone else's house, so when Evandro arrived and saw her chatting with such enthusiasm, he asked his wife, "Who is Olmeda chatting to?"

Zuly, trying to cover for her, replied, "With a schoolmate."

This situation would make Evandro begin to question the fidelity of Olmeda. This doubt would only increase during the week when he would unexpectedly see her three more times doing the same thing.

When Evandro didn't find to Olmeda using the family computer, he found her talking with that alleged classmate on Zuly's mobile phone.

Soon after, Evandro and Zuly, due to the sudden illness of their youngest son, couldn't attend their classes.

That morning, the three arrived at the emergency room, where after an examination, the doctor told them not to worry as it was just a simple allergy. Once the diagnosis was made, they obtained a prescription and went in search of the medication. However, after failing to find it at the local pharmacy, Evandro went to the shopping centre instead.

Evandro not only found the medicine but also confirmed his suspicion of Olmeda. From a distance, he observed as Olmeda said goodbye to a supposed friend with a passionate kiss.

Feeling deceived, he returned to the apartment but didn't mention anything to Zuly about the betrayal of her friend Olmeda. He decided to wait until Olmeda visited Zuly to say the truth in her face.

The night that Olmeda came to visit them, Evandro, in determined tone, forbade her to return to his apartment and, above all, asked her to stay away from his wife. Due to this reaction, a total silence came over the room; Zuly, fearful that her husband had discovered her friend's truth, didn't dare to intercede for Olmeda, since she knew that if she did, Evandro would take actions against her.

Olmeda, surprised and not understanding the reaction of his neighbour, acted as the victim and told Evandro that, whether he liked it or not, Zuly would always be her friend.

Hours after that embarrassing episode, Olmeda and Zuly received invitations for her best friend's bachelorette party.

As both women were out from their houses, Evandro and Zeledon would receive the invitations.

Each one of them, when observing that the envelopes had an arrowed heart and that it was addressed to their wives as confidential information, became curious. So, very delicately, they opened each of the envelopes, finding inside each, a picture of their wives next to a naked man coming out of a huge cake.

They would also find on the envelopes a small note in which her friend indicated that to enter, they had to present that photograph at the club entrance.

In another paragraph, she clarified that as it was an informal bachelorette party; there would be only women and so they were required to only wear casual clothes.

Zeledon and Evandro, after satisfying their curiosity, sealed the envelopes again and returned them to the mailbox.

Hours later, when Zuly and Olmeda opened their mail and read the invitations, they realised that the date of the celebration coincided with their next clandestine meeting. They decided that although it was their best friend, they wouldn't be present, but both would take that invitation as the perfect excuse for their next outing.

While Olmeda would follow the recommendation of casual clothes written in the note, Zuly started to do her makeup hours earlier. Then, in front of the mirror, she tried each of her best dresses more than once until she chose the most elegant. Evandro, who was watching her, saw his wife's enthusiasm as suspicious, since the invitation stipulated that the guests should wear casual clothes. His mistrust led him to talk to his sister, who offered to help him. So, she waited in the back of the building. When Zuly went looking for Olmeda, her sister-in-law came in to take care of the children so that Evandro was free to follow Zuly.

Ten minutes later, as Olmeda and Zuly took a taxi, Evandro continued his chase in his car.

After a quarter of an hour, both women got out in front of a nightclub. There in the parking lot, two men waited for them. They, upon seeing the two women, greeted them with a romantic hug and a passionate kiss.

From across the road in his car, Evandro recorded the scene on his cell phone. Angered, he continued to watch his wife being caressed by another man. He watched as her lover, after touching her private parts, took Zuly by her hand and walked to a Latin bar, from where, after a few drinks, they left without any direction in mind.

Evandro, who was still following them at a distance, pursued them to a motel. There, he waited until they both entered their room. Next, he went to the window and through a small slot, watched as the two threw themselves on the bed. When they started to have sex, he delicately opened the door of the small room and filmed the two.

After filming, Evandro launched himself on both of them and began to punch Zuly's lover, unloading all his fury on his rival. At the same time, Zuly cried desperately disturbing the calm of the entire motel.

Enrique, who was with Olmeda in the next room, came to see what was happening. Realising that his friend was being attacked, he immediately intervened. When the police arrived, they saw the two men beating the husband.

The five of them were taken to the police station. While they filed reports, the officer confirmed that both Mexicans had their student visas expired. Thus, they were violating the laws of Canada. Due to this, they were detained to be transferred to immigration, who would be responsible for deporting them back to their country of origin.

Evandro, based on his wife's betrayal, stated in his report that he didn't want to see his wife in their apartment. So, officer advised Zuly to spend the weekend in a shelter. For the time being, Evandro would have the custody of their children until a judge decided which of the two would be their guardian.

That news and the loss of her lover overwhelmed Zuly with sadness. Although this sadness also affected Olmeda, it wasn't as noticeable as her neighbour, considering the temporary absence of her children. The few days that she would be without them would make Zuly understand the pain of her betrayal. Eventually, Evandro, seeing the sadness in his children due to the absence of her mother, let her return home. However, before her arrival, he warned her that he didn't want to see her talking again with her friend Olmeda.

Evandro, trying to get as far away as possible from the person who had destabilised his marriage, decided to move to a new apartment. Even so, that wouldn't be an impediment to the friendship between Zuly and Olmeda as they would continue to meet in secret.

A week after humiliating incident, Evandro received a subpoena for his hearing. On the date stipulated by the judge, the couple would be present at the court.

As they arrived, Evandro thought about showing the judge the videos. However, he knew that if he did that his wife would lose all rights to their children, and he didn't want to make them his children suffer more. So, under a sworn agreement before the judge, both he and Zuly committed to improve their relationship.

Once the clause was settled on their personal files, the magistrate warned them that if either of them were violent towards each other, the government would take custody of their children. As the sentence was announced, the judge commanded them to attend fifteen sessions of family therapy.

As Evandro wanted to avoid gossip about his wife and Olmeda, he decided not to tell Zeledon about what happened. Even so, sometime later, rumours of the infidelity of the two women would come to Zeledon through street conversation. However, as nobody had conclusive evidence, he didn't give the rumours any importance.

Zuly's Relapse and Zeledon's Hell

Forgiveness in love never produces a good result if the forgiveness is not true.

Six months after the couple's agreement in court life would give them a new setback. As Evandro was still hurt by his wife's betrayal, he was no longer having sex with her.

Zuly, overwhelmed by the degrading treatment and her husband's indifference, locked herself in her own world, and although she felt guilty for that behaviour, she was still a grown woman with sexual needs. So, carried by her passion, she wanted to feel alive again. So, she would look for someone to calm the fire burning inside.

That uncontrollable desire in her would provoke, in her partner, a new conflict, since Evandro would find her caressing another man. However, this time he wouldn't take out his anger on the man; instead, Zuly would take his beating.

After beating her, Evandro, warned her, "If you want to lose our children, take me to court."

Although that was Zuly's greatest wish, the bond signed before the judge months ago tied her hands.

Soon after, Evandro left the apartment and got a secret lover, while Zuly decided to return with her children to Brazil. However, without the father's signature, she couldn't get them out of Canada.

She thought that as she is a woman, she had every chance to win custody, so she went to court and with a false story and asked for permission to leave Canada.

The judge, a little confused at Zuly's story, stated that he could not give permission without hearing the father's side.

So, on the witness stand, Evandro, in revenge for the audacity of his wife, showed the video to the judge. When observing the scenes of betrayal, the judge determined that Zuly didn't meet the requirements to keep the children and ordered that the two little boys go to an orphanage to receive foster parents.

Evandro's secret lover, without the judge realising the connection between them, would be the first person to apply for custody of the boys in court.

While the days passed, other people would also apply, but she would be successful as the most qualified person to care for them.

With custody in Evandro's lover's hands, the loser in the end would be Zuly, who, sad, abandoned and without any other options would have to travel alone to Brasilia.

Zeledon, through the grapevine, was informed of the situation between Zuly and Evandro, which would also confirm to him of his wife's betrayal. That night, with Zeledon's macho ego injured, he would admonish Olmeda for her bad behaviour. She, as always making herself the victim, knelt and with tears in her eyes, swore that she would never be able to betray him. This was all slander from jealous people, she added.

Olmeda, resentful towards her husband for his accusations, retired to sleep elsewhere.

Due to his disappointment, Zeledon no longer liked to stay in his apartment in the afternoons. When he had nothing to do, he would leave the house with some excuse and stay there for hours.

One morning, while walking around the community, Zeledon saw a notice where an owner urgently needed a couple of cleaners for his restaurant.

After calling and an interview, he got the job. Immediately when they agreed on the payment method, Zeledon thought of Laura, his best friend, who, after listening his proposal, accepted to be his cleaning partner.

When Olmeda learned about her husband's decision, she became jealous. So, she decided to go back to sleep with him in the same room.

The night that Olmeda changed her mind, Zeledon, when seeing her arrive and throwing herself on the bed, didn't acknowledge her. For a few days, he controlled his erotic desire and didn't seek her for sex; in fact, when she asked for it, he rejected her.

That disinterest of her husband led Olmeda to look for sex toys and masturbate in his presence. She knew that Zeledon wouldn't resist so much eroticism and would fall head over heels in the middle of her legs.

Successful in her goal, Olmeda threw the mattress on the carpet, because the physical task upon them would be loud, and they didn't want to disturb their children.

From that night on, Olmeda would begin to play with Zeledon's weakness; she would devote herself completely to saturate him with pleasure.

Her behaviour in bed would make Zeledon forget all the suspicions that were circulating in his mind. With this, she would stir up the fire so that it would keep burning and allow for Olmeda to proceed with the second step of her original plan that she had thought in Brazil.

Olmeda, unable to have relations with Enrique again, focused her thoughts again on her young lover of Bahia and began to contact him through text messages. However, to fulfil the promise made to him years ago, she would need to catch Zeledon, in a moment of despair, committing something atrocious and above all, she needed record evidence of it. Thus, she planned to accuse Zeledon of sexual harassment and domestic violence.

Olmeda wasn't afraid to receive a violent reaction from Zeledon because she was sure that even though he had many reasons to do, he wouldn't dare to hit her.

When discarding that possibility, Olmeda opted to press him psychologically and with that, she was an expert. From that night, she started to reject Zeledon again. When he looked to her on the bed and tried to caress her, she ignored his desires. For several nights, she would do the same. This caused that he satisfied his needs by himself. For a few seconds, she watched as her partner masturbated, then, without caring, she continued to ignore him and continued her sleep. Her rejection and apathy would fill Zeledon with fury and make him get up from the mattress and kick the furniture around the room. The noise, although woke up their children, didn't alarm them, since they couldn't hear any verbal arguments.

When the morning arrived while Zeledon took a shower, Olmeda put the objects back to their places. However, before doing it and without him noticing, she took several photographs.

The coldness shown by Olmeda would continue week after week. After Zeledon didn't receive the intimacy to which he was accustomed, he lost control.

One night, after searching for her insistently to have sex with her, Zeledon became so frustrated that he walked to the kitchen, took a knife, and returned to the bedroom.

Olmeda, when observing the anger in Zeledon's eyes from a distance, retired to sleep with her eldest daughter.

Seconds later, when Zeledon returned and saw that his wife was not there, his anger increased. Wanting to take revenge, he vented his rage at the mattress, destroying it with numerous stabbings.

His behaviour was recorded by Olmeda, who had finally found the perfect opportunity that she was looking for. With that proof, Olmeda could easily accuse him of sexual harassment or psychological torture in front of the judge, which she had always threatened if he ever touched her, even in the slightest.

Realising that she had him in her hands filled Zeledon with insecurity and anger, which naturally caused vulgar words to spring from his mouth in front of his children. He admonished Olmeda for being a shameless vagabond. Zeledon's violent shouting caused his children to retaliate against him, refusing to accept his accusations against their mother.

One day, the two, hurt by his behaviour, threatened to call the police if he didn't leave the apartment forever.

Zeledon, knowing the genuineness of their threats, retired to a shopping centre. There, when wanting to use his family visa card, he saw that his account had been cancelled. Realising he couldn't access any money to pay for a hotel, he had no other choice but to return to his apartment.

As time passed in the hostile home, Zeledon retained hope that things would improve between his wife and him, and although he tried his best to achieve it, it wouldn't be possible. Although the household seemed to be calm, he was living in a world of mistrust and deception, which he wanted to pretend didn't exist. But, of course, that would not last and, eventually, it would collapse.

Days after the temporary calmness, Olmeda, showing fictitious interest, got up one morning and very affectionately told him that she loved him.

During that expression of affection, she also proposed to get married. Zeledon, who had gone too long without hearing a loving word from her mouth, was not interested. With a resounding no, he rejected her offer. Zeledon clarified to her that if he didn't have confidence in her, then there was no point.

His rejection didn't anger Olmeda who was so sure of herself that she reminded him that all were innocent until proven otherwise. In addition, she remarked that love knows no barriers. If her friend Eliana, a prostitute, got married, why not her, a woman of just one man?

Zeledon, with the intention of not arguing, didn't say anything else. He just took his bag and went to school.

That afternoon, upon arriving at the apartment, Zeledon found Olmeda weeping. He thought that his tears were due to their argument hours ago. However, the reason for his wife's lament was due to a call from her sister who informed her that her grandfather, the person, who, in the past, was always in charge to care for her was seriously ill and her duty as a granddaughter was to be present. Zeledon, saddened by the news, immediately recommended that Olmeda call the travel agency and book departure date.

Soon after, she asked him to sign in front of a notary a permit for her son to leave the country.

After confirming their departure, Olmeda informed their schools that both she, and Henry will be absent for a few weeks; that estimation would be a mistake, since their stays would last for three months.

Without planning, Olmeda's family emergency would coincide with her daughter Karen's vacation trip to Mexico.

Although it just was for two weeks, she decided to stay at her friend's home.

Loneliness and the doubt about his wife would make Zeledon depressed. Due to that, when we would meet in the school, I would improvise some casual conversation and try to get him out of his affliction. However, Zeledon always managed to deviate from the subject, and we always ended up talking about his life.

A day before that Olmeda returned from Brazil, Zeledon made the decision to leave the apartment, because he sensed that his wife wasn't taking care of her grandfather in São Paulo and that, perhaps, the illness had served as an excuse to spend the time in Bahia with her young lover.

Zeledon wasn't mistaken, his hypothesis was reality. Olmeda, when arriving at her grandparents' house, would do so accompanied by her lover. There, she convinced everyone that the young man was one of her husband's best friends, convincing them to lodge him with confidence and to provide him with food and shelter for as long as they thought fit.

After three months of their stay in Brazil, Olmeda returned to Toronto. When she arrived at the apartment and didn't see Zeledon's things, she assumed that he had abandoned them, although she had no idea where he had gone. Olmeda searched for him for everywhere, sending him messages and calling his cell phone, but Zeledon was determined to hide from her. When he saw her number on his phone's screen, he didn't answer.

One night, while Zeledon contacted their children through his mobile phone, he heard his wife crying like a girl. As she cried, she commented to her children how much she missed Zeledon. Through them, she begged him to come back. As he heard her plea, Zeledon wasn't surprised by her tears. By this stage, he knew that she was manipulation expert. However, the reason for her request confused him, since she had supposedly spent her 'honeymoon' with a young man. She must be saturated with sex, Zeledon thought, so he didn't understand her insistence to be together again.

Her perseverance succeeded in bringing back Zeledon a few days after; he swallowed his pride and came back to sleep under her sheets, although, according to him, this would be more for intrigue than pleasure. His curiosity to know if she had been unfaithful had that had become an obsession; his desire to see her have the courage to tell him the truth to his face led him to create an entire scenario. That night, both sitting on the bed, Zeledon repeated again that he didn't trust her because everything about her was suspect. Also, he clarified her that he hadn't been a saint and that, during his stay in El Paso, he had several women as lovers, including a minor who was Henry's babysitter.

Zeledon's intention was to trick her into resentfully telling him the truth. He thought that Olmeda, in her pain, would react and end up responding to his betrayal in the same way. However, it wouldn't be so. She, making herself a victim, resorted to weeping and shouting degrading words to him.

Secretly, she would accuse him in front of their children as a maniac and depraved deviant.

The next morning, when Zeledon returned from school, he found his suitcase on the patio and noticed that the locks had been changed. Although he tried many times to open the door, he didn't succeed. Without other options, Zeledon resorted to asking for my help.

Days later, at Olmeda's request, he would be taken to court, where a judge would declare them legally separated. To his surprise, Olmeda gave him a copy of the key and gave him the freedom to visit his children whenever he wished as long as his children wanted to talk with him.

From that moment, things between them changed; although they separated, they continued having sex. Olmeda, from a wife, became his lover.

When Zeledon came to visit his children, he rarely spent time with them. Olmeda would take advantage by inviting him to wait for them on the second floor of the house.

In doing so, her intention was to excite him by wearing a small miniskirt without underwear, so that when she walked up the stairs, Zeledon would see her intimate area.

Zeledon, still clinging to his addiction for her, couldn't control such a temptation and both ended up wallowing in the basement.

This arrangement lasted a couple of months. During that time, although Olmeda was still in a relationship with Zeledon, at the same time, kept in touch by phone with her young lover from Bahia. They planned in secret to have a wedding that would take place next December.

Her desire to keep Zeledon deceived and the fear that her grandfather would oppose to her betrayal forced to Olmeda to make that decision.

Weeks before the marriage, her grandfather, who was struggling with a serious illness, died. Olmeda, due to the circumstances, returned to São Paulo where her young lover was waiting for her and together, they attended the funeral.

Despite the sad circumstances, with the death of her grandfather, Olmeda was free to do what she wanted and so, she continued with her original plan.

The Wedding and Gustavo's Odyssey

In Toronto, the lonely days felt longer than usual. As December arrived, Zeledon spent the nights alone again at home. Sitting on the living room sofa, he felt nostalgic remembering the three people who, until that moment, were the most important in his life: his wife, his son, and his daughter. Particularly his daughter, who didn't talk with him anymore.

Along with Karen's silence, she soon unexpectedly decided to travel to Bahia.

Although Zeledon loved them, he would show them the opposite due to the pain that his soul felt, which darkened his sentiments. He assumed that his wife, for many years, continued to betray him in love, and his children possibly were her accomplices.

Regardless, Zeledon continued to delude himself such that when she would return and he would see her again, they couldn't contain their desire to kiss and make love, since his body still had an addiction for her touch, and he needed her touch to calm it again. Because of that, Zeledon knew that eventually, he would end up begging her, hoping that she would come back for a night under his sheets, even for only a few minutes together.

He no longer cared that his beloved wife was 'a complete bitch' according to his friends, especially because he hadn't yet verified the rumours that circulated in the mouths of his friends. So, he still believed that the gossip was only speculation, particularly since Olmeda always had the perfect alibi with her planned absences and trips. And although some of it seemed suspicious, Zeledon turned a blind eye. However, with time, truth always reveals itself.

Zeledon's destiny would have a surprise for him, a surprise which Olmeda had already revealed to her children. However, they refrained from telling their father, to keep their mother's secret. With this, the two had betrayed their father again.

Hours before finding out the truth, during another night of solitude, Zeledon approached his living room window. There, for a few minutes, he entertained himself by watching the snowflakes fall on a tree in front of his house. He watched and concentrated on how a branch caught the tiny flakes of snow. After a few seconds, he watched as the branch, overloaded by the weight, was torn from the trunk and fell to the ground.

Instantly, Zeledon remembered the reason why he had originally moved from the couch that he had been reclining on minutes before. Karen suddenly left a message on his cell phone, writing:

'Dad, please call me, it's urgent.'

Immediately, Zeledon spun his body around and to return to the living room where the phone was. But before taking the first step, suddenly the silence was interrupted by the telephone's ring.

Surprised, he looked at his watch and seeing that it was midnight, he imagined that this call was not good news.

As he answered the call, Zeledon heard the voice of his daughter Karen, who, between cried, said, "Dad forgive me! You were right when you questioned my mother's reputation. Today, with pain in my soul, I must admit that trusting her was my biggest mistake."

During her momentary anger, Karen explained to Zeledon that, for the past few weeks through her Facebook friendships, she began to listen to the gossip of her mother's infidelity, and wanting to confirm the truth, she travelled to Bahia.

There, she would discover that during the time that Olmeda was living in El Paso, she had many secret lovers, one of whom she would marry in secret next Friday.

After the revelation, Karen added that although at first, she had doubts, lately, her suspicion increased.

Karen divulged that at night, due to the mid-term exam the next day, she was studying late with her friend. When she got home, she found her mother with a young man in the master bedroom.

As soon as he saw her arrive, he left. When she demanded an explanation from Olmeda, she fell to her knees crying, and swore that there was nothing between them, that the neighbour's son was just showing his video about his graduation party. Karen, thinking that she was sincere, believed her at the time, but it was all false.

In middle of her pain, Karen continued and told Zeledon that the previous year, when Olmeda supposedly travelled to Bahia to visit her dying grandfather, it was just a lie to meet her lover. Through my Facebook contacts in Toronto, I already knew this. It was from someone who I least imagined that told her that her mother didn't travel to Bahia, but to São Paulo to meet with her lover in a resort.

In addition, she knew that her mother had left her brother Henry in the care of her aunt and niece who were aware of that romance and supporting her decision.

Karen, based on hearing this, called Olmeda from the house of her maternal grandmother, Matilde, in Rio de Janeiro. Through the phone, Karen chastised Olmeda for being a vagabond and an irresponsible scoundrel. But Karen, for two reasons, didn't say anything to her about her discovery, and allowed Olmeda's plan to marry in secret to continue.

The first reason was because she wanted to confirm Olmeda's brazenness with her own eyes.

The other reason was because she wanted to have the pleasure of rubbing the truth in her face, stripping her of her cloak with which she pretended to be a lady.

According to Karen, the rumours of infidelity heard about her mother in the recent weeks through her Facebook contacts pushed her to advance her trip to Brazil, since the wedding would be taking place on December 23rd.

Once there, Karen began making her own inquiries. In Bahia, she confirmed the sad reality and other things more painful to accept. Unfortunately for her, these rumours were the truth that she could no longer avoid.

At first, in Toronto, Karen refused to believe the comments, because she thought that they were just an exaggeration from envious people. So, now knowing the truth, she visited Marina, her mother's best friend, the only person capable of telling her the truth.

Marina, knowing everything about Olmeda's past, had been an accomplice of her affairs. Although until that time she maintained her loyalty to Olmeda, seeing Karen's despair made her conscience and the weight of her guilt divulge the truth.

Thus, Marina knew that both the husband and daughter should know of Olmeda's betrayal. Regretting her lies, she apologised to Karen for being her mother's accomplice and assured that all gossip about Olmeda were a harsh reality.

After her revelation, Marina added, "You can tell your mother, with my own name, who was the person who told you the truth."

However, Olmeda would never know that her friend was the one who betrayed her.

Karen, even with that certainty, wanted to hear a confession of her deception straight from her mother.

Achieving this goal wouldn't be so easy, since Olmeda was very clever. So, Karen would have to come up with a plan.

That same afternoon, without Olmeda having any idea of her presence, while Olmeda was driving the rent car, Karen began to follow her.

Minutes later, she watched as Olmeda parked the car in front of her new family's house. There, they received her with hugs and kisses, to which she responded with a gift for each one of them.

When the future husband of her mother appeared, Karen confirmed that he was the same young man that she found in the room with Olmeda five years ago; the man who Olmeda insisted was only a friend. Once confirmed, Karen went back to her paternal grandmother, Carmelina, and from there, she told her mother that she was in Bahia.

Then, there, Karen waited for her, since she knew that Olmeda would look for her from the moment she told her she was in Bahia.

Karen thought of a lie about the young man her mother had planned to marry. Karen, very emotionally, told her mother that when she was in El Paso visiting Zeledon, her young friend, Albeiro, came to look for her, but when he saw that she was alone, with the pretext that he is loving her from when they are studying together, he tried to rape her.

Olmeda's reaction to supposed slander was instantaneous, and like a dictator protecting his empire, defended him with her own arguments. Hysterical and very confused by Karen's comments, Olmeda expressed, "That is impossible because he is my lover for years. I trust his love so much that under no circumstances could he do such a thing. I am the reason he lives and the reason for his joy. I am in Bahia with him because next week, we are getting married."

As Olmeda revealed the truth, Karen's blood boiled inside of her veins. Even considering that she was talking to her mother, she burst into a fit of rage and shouted, "Shameless woman, vagrant, you are not a lady. How could you cheat on my father for so long?"

Olmeda, incredibly surprised by such a reaction, responded, "There is no doubt that you are a worthy daughter of Zeledon, and you inherited his violent DNA."

Karen, angered by her comment, replied, "It's better to carry my father's genes and not the disgraceful blood that you carry in your veins.

"In the past, you had no shame with Henry; one night he found you and your lover in bed having sex. Although he discovered this truth a long time ago, because of his youthful age and naïve mind, he let himself be manipulated. You made him believe that if he told anyone about what he saw, he would lose you forever. You instilled in his mind that he never saw that other man having sex with you, that the man that he saw was just Zeledon."

Karen, reflecting on her bad treatment of her father in the past, acknowledged, although late, that he had always been right when he accused her mother of bad behaviour.

Karen, from that moment on had no doubt that her mother was a shameless woman, particularly since she intended on getting married without saying anything to her relatives in Toronto and continue being the lover of Zeledon, despite being married to another man in Brazil. If it had not been for her wit, Olmeda's plan would have succeeded, Karen concluded.

Olmeda, realising she had been discovered, knew that it didn't make sense for her to continue with her secrecy. So, on the eve of her marriage, she made her invitations. When she invited her mother to the wedding, she, with much disappointment, told her.

"I'm sorry, Daughter, but I will not attend your wedding! I know Zeledon, and I don't have any doubt that he is a good man. So, I don't agree with you betraying him. I, as a wife, have lived with a man who gave me a bad life until moments before he died, and even so, I was at his side until the day of his death."

Others would also turn their backs on Olmeda, including her brothers. They, after echoing the comments that were being said about her, referred to her as a bitch who didn't even deserve a response.

The only relatives to attend the wedding would be her sister and niece, as well as Marina, her best friend from São Paulo.

When Zeledon learned that Olmeda had married in Bahia with the young man who he had once caught chatting with his wife and who he assumed was only Olmeda's friend, he realised that for many years, he had been a cuckold.

In that moment, he could finally understand the revelation that his youngest son once told him in El Paso.

One afternoon, his son arrived to visit him. Within five minutes of his arrival, exclaimed, "Dad! I know what is having sex!"

Zeledon recalled the question that immediately came from his mouth at that moment.

"Is that what you are being taught at school?"

"No, Father!" replied the boy.

"I say this because one night, I saw you and my mother making love."

This surprised Zeledon, since he had not visited his home in São Paulo for years. Even so, he never thought that what his son observed was a betrayal by Olmeda.

That security in his son made Zeledon confuse the reality with a premature vision created from the innocence of his child.

As sadness began to overcome Zeledon in response to Karen's revelation, he started to analyse the facts of the past and connect them to the adultery of his ex-wife, which only increased his shock. But the most degrading thing for him was discovering that Olmeda intended to marry in secret with the intention of betraying her new husband and, at the same time, would continue deceiving him with a false love.

That discovery, although too late, led Zeledon to think about his dignity, for which he thought to repair with blood.

For several weeks, due to his pain in the soul, Zeledon couldn't sleep well. Although it was clear that Olmeda was only his temporary lover and that, eventually, she would marry another, he always thought that if this happened, he expected that it would be with someone that she knew in Toronto; that would have made her betrayal less painful.

As the days passed, the mood of Zeledon worsened. Little by little, the depression and the anxiety of wanting revenge pushed him to rock bottom.

His habit of taking refuge in his solitude and thinking of memories with Olmeda made his life lose meaning. His critical situation was further complicated when, through Marina, he discovered in detail of the different betrayals of his ex-wife.

This would cause Zeledon, for two weeks, to leave school, block his Facebook account and not respond to my calls. His attitude warned me that he was in serious trouble.

Concerned about such behaviour, I called him at home, but upon hearing the voicemail stating that the number was disconnected, I confirmed that something unusual was happening to him. Worried, I devoted myself to look for him everywhere he usually visited, but I was unsuccessful. What I didn't know at the time was that Zeledon was in another city entirely.

He, trying to forget the sad memories, had embarked on a trip without any destination.

On this trip, Zeledon was minutes away from losing his life. That day, in a certain way, luck was on his side, since the bus in which he was traveling in had a fatal event take place only hours later.

According to the Zeledon's story, that day during the first hours of his trip, everything went relatively smoothly, but death was soon approaching.

Nobody inside the bus thought that the small person of calm appearance sitting in the first seat of the bus was a psychopath preparing a terrifying plan in his Machiavellian mind.

The man, despite leaving every quarter of an hour to go to the bathroom, didn't arouse suspicion, since with his submissive attitude, he confused everyone inside the bus.

While the psychopath stepped through the vehicle, he observed the occupants one by one. That routine continued until the night arrived, when most of the passengers settled down for the night. Taking advantage of the fact that most were either distracted by watching a movie, reading a book, or sleeping, the psychopath would start his attack.

Ten minutes before his fatal attack, he chose his victim among those present. At that moment, his most viable option was Zeledon because he was asleep in the last of the seats, but as the attacker approached his target, Zeledon woke up with a startle.

The psychopath, seeing that his future victim was an immigrant, with a seemingly disgruntled mood, opted for a second alternative: he turned to a young man who was a few metres from Zeledon instead.

The attacker, after his second analysis, retreated to his seat and from a drawer of the luggage carrier took a small backpack from which he extracted a saw knife and proceeded to unleash his chaotic imagination. As stealthy as a feline, he reached over his victim, pressed his hand against his mouth and slid the knife quickly down his jugular.

The young began to convulse while the blood gushed out and his hand feebly tried to save himself, as he instinctually clung to the arm of his murderer.

Immediately after the fatal attack, the young man's life escaped from his body.

Those who felt tiny drops of blood fall on their heads initially assumed that these were drops of water emanating from the bus's heating, but the cries of terror emanating from those who realised what was happening alerted all to the reality.

The driver, upon hearing the collective hysteria, parked the vehicle, activated the alarm, and turned on the emergency lights to reveal what had happened.

Immediately, they saw the psychopath with a bloody knife in his mouth, and in his left hand, a firearm with which he was pointing to the victim's head.

Instantaneously, the passengers stormed off the bus as they screamed in terror. Only two would remain in the bus: the attacker and a young woman, paralysed to her seat due to fear. Her legs felt as if they had been glued to the floor.

Despite coaxing from everyone outside, helping her overcome her anxiety, no one would come to help her.

Because of their impotence, she was forced to witness the disturbing acts coming up.

With nearly all the passengers safe, the bus door was locked, and the police were notified.

While the authorities arrived, the psychotic attacker finished detaching the head from the body of the victim and began cutting his organs. Then, he took the nose and one ear to eat.

After that act of cannibalism, he continued with his macabre ceremony, taking the head, and amputating his right ear, before putting it into his pants' pocket.

That creepy behaviour continued to terrorise the passengers who feared that the woman would suffer the same fate as the young man.

The distress of the onlookers caused other travellers to want to intervene to help the lady. But as they wanted to act, the killer ran the bloodstained curtain and exhibited the decapitated head like a trophy, whilst pointing at it with a pistol. Thus, the onlookers abstained from intervening.

Minutes later, an anti-terrorist squadron stormed the vehicle, rescued the woman, and apprehended the killer. After medical analysis on the recommendation of the doctor, all passengers, except for Zeledon, would receive psychotherapeutic treatment. Although Zeledon was also recommended, he wouldn't attend any treatment, since mentally, he was already living his own trauma.

Zeledon was still fighting to overcome the consequences of his own disappointment.

Several days after that terrifying event, one Sunday, walking through a shopping centre, I found Zeledon sitting on one of the aisle benches. His appearance surprised me, because I had never seen him with dishevelled hair, unshaven and poorly dressed; he practically looked homeless. I was even more alarmed to see his emaciated face and the trembling in his hands due to insomnia and days without eating any food.

Zeledon's circumstance was not due to him not having money for sustenance, but rather because of his desire to finish his life; he was so consumed by depression that when I saw him, it was hard for me to accept that it was him.

Very worried, I stayed by his side, willing to listen and help him get out of his emotional state; I knew that, at that moment, Zeledon needed a person to whom he could vent all his sadness.

Realising my presence, I again became his confidant like weeks earlier, and after telling me about the terrible event he had experienced in the last few days, he began to express his feelings that he had kept in his mind.

In detail, he recalled the hints that warned him about Olmeda's hidden life, but that he, at time, perceived this as normal.

He understood why that day, before leaving Brasilia, Olmeda disappeared for several hours. That afternoon, after hours of uncertainty and having searched for her around the neighbourhood, he saw her get off a motorbike driven by a young man. When he asked where she had been all afternoon, she replied that when she went for a walk to a park, she became lost and thanks to the boy who picked her up, she found her way back. Zeledon, grateful for his kindness, even gave the young man some money that he had.

The fact that Olmeda had the perfect excuses for her absences prevented Zeledon from ever suspecting anything suspicious, but it turned out that this teenager was the same man with who Olmeda would marry years later.

"How ironic," Zeledon told me at that time, "that afternoon I was worrying for her safety, while she, in a hotel room in Brasilia, found comfort in her young lover."

But not only had Olmeda betrayed his confidence but also, would those who Zeledon believed were his friends. One of these friends was Carlos, who knew that Olmeda was cheating on him with Sergeant Leão but decided to keep her secret.

However, the day when Carlos thought of telling Zeledon about Olmeda, she discovered his intention.

So, before he was able to disclose her betrayal, she shut his mouth by inducing him to have sex with her.

Carlos, already seduced and with no other option, decided to hide the truth from Zeledon.

Some were for love or maybe for convenience, Zeledon said, but for Olmeda, they were only a boast of her arrogance. Every man that was in her sights couldn't resist her power of seduction.

At this most, Zeledon would understand why, when both were in El Paso, she was always desperate to be in Boa Vista. The reason for her behaviour was the desire that she had for Sergeant Leão. Her desire to seduce him was so intense that Olmeda didn't care that it was the eve of his marriage.

Olmeda, sure that she would successfully seduce him, arrogantly told her friend Marina that the sergeant will have sex with her.

The frustration of not having noticed the betrayal was breaking Zeledon's soul. I, feeling sorry for his turmoil, expressed to him, "Okay, Zeledon. Please, shut up and calm down. Please try to see that remembering this will only cause more pain to you. Pretend that she died or left to somewhere in the world so far away that you never will find her. Think that she was never worth it."

After that long talk, I practically forced him to accompany me to see a psychologist.

His first consultation would be greatly beneficial, although as he was retelling his past, the sadness from his nostalgia sharpened again, as he ended his story tears streamed down his face. The psychologist, after listening closely to Zeledon's situation and all his memories, took a small elastic band from a drawer in her desk and placed it on Zeledon's left wrist. While she was doing that, she instructed him that whenever he thought fondly of his ex-wife, he must pull the elastic and let it snap against his wrist.

Soon after Zeledon finished his first therapy section, the psychologist instructed him to follow the steps given and to return to visit her next week.

But that appointment would not be necessary, because from the moment that the appointment ended, Zeledon would leave the psychologist office with a very different spirit than before.

As the hours passed and Olmeda's memories came into his mind, Zeledon snapped his wrist again and again. That pain produced would overcome his thoughts and a week later, although with his arm inflamed by this voluntary torture, Zeledon had forgotten Olmeda and all their shared memories.

That punishment also produced in his mind a sort of defence mechanism that caused him to forget his love for her and fill the emptiness in his heart with pride instead.

Already recovered from his heartbreak, Zeledon, with the intention of fighting for custody of his son, went to a legal aid lawyer. However, after days of contemplating what to do, he realised that even if he won the battle, the one who would lose would be his son.

The reason for this realisation was that Henry was dependent on his mother's love. In addition, she, as her guardian, would have more time to care for him. So Zeledon, recognising this, gave up the custody battle, since he didn't want to see his son suffer at his side.

With this decision, Zeledon also relinquished the guilty feeling from himself that had been rooted in his mind and was affecting him greatly during his crisis.

Months after unleashing his mind from the pleasurable memories that Olmeda had left in him, Zeledon decided to give himself another chance at love. He wanted his broken passion in his soul to become whole again so that he could share it with another woman's heart. That wish would become reality three years after having seen Claudia last, when in an unexpected way, she crossed his path again. With that meeting, the two confirmed that the arrow thrown by cupid in the past was still in the air, waiting for both.

Since Zeledon was no longer spoken for their desires to be together continued to increase during Claudia's birthday, the date which fate would allow them the opportunity to express their true feelings in their souls.

After a short romance, they became lovers, and although their adventure would last a few months, it would be very emotional.

At first, they were so in love that I thought that they were made for each other. However, Claudia continued to carry with her the burden of her ex-boyfriend's betrayal; her frustration led her to belief that with Zeledon's affection, she would overcome the memories of the man who kept her awake at night, but that wouldn't be the case.

After a few weeks of trying to get over her past love, Claudia fell back into her fond memories of her former lover and changed her mind. Nevertheless, despite the fleeting coexistence between the two, Claudia became the fundamental basis for Zeledon to close his previous wound forever.

Ironically, the absence of this new love encompassed all his feelings, beginning an even greater sorrow, with the only difference being that Zeledon missed Claudia too much, and every time that he remembered her, he did it fondly, with respect and admiration.

As the months passed in Toronto, life would give me new surprises, and the meeting with Zeledon wouldn't be the last of them.

One day when I returned from school, a few metres away from me, fate had already begun to forge another new surprise to me.

That afternoon, I was surprised to hear the barking of a dog and the footsteps of high heels on the second floor, as if someone was dancing. No doubt, in that apartment where pets were not accepted, a tenant had managed to change the mind of the owner.

Intrigued to meet my new neighbours, for several days, I tried to make contact with them, but I wouldn't have the opportunity. In the afternoons when I returned from my classes, I always heard voices of two teenagers and hip-hop music at a high volume. That inconvenience always stopped me, since my intention was to chat with the adults; however, the parents always arrived at the last minute, precisely when I was sleeping. In the morning, they left the home before I woke up.

Despite this, a day that I woke up early, from the windows I could see the two teenagers as they left to take the bus. At that moment, it didn't cross for my mind that were the children of Gustavo, my best friend from El Paso, since they always spoke in English and, due to the bulky winter clothes that they were wearing at that moment, it was impossible for me to recognise them.

Five days after their arrival, I left the house with the intention of complying with my usual routine. In that instant, I remembered that I had an appointment at the immigration office. This commitment made me rush home and call to cancel my morning English classes. After leaving a voicemail message, I continued to the appointment.

When I arrived at this building, I lined up and waited to enter the office. While I was waiting in line, questions began to pass through my head. There, all the experiences that I had experienced up until that moment flashed before me. I remembered Sotomayor, Larissa, and the unexpected disappearance of my compadre, my closest friend, and his family. I had hoped that the latter had a better fate, although I never contemplated the possibility that they were here in Canada. However, my compadre and his family happened to be living in Toronto, and so the most logical thing was to find him in this office, because despite how immense the city is, this place was a necessary to visit, since every immigrant has the same governmental obligations to follow which can only be carried out in the Municipal Palace of Toronto.

That day of the unexpected meeting, as I was called up, I went to the window and paid my bills. At that moment, I observed, from a distance, a person leaving the premises. Immediately after I saw his silhouette, I immediately realised it was my closest friend despite how implausible it seemed. Regardless, I was curious, so after receiving my receipt, I hurried to reach him and confirm if my mind had fooled me.

I turned around and backtracked in order to get this person. When the both of us recognised each other, Gustavo was astonished at my presence and couldn't control his immense joy. His spontaneous emotion was evident all over his body within a few seconds. I reacted similarly, upon seeing him alive and safe.

Motivated by such a hard to believe circumstance, Gustavo exclaimed with disbelief, "No, no, I cannot believe it! My buddy is here?"

After his initial surprise, with more exclamation Gustavo added, "This world is not as cruel as I imagined it!"

After the initial emotions, we embraced and conversed with so much exclamation and joy that we looked like wet parrots.

As our conversation continued, my compadre surprised me with his stories. Afterwards, we left the building and went to the parking lot. After getting in the car, I asked for his address, and he told me the community and the house number. My astonishment would increase even further when realising that he and his family were my second-floor neighbours.

When we returned home, his children were already there. My godson, Raul, excited by my unexpected arrival, shouted, "Godfather, godfather!" before running to me and giving me a big hug.

Moments later, Juliana approached slowly and said to me, "Hi, Poet! How are you?"

I responded, "I am good, thanks, and you?"

She answered, "Not bad."

Then, the young woman asked a second question, "What are you doing in Toronto?"

"I am living here, on the first floor, actually."

"Really? Oh, this is great!" the teenager replied. After this, she refocused on her mobile phone game and said no more.

At that moment, I remembered the introduction talk by the psychologist at the reception house. She warned us that, in some people from developing countries, the psychological pressure would be more evident than in the others, especially for those young people who in had been brought up without the many comforts of a country like Canada and submitted under the parents' strict rules.

These adolescents, she added would undoubtedly be the most vulnerable, as they would find it challenging to assimilate to the new change of life and they would be influenced by the consumer market and the freedom that the new culture offered them.

Immediately after, I got the impression that Gustavo, in Canada, was losing that control exercised over his children back in El Paso. Even so, he was trying his best to be a good parent, and so he focused on Juliana, the most rebellious of the two teenagers, trying from all reasonable ways to be a responsible parent.

He didn't allow to her have a boyfriend, get a piercing and even more so, let her get tattooed.

His rules, until that moment, would achieve the desired result, but such repression began to create a need to rebel in Juliana, which I was sure would erupt at any moment.

Juliana, resenting her father's antiquated parenting method, soon began to show her disapproval.

In retaliation, Juliana felt embarrassed that her friends at school knew who her parents were.

She was particularly ashamed of her stepmother who found it more difficult to learn English, since she scarcely even knew how to write and read in Spanish.

Juliana, taking advantage of that, spoke to her only in English to annoy her.

As the days passed, the young woman would manage to mislead her father. That weekend, Juliana patiently waited until both were asleep to escape through the apartment's fire exit.

When she returned home, she did it in the early hours of the morning, totally drunk.

Her behaviour, although caused concern in me, didn't warrant me telling her father yet. I was sure that, eventually, Gustavo would notice her continual escapes.

A week later, the fire alarm was unexpectedly activated. Immediately, Gustavo, his family and I, startled by the deafening noise, started to run out towards the street.

Everyone was seemingly safe, except for Juliana, who wasn't around. Gustavo, increasingly worried, returned to the apartment. On returning and not finding her in her room, he was filled with anguish; however, upon seeing the emergency window open and without a lock, he realised that his daughter was far from danger.

Confirming her absence, although it left him less worried, his increasing anger took over and only with my advice, he managed to calm down. With no other option, Gustavo returned to the street.

Minutes later, firefighters arrived and controlled the situation. Regardless, he remained hidden waiting to see her arrive.

When she arrived, Gustavo, very cautiously took his daughter by the shoulders, and with strict scolding ensured that she understood her mistake. In addition, he warned her to not act so irresponsibly, because in the long run, she would be harmed. He reminded her that the simple fact that she was in Canada didn't ensure her future.

Gustavo, still worried, continued to explain to her, "We all need to put in effort and make sacrifices to get ahead." Although Canada is a country with many opportunities, she would have success if she studied hard and learned English perfectly because, English is the only necessary tool to gain a good profession. If she didn't take advantage of this opportunity, Gustavo added, fate would make her look like a loser.

Juliana, pretending to have understood the message, expressed, "I'm sorry, Dad, I promise that I won't do it again."

Several weeks later, Saint Patrick's Day arrived.

That afternoon, Juliana was invited by one of her friends from high school to a sleepover at her home. When her stepmother discovered that boys would be going too, she refused to let her go, which made Juliana lose her mind and begin shouting at her, "Stupid woman! You aren't my mother, remember that this is Canada and here you cannot infringe my rights."

Gustavo, hearing her insults, was filled with anger, and slapped her. Juliana's reaction was the least expected. She ran, taking refuge in her room. From that moment, Juliana didn't speak with any of them, in any languages.

A few days later with no more disturbances, Gustavo thought that the anger of his daughter would pass soon, as would her disrespect. However, that was not the case. One night, Gustavo, overwhelmed by an English test that was approaching him, stayed up all night.

His insomnia and the anxiety from smoking pushed him to take a tour of the block. As his walk ended and he walked through the patio, he heard the basement window closing. Immediately, he imagined that it would undoubtedly be his daughter, who was probably drunk.

Gustavo, wanting to confirm his assumption, went into his home and went straight down to the laundry. Shortly after, he heard moans of passion that Juliana emanated from the laundry, which would immediately worry Gustavo.

Without thinking, Gustavo broke into the room to find Juliana having sex with her boyfriend.

Outraged by the depraved action of his daughter, he took off his belt and began to whip her far too severely, leaving deep wounds on her body. Not satisfied with that, Gustavo punched twice on Juliana's boyfriend face.

Immediately, Juliana's boyfriend called 911. This would complicate his situation more because days before, my buddy Gustavo, obsessed with protecting his daughter, had taken, by the neck, more than one of her suitors, whom he threatened to beat if he saw them near her again. This had caused that a judge would make several warnings for his violent acts and applied him as punishment, monthly presentations in the court.

Soon after, two officers arrived and arrested Gustavo. Then, Juliana, showing her scars to the police, accused him of physical violence and violence against a child. Under those charges, Gustavo would be taken to prison to await the decision to either release him or possibly deport him.

While the verdict was taking place, Juliana discovered that she was pregnant and that her young boyfriend wouldn't be there for her, and although abortion was an alternative, Juliana didn't see it as a viable option. She didn't want to increase the tragedy of her situation with the death of an innocent. Sad and disappointed, Juliana realised that with her mistake, she would practically be abandoned, because both her brother and her stepmother would be at the side of her father.

This undoubtedly left her without options, and the baby that she carried inside her due to her age would be placed into the hands of government entities, which would place her in foster care, until she became an adult, since the government wouldn't authorise her to travel without the permission of her new parents, and even less if she was pregnant. The laws forbade her from leaving the country without the father's permission, as the baby had been conceived in its jurisdiction. Thus, if she did want to travel, she would have to wait until she gave birth, leave the baby with the government, and take the trip alone. However, what hurt Juliana the most was knowing that, despite her remorse, she couldn't do anything to stop the possible deportation of her father.

Fernanda's Contact, Olmeda's Return and Zeledon's Plan

With everything going on in the lives of Zeledon and my closest buddy Gustavo, my enemies in Brasília and my friends in El Paso used every possible means to find me.

One day, after years of still searching, Fernanda managed to communicate with me through Facebook. She explained that she didn't want to contact me before for the safety of both of us.

Regardless, the fact that she successfully found me would be more by chance than anything else because Fernanda also assumed that I was dead. But one afternoon, Fernanda, when trying to find her better half, sent an invitation to my new profile without realising that it was me.

The reason for this confusion was that the photo and the personal information that appeared on my profile was false.

After greeting and seeing each other's faces again, Fernanda was surprised. Excited and happy because her friend was alive, she updated me everything that had happened during my absence.

Via the internet, she told me about the murders of Ludiela, Santos and detectives Baena and Guerrero, as well as the disappearance of Gustavo and his family, the death of Sertino and his responsibility in the robbery of the Poppy Cartel.

As well as this, she told me that, she had kept an envelope for me for a long time, left by the late Santos. Also, she told me that only I could receive the envelope in person, as she promised to Santos days before he was killed.

After, I informed her of my situation and told her about meeting with my compadre, Gustavo, here in Toronto. As well as that, I told her about the ordeal experienced by our friend Zeledon and confessed to her my secret identity.

In prevention of an imminent danger, I made her commit to keep the secret envelope in a safe place until our meeting in El Paso. As I had an idea of its contents, I warned to her that the envelope could contain strong evidence against the politician, Tancredo Moreira.

In our conversation, by chance, I would learn that Tancredo as governor had been visiting around the state for the last few days. Knowing this made me think, and although this was a great opportunity I had wanted, I also knew that it was not the right moment for my revenge and decided that I would leave in search of the evidence while the politician was distracted in the middle of his campaign.

While I waited, Olmeda, already married, was returning to Toronto. There, without the love of Zeledon and her daughter, she felt nostalgic, with the harsh cold and loneliness of winter aggravating her sadness even more.

Those circumstances and her cynicism would lead Olmeda to a Christian church in search of God. There, she met Ramiro, who with his affection made her forget her hesitation as a married woman and take refuge in his arms.

Olmeda, already engaged with her new aberrant relationship, would introduce her lover to her son as her best friend from school.

This man, who knew very little about Olmeda's past, didn't know that he would fall prey to her deception. With his innocent mind, he let himself be wrapped up in her sensuality and fell in love with her. The behaviour exhibited by Olmeda in bed would turn his passion into a sickly love. With her ability to make all his sexual fantasies come true, he became so delusional that he became a darker version of himself. His possessive natures increased, and he didn't want to give another man the opportunity to come into Olmeda's life.

Ramiro, with the intention of earning Olmeda's eroticism forever, began to fulfil all her wishes and sometimes even helped her with money that supposedly she was sending to her parents in Brazil for their living expenses. But this money was going directly to Olmeda's young husband.

Without knowing, Ramiro was unknowingly paying for his rival's arrival to Canada.

After the first weeks of her betrayal, Olmeda kept her furtive meetings secret. However, as time passed, the feelings in both grew and from time to time, they display a subtle kiss or caress in public.

When these rumours reached Zeledon, he didn't mention anything to his daughter Karen. He, thinking only about revenge against his ex-wife, wanted to take advantage of this mistake.

Taking advantage of the fact that he was travelling to his country, Zeledon took photos and videos of Ramiro and Olmeda together, with the sole intention of giving them personally to Olmeda's husband in Bahia, so that he would realise the kind of person he had married.

So, the night before his travel, Zeledon told me the plan that he had in mind. When he asked me for an opinion, I recommended him to forget the revenge against Olmeda, as the problem wouldn't be solved. The best for him, I said, was to leave her betrayal in the hands of fate. Without doubt, destiny would know how to punish her in the best way.

Inevitably, my opinion would lead Zeledon to change his objective.

After our talk, he said goodbye and promised me that he would follow my advice precisely, and that he would be in touch with me from Colombia.

Although I was also travelling on the same date, I didn't want to let him know. However, this was not due to distrust, but for his own safety.

Hours later, the departure of our respective trips would arrive, and we both left on the same day, but in different flights.

For my arrival in El Paso, I took the same precautions as when I left the country years ago.

My first stop would be in Montevideo, and from there I would cross the border by mountain trails to the territory of Brazil. Here, disguised with a false identity, I would manage to evade the authorities, arriving without any impediment to Fernanda's house.

My visit there would be without much fanfare, unexpected and fleeting.

Almost immediately after I picked up the envelope left by Sotomayor to my name, I headed for Brasilia. During the uncomfortable trip, I reviewed the envelope's contents, finding within it an account under the second name and surname of Sotomayor, as well as the address, name of the bank in Ipiranga and the keys and the combination of a security box.

In addition to this, I found an extra document with his signature authenticated by a notary, in which he authorised Dirceu Figuereiro as the claimant of the deposit in the safe deposit box under the name of Eliécer Dongón.

Upon seeing this, I diverted my original route and went towards the border city. Upon my arrival at the bank, I assumed I would encounter many obstacles, but when speaking with the manager and showing him the authenticated document, he only demanded my identification as a requirement to obtain access to the security vault.

Afterwards, I finally had on my hands the SIM card and the mini cassette for which Moreira was willing to pay a fortune.

After looking through the information, I decided to make the best use of them and contact the attorney general of Brazil.

When I heard her voice, I was instantly taken by surprise. I didn't expect to hear Larissa, my former girlfriend and comrade in arms from years ago, who I had loved dearly. When I heard her voice again, I was overwhelmed with emotion and thick saliva slid down my throat, which unintentionally made my voice sound deeper and slower. Then, without telling her my name, I assured her that I had very compromising evidence about a very important politician who was directly involved in cocaine trafficking.

She, eager to hear my evidence, gave me her private phone number and multiple locations of their maximum-security offices so that I could choose with who I could make my statement. After hearing her instructions, I clarified that if she wanted to obtain the evidence, she would need to see me herself, because the information that I possessed was very dangerous and I could only leave it in her hands.

For a few seconds, Larissa doubted my word and thought that I must have been bluffing, but when I informed her that the case had to do with the death of her brother Vinicio, which occurred some years ago, she changed her mind and confirmed an appointment with me for the next morning, as well as giving a five-digit protection code to declare to the first level of security in the detective's office.

Although I trusted her entirely, I wanted to be as cautious as possible. So, to be safe, I sent a copy of the video to my ex-brother-in-law, Matheus, Tancredo's opponent candidate.

At that moment, I thought about going straight to the detective's office and show Larissa proof to the evidence which many, including her and her brother, had used to incriminate me years ago when I was totally innocent. Even so, I decided to wait a few more days to give Matheus enough time to receive my mail.

Once calculating that the envelope had reached the campaign headquarters, I went to the detective's office.

At that moment, when Larissa saw me, it was as if she was seeing a ghost. Behind the safety glass in the waiting room where a detective escorted me,

Larissa couldn't hide her surprise. Excited to see that I was alive, I could read from her lips as she happily exclaimed my name, "Dirceu Figuereiro!"

When Larissa confirmed my identity, she ordered for me to be taken to her private office.

If she was surprised, I was in complete shock. The fact that I was seeing her again was unexpectedly reopening the wound that I thought had healed in my heart.

After our spontaneous greeting, our souls, from deep inside, emanated an even more passionate desire that we had experienced in the past. However, both of us were overcome by pride. Aware that we couldn't mix work with our feelings, we found the perfect excuse to maintain distance, and both she and I knew that there wouldn't be time for that sentiment. So, we focused on the priority of the moment, the videos, and my statement.

When Larissa saw the recordings, she realised her unfair treatment of me. Embarrassed, her eyes became cloudy, and although she tried to conceal her mistake, she would be betrayed by her tears.

Simultaneously, while we were analysing the evidence, Larissa's mobile phone began to ring.

Upon her answering, I noticed that the person calling her was my ex-brother-in-law, Matheus, who, exalted by the package in the mail he had received, thought to surprise her. But his emotion would be suspended when Larissa notified him that I was in her office. Immediately in response, Matheus came to the detective's office. Fifteen minutes later, the three of us were talking face to face.

Matheus, saddened by his mistake of the past, simply greeted me without much fanfare. He knew that both owed me a great apology, which he didn't want to approach with a tone of cynicism. Although I was the hardest hit of the three, we had a common goal that would unite us to the same cause: revenge against Tancredo.

With my presence, and the evidence that I provided to them, I had basically served Tancredo's head on a silver platter, the person who for months had been threatening to kill Matheus. Although they very well knew the origin of such aggravation, for not having the evidence against him, the detective and the candidate had remained on the defensive.

That afternoon, after meeting at a kind of round table, we agreed to strike to Tancredo on the day of his televised debate.

The reason for that wait was that the detective wanted to give him a fulminating and lethal blow. However, to achieve it, she needed some time, since she had to coordinate with the DEA. She wanted to show to the country the false image of and honest politician that Tancredo was showing in front of his followers.

As a reward for my collaboration and in favour to emend their past mistake, I, as a temporary detective, would return to the institution and have the pleasure of being the person who would carry out Tancredo's capture.

By convenience, I didn't object to anything about their plan. So, when the agreement was finished, I said goodbye and promised that one day before the stipulated date, I would return to the bunker to revise the plan and then we would go together to the TV channel station and take the politician by surprise.

At the time of my departure, the detective, thinking of my safety, recommend remaining at the military school or be in custody of personal escorts. Nevertheless, I rejected the ideas, stating that, except for Tancredo, the only other people who knew of the content of the videos were the two of them, and I was more than sure that if I left the evidence under their possession, it would be impossible for the information to leak.

Trusting in their integrity, I left my life in their hands.

Thus, I began my wait from a small town on the border of Uruguay. There, in a public notary office, I would leave a copy of the videos as a testament under the name of Zeledon Lindarte, whom, without his consent, I would involve in an extremely dangerous situation.

After a few days, I sent Zeledon an e-mail, warning him that if any tragedy would happen to me, he must arrive at the address indicated in my message and claim a testament left to his name which he must take to a newscast in Brasilia.

Simultaneously with my arrival to Brazil, Zeledon returned from El Paso to Bahia. There, from the moment of his arrival, all those who knew him began to reopen the wound in the soul. Their intentions were not to incite hatred but looking for his forgiveness as some of them had been accomplices hiding the truth.

Among those included was his mother, Carmelina, who, bereaved of keeping him deceived, told him that she had known the truth for a long time, but to avoid his heartbreak, she didn't tell him. To her, it was better to have a son labelled a cuckold than in a prison or, even worse, in a cemetery!

Carmelina informed him that through the mouth of Dorelyz, Carlos' innocent wife, she knew the rumour that Olmeda had more than one lover, because one night when she went to receive a remittance of money sent by him from El Paso, she let her know indirectly.

After this, Carmelina clarified that even with the two having such a close relationship, it wasn't easy to verify the rumours that were spoken of her daughter-in-law, because Olmeda was always a very cunning woman.

Another reason that saved Olmeda from being discovered was that her young lover had the keys to the house and entered through the back door at any time he wanted. With that cunning approach, her daughter-in-law prevented any mishap and ensured that none of her neighbours noticed her betrayal, maintaining her deception, when in reality, she was a shrew.

Even with such an aggravating circumstance, Carmelina would be forced to keep the secret, since days ago she had discovered that one of those lovers was Carlos, the person whose wife, Dorelyz, believed was faithful and Zeledon considered as one of his best friends.

It wouldn't take Carmelina long to confirm the new gossip circulating about her daughter-in-law.

Without her imagining it, a week after those rumours, Olmeda and her lover were in Boa Vista, where another of the Olmeda's secret betrayals would go to afloat unexpected.

That afternoon, Sergeant Leão's girlfriend and Olmeda started to argue. The young woman, enraged, accused her of being a prostitute, such slander that, without a doubt, would warrant a claim from Olmeda. However, when Olmeda threatened to do so, the young woman warned her that she knew about her clandestine encounters with her boyfriend and if she didn't stop harassing him, she would tell Zeledon everything.

Olmeda became immediately lost for words, simply denying that she knew what she was talking about.

Although Olmeda swore to her that the woman had confused her with someone else, her silence and bowed head left no doubt that this accusation was true.

Another person who would come to Zeledon to clear their conscience would be his brother-in-law. He, regretting not having told him the truth earlier, revealed that when he went to Bahia for a business trip, one of his companions, without knowing the relationship had between them, told him about the extramarital affairs of his neighbour Olmeda. The colleague noted that the husband must be blind because according to most people, the woman with whom he shared his bed was a fraud who disguised her infidelities with a false image of a lady. His colleague was so sure of her infidelities, the brother-in-law added, that he recommends him that if I knew Olmeda's family, he should advise them to pray to their grandfather so that he can rest peacefully in his grave, because due to the shameless actions of Olmeda, he would be wallowing in his grave, having a such shameless daughter, he concluded.

As their conversation continued, Zeledon discovered other hidden secrets of his ex-wife.

In addition to this, he would find out through Carmelina that before Olmeda's young lover visited her at night, she gave her children medication to put them to sleep in order to not have obstacles when they had sex and prevent her children from discovering the truth. But even with Olmeda's reckless plan, one night her lover forgot to lock the door, so when Carmelina arrived to visit her, she was taken by surprise when she found her grandchildren in a deep sleep and Olmeda and her lover enjoying an intimate shower. Although when they heard her arrival, the man tried to avoid being caught, they were too late.

After her most important revelation, Zeledon's mother continued to list the things that she didn't see at that time as suspicious, which is why she hid them from him during the years that he lived in El Paso.

Between the events that Carmelina had not confessed to him before, she would reveal the most peculiar.

She remembered that one night when she arrived at her daughter-in-law's house, she found in each one of the rooms several pink candles set up in a cross. Incredibly surprised by that strange ritual, with slight suspicion, she inquired, "The fire from the pink candles is to repel bad energies?"

Olmeda feigning innocence, replied, "No, this is to scare away the flies."

Her evasive answer couldn't deceive her. Carmelina knew very well that Olmeda was performing a spell. Although she didn't know for sure if the witchcraft was intended to ensure that Karen maintained her secret or if the spell was to subdue her young lover to her whims, but she as a mother, could never rule out the possibility that this was a spell to maintain Zeledon as a fool.

According to Carmelina, this was logical because her son never would notice that Thiago, one of his best friends in El Paso, had also been one of Olmeda's lovers.

As these revelations were new to Zeledon, wanting to know if that was true, he went to talk with Marina again, who upon confirming Carmelina's story, helped him understand the reason for that sudden change between their relationship.

According to Marina, Olmeda's behaviour was due to the jealousy that she felt the night that she learned that back in El Paso, Thiago, the man who was her sexual entertainment at the time, had taken comfort with another female.

Olmeda, confused, thought that this woman was Ludiela. So, seeing her that afternoon in a conversation with Zeledon, she found the perfect opportunity to retaliate against the deception of her secret lover, and at the same time, to pretend in front of the people in the town that she really loved her husband.

That afternoon, Olmeda with a knife in her hand would show Zeledon an impressive scene of jealousy. However, this wasn't jealousy towards Zeledon, but towards the supposed betrayal between Thiago and Ludiela.

Zeledon, overwhelmed by the confessions of his friends and family, decided to travel from Bahia to El Paso. He thought that there his friends, because they knew very little about Olmeda, wouldn't remember her. However, upon his arrival, he would receive an unpleasant surprise when hearing his relatives include his ex-wife in all their conversations.

Zeledon, trying to hide his past, sarcastically evaded any inquiries about her, insisting that he knew nothing about her life. With that, he avoided the conversations that he didn't want to hear.

Zeledon continued to keep quiet regarding his past for many days; he believed that by not touching the subject, his acquaintances wouldn't find out the aberrant facts of his ex-wife, since he didn't want their shock to release the stitches of his healed wound.

Nevertheless, one night that his family saw Zeledon with Thiago and Carlos sharing drinks as loyal friends, they were filled with fury, and seeing them partake in pleasant conversation, they decided that it was their duty to unmask their criticism.

First was Fernanda. She, outraged by the falsehood of these two men, called Zeledon in private and said to him, "One of the things that hate most in life is observing the hypocrisy of people."

Zeledon, surprised, asked, "Are you referring to me?"

"No, no," Fernanda clarified, "it's for those who claim to be your friends, like Thiago and Carlos, because I know that both were traitors who, after having enjoyed your wife, intended to continue their false friendship with you."

Zeledon, showing a smile, took her by the shoulders and said, "Take it easy, my friend, I am aware of their betrayals, as well as Sergeant Leão's betrayal, too, but they cannot know that I know about that, because in my revenge, I have planned to give them a dose of their own medicine."

Because of Fernanda's loyalty, Zeledon felt committed. At that moment, for him, it seemed fair that his loyal friends knew the true story that happened with his ex-wife in Toronto. But for them, that wouldn't be news, because they already knew about Olmeda's infidelities in Bahia. Even so, knowing rumours wouldn't compare to hearing the stories from the victim's own lips. When they heard Zeledon's story, they were shocked. They admired the cynicism with which Olmeda had deceived them, but the most surprising thing for those who knew her was to know that she, the woman who appeared to be a great lady, was a complete sexual nymphomaniac.

Fernanda, a bit indiscreet, asked, "Zeledon, if you had known in those days that Olmeda was betraying you, would you have abandoned her when she first began cheating?"

Zeledon, somewhat dismayed, replied, "If I had noticed her betrayal at the beginning of our relationship, maybe not, because I loved her too much. If I managed to do it wouldn't have been easy, because she was an expert at seduction that turned me into an addict. Although I looked for other women for release, I didn't find one who behaved like her in bed."

"My passion was so ingrained in her body that I compared Olmeda's eroticism with a drug and my body as a drug addict in crisis. Although in my case, the need wasn't cocaine, but sex," he concluded.

After finishing his explanation, Zeledon said goodbye to Fernanda and left for the hotel. When he got there, he collapsed on the bed and began to unleash, in his imagination, all the possible methods of seeking revenge.

As he thought intensely, he tried to find the best form of revenge without resorting to violence, since Claudia, unexpectedly, with their fleeting but substantial love, had patched that wound in his soul. With her departure, she left a bandage that made him immune to the pain in his heart.

Regardless, he still carried a debt of honour which his friends who had betrayed him with his ex-wife had to pay with an exemplary punishment.

Their deceptions at least merited a wake-up call and so, they must to feel the same pain that he had felt.

After a thorough analysis, Zeledon came to a perfect conclusion. Due to this, he would commence a secret investigation, whose victims would be Olmeda's young husband and the wives of the three men he believed were his friends.

Hours after his investigation, Zeledon knew the names of each wife of his supposed friends, being taken by surprise when discovering that he already knew these women from long ago. With that information, he focused his priority on investigating the closest people of his future victims and would eventually discover the intimate secrets of these women. From that, he would try to take any advantage possible.

Convinced that he would achieve his goal, he undertook the difficult task of searching for these women and befriending them.

That same day, I, without knowing the direction of his plan, sent him a message to his mobile phone, asking him to call the number that appeared on the screen.

Minutes later, I received his call.

Zeledon, immediately after our greeting, asked me, "Hey, Poet, where are you?"

I responded, somewhat evasively, "For now, in a small town in Uruguay! But I am planning to travel to Brasilia. However, I don't know the date or time of my trip."

Zeledon, confused, asked me about the testimony that he must take to the newscast in Brasilia if something bad happen to me.

At that moment, thinking about his safety, I told him a lie. I said that this was simply a house document title that I will leave as inheritance to a son that I have with a reporter that is working there.

After the questions and answers, he told me the order in which he was carrying out his revenge. Although it seemed unfair to the three women, I couldn't judge him when I was also using other people in a similar process.

Zeledon, in the middle of his talk, told me that his first attempt was made in El Paso with Anuves, the best friend of Thiago's wife, Bianca. Through her, he learned that Bianca, although in love with her husband, still suffered in silence since the departure of her former boyfriend, who had died in an accident.

In addition to that, Zeledon learned that when she wasn't on a trip with Thiago, who was a travel agent, Bianca took refuge at her parents' recreational farm. That strange hobby, she added, was because in her solitude, Bianca was always reminiscing about her ex-boyfriend's romanticism: the flowers, the gestures on special occasions, his taste for exotic food and good music. All the opposite of her husband Thiago, who didn't like any of that – in fact, he always saw such things as very corny.

After this, Zeledon travelled to Boa Vista, where he would continue his search to find the next person in his list.

Him finding Marlyn, the inseparable confidante of Sergeant Leão's wife, Teresa, was easy. The awkward thing would be that Marlyn accepted to meet with her old friend; however, five days after his invitation, she agreed. After a week of continual outings, Zeledon achieved his goal.

Through her mouth, Zeledon learned that her friend's husband had been transferred to a conflict zone. That circumstance meant that the sergeant could only visit her two or three times a month. The rest of the time, Teresa practically was alone, but despite that, according to Marlyn, Teresa was a very faithful woman, although no one is exempt to temptations. Love can change, especially when one is away from their beloved and their world is becoming sedentary. That obstacle led to Teresa to think that this wasn't the life that she had dreamed for herself. So, with surprise, she would sometimes ask herself, "But if this wasn't my dream, why did I fall in love with a soldier? I have always liked stable men, with strong appearance, green eyes, athletic bodies and with a different vision of life."

Those rhetorical questions made Marlyn, as her friend, ask her again and again, "Why do you stay your husband, against what you actually want?" An answer she is still waiting for.

With that information, the meeting between Marlyn and Zeledon ended.

Having achieved his second objective, Zeledon went to São Paulo in search for Camelia, Carlos' wife, Dorelyz's niece.

During their talk, Zeledon discovered through Camelia that, Dorelyz was a rather libertine woman who liked challenges and liked to prove to herself that she could control all her instincts. Therefore, when her husband was working outside the city, she would go out to have fun with her group of friends. But those outings became more boring than other interests since her greatest hobby was swimming. For Dorelyz, her platonic love was an expert swimmer. Even with her freedom, Dorelyz always felt lonely, since when Carlos was with her, he never dedicated time to her. When he returned from his long trips, he was always preparing the next one. The few days that he was home, he invested his time into consolidating his business. Thus, Dorelyz dreamed to have a husband who was an athlete, who would practice her favourite sport with her. From time to time, she would be aware of her wishes, Camelia affirmed.

After discovering his future victims' strengths and weaknesses, Zeledon confirmed that the three women had one thing in common, their loneliness, because most of the time their husbands left them alone. Although supposedly, they were happy beside them, they knew conscientiously that they weren't the men with whom they dreamed that one day they would marry.

Finishing his initial investigation, Zeledon focused on finding out about the life of Olmeda's new husband, Albeiro. According to him, the young man owed money that he needed to pay immediately.

In his attempt to find his most vulnerable point, Zeledon had discovered that his rival, back in Bahia months ago, was engaged to marry a young woman named Melisa, but eventually, he left her, leaving his pregnant bride at the church altar.

She, after falling into depression for her love's abandonment, decided to leave her parents' house aimlessly. They, for a long time, have not known where she is.

When Zeledon discovered the reason for his absence, he thought that he could take advantage of that circumstance. So, he dedicated a week to search for Melisa. However, ultimately, he had no success and decided that his plan would take place without her and he travelled to the capital.

While he was there, he searched for an academy of performing arts, where he found three professional comedians who displayed the physical qualities desired by the three women. Once the actors were located, he proposed to each of them a plan to act as a character according to what he required. The script required that each of them must achieve having sex with the female protagonist of his imaginary script and, above all, allow him to take a picture each of them when they are having sex.

For his role in the plan, Zeledon promised to protect their identities and ensure their safety.

The offer for them, at first, seemed so dirty that they must not be doing that to a woman. The three of them considered the response that they would have from their husbands, and so they refused to partake. However, when Zeledon explained that they, the people he had considered his best friends, had also betrayed him with his wife, they understood the reason for his actions.

This validation along with the money offered convinced them. Thus, the three would end up accepting the work.

After the agreement, Zeledon taught them the script they were instructed to follow in their plans to seduce the women. Immediately afterwards, he gave them the phone numbers, e-mails, and Facebook pages of the women, so that they could contact each of them.

Then, he recommended that in their profiles, they should describe personal qualities that were compatible with each woman's tastes. Above all, they must present these qualities to them and put in their profile that they are from the neighbouring town.

With the plan outlined, Zeledon gave each one a part of the money, leaving the rest pending until the work was finished. So, they remained in permanent contact to keep him informed of the date, time, and place where he would obtain the evidence.

After the first few days of their difficult challenge, the three future victims accepted the Facebook friend requests of their new contacts.

With the first step completed, Luisão, one of the hired actors, went to El Paso to have a casual encounter with Bianca.

At the same time, Yerson, the man with green eyes, muscular body and strong appearance travelled to Boa Vista, while Neymar, the expert swimmer, arrived in São Paulo.

The three simultaneously commenced their act. Luisão, playing the role of an agronomist, arrived at the Bianca's farm. There, in front of the main house, he caused his car to have a mechanical defect. In his insistence to repair it, he managed to get the attention of the workers, who assured him that they knew a person capable of finding the issue.

Ten minutes later, they arrived with Bianca, who greeted him from a distance and expressed, "I see that you have problems with your car!"

"Yes, ma'am," answered Luisão, "although the trouble is that because I don't have knowledge of fixing cars, I cannot work out the issue, so I need some help. The gentlemen here told me that you know how to fix cars," Luisão remarked. "Could you please help me?"

Seconds after, with Bianca in front of him, she concentrated on the man's face. When she realised the similarity to one of her new Facebook contacts, with surprise she asked, "I have seen you somewhere?"

Luisão, at that moment, raised his eyes and when he observed her face, he exclaimed with surprise, "Of course! Although I never imagined that I would meet my most beautiful Facebook friend in person."

"Are you Luisão?" she asked.

"Yes, my beautiful lady!"

After their greeting, Bianca lifted the bonnet of the car and noticed that the condenser cable was placed in a different slot and that it would only be a matter of putting the cable in the correct place, tightening a screw and the problem would be solved.

Luisão, in gratitude for her assistance, extended an invitation to dinner, a proposal that she rejected immediately, warning him that she was a married woman.

In addition, those who knew her in El Paso, would be suspicious of her if they discovered her in a restaurant sharing a meal with a stranger.

Luisão, embarrassed, apologised for his imprudence and asked for her forgiveness if he offended her with his insinuation. Even so, he insisted that she accompany him, clarifying that it wouldn't be necessary to go to El Paso, they could go to a place in Bahia where they serve exotic food that is an absolutely delicious.

Luisão's insistence convinced her, but only on the condition that each one of them arrived alone, since she didn't want to be seen arriving together.

Once they both arrived, a reserved table was waiting for them, which was adorned with a beautiful floral arrangement as romantic melodies played on piano that embellished the moment.

Luisão, very gentlemanly, pulled out her chair, and when she sat down, he poured her a glass of wine and with soft whispers, he made her feel flattered.

After dinner, he politely escorted her to the parking lot and opened the car door for her while she settled down. His courtship reminded Bianca of the ideal man in her fairy tale.

While this was happening in Bahia, back in Boa Vista, Yerson, would enter Teresa's life.

That afternoon of the planned accidental meeting, the two were walking around the same park, opposite each other.

He, seeing Teresa from a distance, hid behind a statue and calculated her arrival. So, the moment that she passed, he came out in front of her, making their collision inevitable. Teresa, surprised by the unexpected collision, intended on insulting the cause of such stupidity, but while the aggressor apologised sincerely for his coarseness, the two looked at each other's faces for a few seconds. After a few seconds, in a simultaneous reaction, they exclaimed each other's names in unison:

"Yerson!"

"Teresa!"

Yerson, motivated, exclaimed, "This is a strange coincidence, I never thought to meet with the most beautiful friend on my Facebook in such an embarrassing situation."

Teresa, a little flushed by the gentlemanly comment, said, "Don't worry, everything is fine."

After that little accident that same afternoon, Teresa would bump into him again at the gym, where they had a short talk again.

The following mornings, they would run into each other at the stadium, where he was practicing on his bicycle.

The constant casual encounters led them to share a coffee, and then continue with romantic dinners and discreet outings. Undoubtedly, Yerson would become the man who began to confuse Teresa's feelings.

In São Paulo, Neymar was trying to seduce Dorelyz, Carlos's wife, by visiting the places that she and her niece frequented.

As a result, in the gym, he achieved his first encounter, where his unexpected arrival caught her attention. For Dorelyz, it was very confusing, because it was the first time that a man, apart from her husband, physically attracted her and drew her attention. Even so, she challenged herself to control her impulse. However, this impulse, only a day later at the sports Center, would grow even more when she saw the abilities of the same man in the swimming pool.

Dorelyz, intrigued to know if it was the new Facebook friend that she had accepted weeks before, found an excuse to approach him. But the true reason was her sudden attraction that started to control her mind. She, carried by her curiosity and admiration of his skills, would be the one to take the initiative to introduce herself her niece to him.

At that moment that the three were introduced, Neymar, with admiration, told her, "Wow! You are more beautiful in person than in your photos!"

She, surprised, asked, "What photos are you talking about?"

Neymar, feigning embarrassment, replied, "The photos of you on your profile."

After the clarification, a small smile came from Dorelyz's lips, who said, "I see that the world, despite seeming so large, really is small because I never imagined finding, in one of my Facebook friends, the qualities that I always longed to find in my husband."

After a few days of their casual meetings, Dorelyz received a surprise from him. She saw him arrive at her local club with friends, invited by Camelia, which pained her to watch.

The night that Neymar arrived at the establishment, Dorelyz's female friends focused their gazes on him. To see a handsome man looking for Camelia immediately caused great confusion for the women in the group.

All of them envied the luck of the ugly woman, since Neymar, from his arrival until closing time, would be by her side. The two enjoyed their time together to the fullest.

Dorelyz, on the other side of the bar, concentrated on them all night. Observing how they enjoyed their time together made her burn inside with jealousy. But Dorelyz knew that with her being a married woman, that response wasn't right.

Even so, she kept telling herself that Neymar was the person that she had dreamed about all her life, and although she wanted to bury that feeling, she was already captivated by his presence. And so, their encounters became more frequent and crossed the line from casual to forbidden.

A few weeks after Zeledon's revenge plan started, he became a little overwhelmed. His attitude wasn't due to feeling remorse for involving these three innocent women and not even because of his disappointment from not finding Melisa. However, fate had prepared him a surprise in a place that he least expected.

The afternoon of his surprise, Zeledon was at the stadium for the women's soccer final between Brazil and the United States.

He was very eager to stand up to exclaim his support to the players when the Brazilian team had some success.

With his passionate responses, he unintentionally continued to block the vision of those sitting behind him.

One of them was a lady who, annoyed by his fanatical way of expressing their emotions, shouted offensively in English, warning him that his antics were bothering her.

Zeledon, somewhat bothered by her complaining, turned his head around and said, "I'm sorry; however, you must understand that I'm a Latin man and I am very excited to see my favourite team playing."

The woman, embarrassed by her aggression, responded, "Sorry, dear. Do you speak English?"

"Yes, I do. Can I help you?" he asked.

With a calmer disposition, very politely, she requested, "Could you please switch places with the girl beside you?"

"Why?" he inquired.

"Because you are blocking my view," she answered.

"For me, no problem," he replied, "but let me ask her if she wants to change seats."

Zeledon, then, asked the young woman, "Excuse me, are you okay changing seats?"

"Of course! I have no problem with it," she replied.

With the young woman's approval, Zeledon turned to the woman behind him, saying, "Okay, the problem is solved, excuse me for the inconvenience."

Afterwards, the match entered a fifteen-minute break. So, the young woman, wanting to listen to an opinion about the first half of the match, engaged in a pleasant conversation with Zeledon.

During their talk, they started discussing soccer, but eventually, they would start discussing their personal lives.

With the second half underway, both concentrated on the game and continued to support their team.

Once the game was finished, they attempted to leave the stadium together, which, due to the extremely crowded exits, made their exit terribly slow. So, Zeledon took advantage of the circumstances and invited her to share a coffee and continue with their talk. She, delighted, accepted his proposal, and even recommended to him the best place in the city to have a coffee.

After finally leaving, both reached the exit and walked to the other end of the street to wait for a taxi. While they waited, the two introduced themselves. Zeledon, upon hearing her name, took it as a coincidence and thought that it wasn't the same Melisa that he sought for so long.

However, the curiosity in both would eventually lead them to scrutinise the point that most interested them.

After several minutes of talking about the game in the taxi, they arrived at their destination. There, from the moment they entered the building, the exquisite aroma and romantic atmosphere encouraged them to change the topic of their conversation. So, as they tasted their cappuccinos, the dialogue became more personal.

Unexpectedly, the subject of the pleasant talk would be changed by Melisa, who, intrigued about Zeledon's past, asked, "Where did you learn to speak English?"

He, showing a small smile on his face, replied, "The little that I know was due to my residence in Canada."

"Why did you decide to immigrate so far?" the young woman asked.

"The truth," Zeledon began, "everything was a mistake planned by my fate or I was in the wrong place, because a coincidence with a man's death, that I wasn't involved in, would carry me there."

"Ironically," he added, "having managed to reach Canada alive, carried me to think that I would never abandon my family, since my priority was to protect them, and with that process, we would be more united than ever. However, a year after my arrival, that joy would collapse like a house of cards. When I learned that the woman with whom I had shared my life with was secretly marrying in Bahia with a young man who had been her lover for so long," he continued.

"Her deceit meant that from one night to the next, my world collapsed over me, causing my dream to end in the middle of a nightmare in where her betrayal would leave me at the mercy of chronic depression, alone and empty-handed."

For Melisa, Zeledon's comment seemed a great coincidence, since something similar had happened to her. So, Melisa, intrigued to know everything that happened in detail asked a new question, "What was the young man's name?"

Zeledon, without evading, responded, "His name is Albeiro."

At that moment, smile grew on Melisa's face. Her ironic gesture, accompanied with admiration, was followed by her exclamation, "Today, I see that the world is simply a handkerchief!"

Her expression confused Zeledon who, with surprise, asked her, "Woman! What is the reason for your tone?"

Melisa, still hurt by the betrayal, with nostalgia responded to him, "My sarcasm is because the man that you are talking about is the same man who, years ago, swore to me an eternal love. But he, knowing that I was with his child, sought the excuse to deny his fatherhood and run into the arms of the woman who, today, is his wife."

Melisa, becoming sadder, added, "In those days, with my feelings destroyed by his deception, I left my family and went to another city with no direction in mind. After a few months, the woman that Albeiro married travelled abroad, so when he was alone, he wanted to find me and make me return to his side. However, when I learned of his intention, I decided that I wouldn't want to know anything about his false love."

There, at the café, they both were amazed; the surprise that fate offered to them was hard to believe, because the woman that Melisa was talking about was Olmeda, the same woman who betrayed Zeledon.

After finishing their cappuccinos and becoming lost in their extended conversation, the two concluded that their meeting wasn't random, and so both must join to take out revenge.

After their agreement, they would take their first step towards revenge. As a result, Zeledon promised to marry her civilly and give his last name to his stepson. In addition, he would process visa forms to migrate his future family with the Canadian embassy.

They also stipulated that during their strange relationship, the commitment of the two would be fictitious, with the exception that Melisa could change that rule if she thought it convenient.

One week after making their agreement, the wedding was held. Then, Zeledon went to Brasilia to fulfil, in front of the embassy, the remaining part of the agreement between the two.

Weeks after their marriage, the three actors hired by Zeledon would eventually achieve their objectives, one by one.

Following the arrangement, they communicated with him to give the locations where they planned to have sex with the women, so that he could take the photographs.

When their tasks were completed, Zeledon would reveal six photos, with the actors' faces covered, to protect their identities.

Afterwards, Zeledon met with the three actors and destroyed the remaining photograph negatives. As well as that, he cancelled the rest of the money. With this, the agreement was completed and each one would return to their usual routine.

Zeledon, with the photographs at hand, returned to his hotel room.

There, he took six envelopes and in each of them, he put a small note and the photo of their respective wife's affair.

In the three envelopes addressed to his former friends, with a mocking tone he wrote to them: *'Revenge is sweet, from your friend Zeledon who will never forget you.'*

Zeledon sent the rest of the envelopes with their respective notes to each wife of his supposed friends, clarifying in a small paragraph that they shouldn't feel bad about what happened, since their husbands were having an affair with Olmeda, his ex-wife. Thus, they were also traitors, and so none of them had the moral superiority to condemn their partner.

'Sorry for the circumstances, but I needed to give your husband a taste of his own medicine.'

With his revenge, Zeledon taught his former friends a good lesson and, although this would unleash great arguments with their wives, this didn't separate them. Even with their egos of wounded males, they understood that loneliness wasn't conducive to a happy relationship, and so, their wives had understandably fallen into temptation. Without other options, they, as well as their wives, would end up forgiving their deceptions and from that moment, the three husbands dedicated more time to their partners.

Zeledon, who had already completed eighty percent of his plan, returned to Toronto. Immediately upon his arrival, he began to expedite the immigration procedure for his new wife and her son.

The Politician's End and the Arrival of Zeledon's Wife to Canada

While Zeledon was arriving in Canada, I returned to Brasilia. That day, Larissa called me to tell me that everything was ready to initiate the lethal blow to Tancredo.

According to Larissa, the plan wouldn't be changed, so with the approval from the Ministry of Justice for my temporary reinstatement to the detective's office, I was instructed to be at the office as soon as possible to sign the required documents to receive my weapon and badge, where Larissa would credit me again, as a detective.

After our conversation, not even an hour had passed before I was already in the bunker fulfilling her request. There, we, and her subordinates, agreed on the final instructions of the plan.

After re-examining the plan, a final time, Larissa as the head detective, sent an order to Interpol to begin the dismantling of the traffickers' network and the international figureheads that Tancredo was connected to in other countries. As this was happening, the SIB was escorting Tancredo to a television studio, where he was due to speak with his supporters.

So, his political advisors and personal escorts, having no idea of the plan forged against him, were making the final touches to his future presentation.

With the signal on air, the debate between the two candidates began. There, each one, with proposals and objections from both sides, fought for the reasons why they must be elected.

As the debate was ongoing, international TV channels began broadcasting the news of the dismantling of a Brazilian drug trafficking network led by the well-known politician, Tancredo Moreira.

Upon hearing the report, Moreira's supporters assumed that it was a dirty trick of his rival. So, outraged, they called the head of their campaign and together they protested in front of the television station. The protestors were not willing to allow the success of the dirty tactics of the opposition leader against Moreira.

The director of programming, seeing the angry crowd and the detectives with their faces covered invading the studio, immediately tried to cut the TV transmission. In response to this, Matheus, took out the ace under his sleeve and expressed, "Mr Tancredo, I would like you to explain this video to the public!"

Immediately upon his request, the audio engineer played the violent images.

Tancredo was immediately speechless. However, his silent trance immediately changed to confusion the moment that I took my balaclava off and with a victorious tone, declared, "Tancredo Moreira, you are under arrest for the crimes of drug trafficking, conspiracy to commit crimes and for the murder of Falcão and his men, as well as the death of my colleague, Vinicio Braga, the detectives Baena and Guerrero, my friends Ludiela Cochaeira and Jorge Sotomayor."

Immediately after declaring the charges, I proceeded to place him in handcuffs and clarified that he had the right to a lawyer and to remain silent. Regardless, Tancredo knew that even with these rights, it was too late for him, since the evidence had spoken for itself.

As he was detained, his security present that were also a part of his murderous dirty work were also arrested.

All together, they were taken to the dungeons of a military garrison, where they would be held without communication until the trial date.

As they were detained, I felt so grateful that even though I was forbidden to show my identity, I took off my balaclava. I wanted him and his thugs to see on my face, the immense satisfaction of being able to crush them like they cockroaches they are.

My mistake would force the detective's office to provide me with maximum protection, because, although Tancredo was behind bars, he continued to have great power. So, I would only be safe in the detective's bunker, where I would remain until he was extradited to the US.

During my stay with the detective, I learned that she, from my cruel separation with her, hadn't found love with anyone else. This, although it could have been because of her work, also left me in doubt that it was for even more powerful reasons, including the possibility that, in the depths of her soul, immense love that joined us in the past was still rooted in her.

My assumption that Larissa had managed to get me out of her mind, but not from her heart seemed possible, considering the same thing was happening to me.

Being around her again made me realise that despite the brutal farewell and the years that had passed, I still felt the repressed feelings within me, which invited me to vent all that emotional energy that I had subjected them to. In silence, these feelings screamed to me that if I try, I lose nothing, but I could win something – the possibly that she is still waiting for me.

However, the moment that I thought of staying by her side and trying to recover her love, I realised the possibility was unlikely, especially considering that I was being constantly escorted by a squad of bodyguards, making me feel like a prisoner in my own world.

In addition to this, I knew full well that Larissa wasn't willing to leave her position to run into my arms. So, she would rather continue carrying this possible love for me in silence.

After discovering that Tancredo would be extradited to the US, I cut contact with Larissa and returned to Canada. With this, I would move far from her life again, in the same way that I did in the past.

The day of my departure, I took my own security measures in order to not only avoid Larissa but also, any possible pursuers from Moreira. For this reason, I arrived in Argentina, where I then bought a ticket to Québec and telephoned Zeledon to pick me up.

After arriving to Québec, we travelled to Toronto by land. With this, I buried the possibility of rekindling my story of love with Larissa and, at the same time, confused my pursuers from a possible attack.

On the day that they notified Tancredo of his extradition, his lawyers, trying to ensure that he wasn't extradited, accepted the anticipated confession and cooperated with the prosecution regarding the other charges. With that, they thought that he would be tried in Brazil. But his crimes abroad would prevail over his most recent murders and, ultimately, his trial would take place in a San Francisco court, where he would be sentenced to fifteen years of prison without bail. After completing this, he would be awaiting a life sentence in Brazil.

While this was happening in Tancredo's life, in Toronto, Olmeda had received news of the date of her husband's arrival. That same day that Olmeda was notified, the Brazilian embassy notified Zeledon that he must cancel his flights, as next Sunday, his family would be in Canada.

Immediately upon hearing the news, Zeledon was elated, because he knew that with their arrivals, his revenge was coming to its climax.

Motivated by the good news, he went to the bank and made the transaction. With this, the arrival of his new family was only a matter of days away.

Upon realising that the visas were approved in such a brief period made Zeledon become overwhelmed with joy and contact me.

Upon hearing the news myself, I congratulated him for his effort, since obtaining family visas to Canada in just six months must have been a new record.

After praising his efforts, we continued with our small talk where he asked me to pick him up from the airport on the date and hour that was stipulated on the ticket.

Although I didn't agree with his behaviour, I wouldn't refuse his request, because I knew that if I had been there for him during the most difficult moments of his life, I should also accompany him in his moments of rejoicing.

On the other hand, with Olmeda's husband in Toronto, she was forced to break the relationship with Ramiro, forbidding him from visiting her home, claiming that her son was bothered by his presence and she did not want to risk losing her son because of him. With this, Olmeda gradually drifted away from Ramiro. From that moment, their encounters became scarce and only took place when Olmeda wanted it, but Ramiro's obsession of not wanting to lose her turned his feelings sinister, which caused him to constantly call her and harass her each time she was alone.

Ramiro even resorted to threatening her that his unbridled passion could make him do anything, even kill. This unleashed fury from Olmeda, who threatened to go to the police if he didn't stop bothering her.

The suddenly cold behaviour of his beloved confused Ramiro, leading him to think that there must be something else going on, so he began to investigate.

Only a few days later, he discovered that two years ago, Olmeda had gotten married in Bahia, which explained why she was playing with his feelings, and her husband had recently arrived in Toronto.

Her betrayal turned his love into unending hatred, so he stopped talking to her and began to harass her in silence. No longer did he want to continue satisfying her needs and swore to himself that Olmeda would pay for her deceit with death.

At the same time, Zeledon and I were picking up Melisa and her son from the airport, before welcoming them with great enthusiasm.

After greeting them, we drove Melisa and her son to their new home. When we arrived, I said my goodbyes and returned home, since I felt that the couple would want to be alone – forgetting that the marriage agreement between the two of them was only for appearances.

Having successfully arrived in Canada, Melisa became overjoyed. To her, Canada would provide the opportunity to have her revenge and provide a better future for her son. Despite her joy, her arrival caused her some fear, because she was anxious at the idea of being in a strange country, adapting to the language and the low temperatures. Besides that, she had to live with Zeledon without having sex, and she wasn't sure that he would stick to the agreement, since Zeledon could hold his legal status as her husband against her.

This continued to produce great anxiety in Melisa because she wasn't comfortable with him becoming her life partner.

Another fear of Melisa's was her stepdaughter finding out about the true reason for their marriage, because for Karen, it would be very suspicious that her father had married her stepfather's ex-wife. Logically, this would make her assume that their relationship had ulterior motive and Melisa wouldn't want to have Karen's disapproval. However, Zeledon calmed her by telling her that except for the judge, the witnesses, the immigration staff, and me, no one knew about her marriage. To Karen, Melisa was merely a tenant whose rental payments was helping him to pay for the apartment.

As the days passed, the fear that haunted Melisa's mind slowly disappeared, little by little.

Zeledon's behaviour over time eventually stopped any doubts of his honesty, since he proved that she could trust him.

The desire to win the affection of the young woman led Zeledon to mix their strategies with frequent romantic gestures. In these days, he did not put any pressure on her, however. In his plan, she was free to leave after they took their revenge. With this, Zeledon hoped that Melisa would develop true feelings, so that she may decide to remain by his side for love, not for interest. So, continually, he introduced her to people of the same age and frequently brought her flowers when he arrived home from work. As well as that, he was always on the lookout for opportunities for her and her son to get to know the city, the surrounding suburbs, cinemas, restaurants, and shopping centres. He tried, in such a fleeting time, to make their coexistence as pleasant as possible. Despite this, he was still not satisfied. So, while Melisa began her full-time English study, he sent her to take driving lessons and private English classes as well.

He wanted her to be so well prepared for her confrontation with Albeiro that she would make him feel like a loser for betraying her.

Becoming more impatient, Melisa longed for the opportunity to take out revenge now. However, Zeledon, ensured her that it wasn't the right time.

After the first five months of coexisting as a couple, Zeledon had succeeding in earning the love of Melisa and even his stepson, who was already calling him dad.

While for Zeledon, all was going well, fate began to forge a different story for Olmeda. She, without having any idea, would be the winner of a tragic surprise. She entered a raffle where her church offered one lucky winner the down payment on a new house if they were legally married in Canada, with proof of the marriage's legitimacy.

When drawing the raffle, Olmeda's name was picked, so that Sunday at church, she was pleasantly surprised when the pastor announced that she had won.

When Ramiro found out that she was the winner, his anger pushed him to speak with the pastor, insisting to him that the marriage between Olmeda and the young man from Bahia had been only for business, and that they are intending on divorcing as soon as they could.

This information raised doubts in the congregation, who acknowledged the age difference between the two as possible evidence that this was true. So, the church placed a condition to the prize – that they must participate in a Christian marriage. A traditional ceremony that, according to the pastor, would take place in front of the altar of this church in Toronto. To the congregation, this would ensure that their union wasn't merely for convenience, as their duty as benefactors was to ensure that the subsidy would arrive in the hands of a genuine family.

After stipulating the conditions, Olmeda agreed that the nuptials would be held on Family Day, a date that the church was celebrating its centenary with a great celebration.

Zeledon, through his daughter, Karen, found out about Olmeda's luck and her future marriage in Toronto. This would lead him to decide that the moment to turn Albeiro's dream into a nightmare would take place in the church.

When the date of the nuptials arrived, the venue quickly began fill. There, everyone involved in this story would eventually arrive.

That morning, Henry, Zeledon's son, arrived with the couple. Melisa, her baby, Zeledon and Karen, avoiding the presence of Albeiro, would arrive after the rest of the guests. After arriving at the church, Karen sat in the pews to the right and Zeledon and his new family opted for the last bench, where Melisa, in all her youthful splendour, thought to surprise her former lover, only she would wait for the admonition of the pastor to make her triumphal entry. So, when the pastor announced the routine phrases, "If there is anybody who objects to the marriage between these two people, speak now or forever hold your peace," Melisa immediately, carrying her son in their arms, rose from her seat and began to walk towards the altar to exercise that right. However, as she took her first steps, Ramiro, with a gun in his hand, entered through a side door and, like a professional hitman, unloaded eight shots of the nine loaded towards the couple, leaving last bullet for himself.

Ramiro's insane act left three victims, including both his own and Albeiro's instantaneous death, as well as leaving Olmeda, his ex-girlfriend, seriously injured.

Moments after the attack, the police and paramedics arrived, took away the corpses and sent Olmeda urgently to the operating room. After the surgery, Olmeda was unconscious for several days. When she woke up and found out that Albeiro had died, sadness overwhelmed her, and she fell into a prolonged silence. In a way, she felt guilty for his death. What was supposed to be a celebration to the couple, the pastor and the guests would end in a tragedy, and without doubt, to Zeledon and Melisa, this wasn't the sweet revenge that they had planned.

In the end, the tragedy of Albeiro somehow involved everyone, including Zeledon and Melisa. Even with their rivalry against him, the two made all the arrangements required by the embassy, so that Albeiro's body would be sent to his home country.

While Olmeda was recovering from her physical injuries, the police concluded the initial investigation, which led to suspect Zeledon as the crime's mastermind. So, they began to harass and interrogate him. Regardless, the police's accusations didn't worry him, he knew that the man assumed to be a hired assassin by the police, had a secret romance with Olmeda, and upon learning of her deception, threatened to take out his revenge with blood.

So, Zeledon informed the authorities and his daughter Karen of this. Sure of his innocence, Karen told her brother of the injustice towards their father from the police. Luckily, Henry revealed to Karen that the murderer and their mother had been more than just friends for a long time.

Although Karen was unaware of their relationship, she didn't doubt Henry. She knew her mother well enough and knew that she was a nymphomaniac. Regardless, she had to prove her suspicions to the authorities in order to prevent them from staining Zeledon's criminal record. So, that same afternoon, Karen visited Olmeda during her recovery.

There, without hesitation, she asked her mother, "What kind of relationship did you have with Ramiro?" Olmeda, weighed down by her guilt, didn't have the courage to deny the close bond between the two of them, and with broken words, she told Karen that Ramiro was her lover and the crime an act of passion. Thus, Zeledon had no relation to the accusations against him.

With that statement in the hands of the authorities, Zeledon would be free of any suspicion. After overcoming the small obstacle, a new surprise waited for Zeledon, but this one would be much more pleasant.

That night, realising her feelings and certain that she would only give herself for true love, Melisa came to Zeledon's room.

There, wearing revealing nightwear and carrying two glasses and a bottle of wine in her hands, she invited him to celebrate his release from being a suspect. Her attitude took Zeledon by surprise, who, during their peculiar coexistence, hadn't had the opportunity to observe Melisa's appealing figure, in all her splendour.

As the wine was consumed, their bodies began to rub against each other. With this, they both expressed words of admiration and affection.

After their compliments, they began feel to each other, before ending their passionate touching with sex, where they finally released their bottled-up passion.

After many months, they consummated their repressed desires during a honeymoon that lasted for several weeks.

A few months after the couple started having sex, Zeledon revealed to Karen that Melisa wasn't merely his roommate, but rather his wife. At first, she saw his confession as a lack of maturity, especially considering their large age difference, but after taking time to think, Karen eventually understood that their relationship could be true love if Melisa was so much younger. Karen couldn't make him feel guilty for true love, so she decided to support them, hoping that as time went on, their union would become stronger and stronger.

From the first months of their unexpected relationship, fate began to welcome them with benevolence. While destiny was smiling to them, on the other hand, destiny was cruel to Olmeda.

The low instincts exhibited by her in the past would make a judge declare her incompetent. With his verdict, Olmeda lost the benefits formerly granted by the court, as well as the custody of Henry, whose guardianship would be taken over by the state. Thus, Zeledon decided to appeal again for the custody of his son, since this time, he had Melisa at his side, so he could already provide him with better emotional stability. Even so, gaining custody wouldn't be easy and Zeledon would have to earn that right in front of the judge.

Regardless, Zeledon remained hopeful, and he trusted in the laws of karma, since sooner or later, those who deserved it would always win.

After successfully achieving a ruling in his favour, Zeledon committed to comply with the clauses stipulated by the judge and, above all, to be rigorous about the mother's visits. However, he wouldn't be selfish and would let Olmeda visit him as many times as she wished, on the condition that Henry wanted to see his mother, too.

Despite this, it still wouldn't be the same as sharing twenty-four hours a day with her son for Olmeda; his absence and the hard blows of life recently would leave her overwhelmed in solitude and under psychological treatment.

While Olmeda's misfortunes were ongoing, the Mennonite Congregation, after learning of the injustices in the arrest involving one of its members, pulled out all the stops to assist. Hoping that they would be able to reverse the arbitrary family law stipulated in the Canadian Constitution, they hired a law firm to take over everything related to Gustavo's defence.

Several months after continuous sessions and appeals in the court, the lawyers' battle to try to stop the deportation of their client would be useless. The judge's final ruling sternly communicated that the case was lost. Immediately after the verdict, an immigration officer told Gustavo that from noon, he would be taken into custody for 72 hours. The reason for this, the officer explained, was to allow him time to pay off any outstanding debts with the government. After this, he would be deported to his country of origin.

Gustavo, when listening to the ultimatum, immediately thought about his daughter and his grandson who he was leaving behind. This filled him with sadness; he knew that although the two were under government protection, he would be abandoned without their blood family since their stepmother and brother, although they were free to stay, would undoubtedly return with him.

The remorse emanating from his conscience made him feel guilty at times, but the reassurance from his friends, relatives and even his church told him otherwise. According to us, he had acted at his discretion, so with our opinions to his favour, we exonerated him from his guilt.

After much travelling and telephone calls of all kinds, Gustavo arrived back to his home country. There, together with his wife and son, he began to look back on his adventure in Canada. He described his arrival as a unique experience that, despite all the troubles, provided him with valuable experience, but even this was not enough compensation for his great loss, his daughter.

During his sadness, he justified his arrest and the way he was morally mistreated. Even so, he appreciated the welcome that, for several years, many Canadian people in their country gave him and his family because at that time, although hurt by the Canadian laws' harshness, Gustavo knew that he had learned several beneficial trades, a new language and, above all, he had made many friends.

With these new skills acquired during his stay in Canada, my dear friend Gustavo would be able to take advantage of many opportunities, including his stay at prison, since his English level provided him a surprising economic profit.

During his time in prison, the luck of being the only person who spoke Spanish would inspire great interest in some of the inmates who wanted to learn the language. Among them was a man accused of fraud that had a difficult online romance with a Mexican woman, and so Gustavo's arrival was like the ring on one's finger for the prisoner.

Thankful for his help, that afternoon before Gustavo left the penitentiary, in gratification for his teaching, the man discreetly gave him a large sum of money.

As the day of his deportation arrived, my great friend Gustavo said his goodbyes to his friends, including his daughter Juliana, who, in her third trimester and with tears in her eyes, bid him farewell.

Larissa's Decision

As the tragic fates of Olmeda and Gustavo ended, my fate, thousands of miles away, gifted me a surprise that was unexpected. Larissa, the cause of the empty feeling in my heart, began feeling the punishment of persecuting Moreira and the drug trafficking network.

The continuous death threats and attempts on her life by the gangs that she persecuted made her constantly anxious, most of the time locking herself in her secure metal vault.

At forty-two years old, she thought to herself that she had lost her youth chasing and capturing criminals who, for their crimes, ensured the whole weight of the law fell on them.

Larissa, with her soul hardened by the events of her past, questioned herself, "Where will all this animosity lead me?"

The vision that came to her mind was the possibility that true love would never come for her, and that with this, she would be imprisoned in her own solitude. However, if she had already managed to eliminate the death threats against Matheus and had successfully put the criminal mastermind that destroyed her happiness behind bars, she saw no point in continuing to harden her soul. Larissa was aware that the capture of the man who had killed her brother only gave her some sense of satisfaction, because nothing would ever bring Vinicio back. Her self-reflection, although possibly too late, led her to contemplate the possibility of getting away from this life. But her remorse could not change the past, which had lost her youth and her love because of her cold antipathy.

Particularly, she yearned for the person she lost because of her arrogance, the man she had tried to kill.

The person who Larissa thought of was me. The remorse she felt pierced her conscience, as she reflected on our coexistence months ago. While being lost in thought about her life, Larissa realised that if I still loved her, even in a corner of my soul, it was because my love for her was sincere.

As she reflected, she promised to herself that if her intuition was true, she was determined to overcome any obstacles and never give up until our old flame was rekindled again.

With her position as prosecutor general of Brazil, it wouldn't be difficult for her to locate me, so she undertook the search for me, finding my residence within a few hours.

A week after finishing her investigation and leaving her resignation letter, Larissa arrived in Toronto. That afternoon, with the help of her colleagues in Canada, she easily found my apartment. Despite this, she wouldn't be successful in finding me, because at the time, I was having lunch with a new friend, Katy. As I met Katy, I was determined to find myself a new love. Although I knew that this was ultimately in vain, because I couldn't bring myself to move on from Larissa. It was still a great challenge to control the feelings that were running through my body.

The image of her from the last time I had seen her was still permeating through my mind, so much so that sometimes when seeing a woman in the distance, I would confuse her with Larissa and would even run out to meet her. For that reason, when my mirage unexpectedly became reality, I didn't give it much importance, since I thought I was merely hallucinating again. However, this time, the one that ran towards me and shouted my name was her. My immediate reaction was to reciprocate and run into her arms.

At that moment, I let myself be carried by my heart, so when she emotionally apologised for her past mistakes, I silenced her mouth with a passionate kiss, communicating more than a thousand words. Although I didn't know her intentions, her proposal cleared all my doubts. She offered to resign from her job if I was willing to share my life with her. Her words immediately comforted my soul, and I responded, without hesitation, with a yes. Without realising, I lost the notion of time and forgot all the damage that she caused me, promising to give myself completely to her love.

One month after our reconciliation, Larissa, through the help from the Brazilian ambassador, successfully found a job and established herself as a diplomatic attaché in Toronto, where together, we started a new life.

END